Praise for *We Are*

'A fierce, poignant and poetic sto...
will linger in your heart long after you've closed the boo...

Kathleen Glasgow, author of *Girl in Pieces*
and *The Agathas*

'I am in complete and utter love with everything Amy Beashel writes,
but this one may just be my favourite.'

Jennifer Niven, author of *All the Bright Places*

'An incredibly beautiful and moving book, as full of twists and turns
as it is heart and compassion.'

Kate Weston, author of *Diary of a Confused Feminist*

'A pacy page turner that explores grief, love, the messiness of life,
and facing up to the past… Brilliant and utterly original. Cannot
recommend highly enough. Bravo!'

Liz Hyder, author of *Bearmouth*

'Amy Beashel is fast becoming one of my favourite contemporary
authors. *We Are All Constellations* is rich and multilayered, funny
and heart achingly beautiful. Iris is a character you can't help
but take into your heart even when you kind of want to shake
her too.'

Ciara Smyth, author of *Not My Problem*

'A raw, beautifully written tale of grief, friendship and the struggle
to open oneself up to others in a world that often times feels like too
much to take. Readers everywhere will connect with Iris as she fights
against the tide and, ultimately, finds her way through.'

Liz Lawson, author of *The Agathas*
and *The Lucky Ones*

'Powered by the pain of grief and the joy of love, *We Are All Constellations* is a deeply compelling coming of age story that deals honestly and unflinchingly with the agonies of discovering your past may not be all that you believed.'

Louisa Reid, author of *Gloves Off*

'A beautiful, nuanced and necessary book, handling difficult topics with great skill and without judgement.'

Gina Blaxill, author of *You Can Trust Me*

'Beautiful, heartwarming, heartbreaking and gorgeously written. Stunning.'

Julia Tuffs, author of *Hexed*

'This beautiful story of grief and love is raw, real and full of heart. Amy Beashel's writing is exquisite.'

Bex Hogan, author of *Viper*

'Gorgeous and heartbreaking… It turned me inside out and put me right again.'

Lucy Cuthew, author of *Blood Moon*

'A truly beautiful book featuring a captivating protagonist who will forever hold a place in my heart.'

Tess James-Mackey, author of *Someone Is Watching You*

'A beautiful story that many readers will connect with; it doesn't shy away from difficult topics but instead portrays them with a stunning realism.'

Elliot Jacobs, early reader

'A piece of art that will resonate with many readers whilst exploring powerful, sad yet beautiful themes.'

Alicia Milligan, early reader

Praise for *The Sky Is Mine*

'A powerful page-turner with giant heart. A book that everyone needs to read. Izzy is my hero, and her voice deserves to be heard around the world. Stunning.'

Jennifer Niven, author of *All the Bright Places*

'Izzy's story is raw, painful, and ultimately one of survival and strength. Amy Beashel holds nothing back when confronting rape culture and toxicity; this beautiful book will floor you and deserves to be on every shelf, everywhere.'

Kathleen Glasgow, author of *Girl in Pieces*

'Beashel joins feminist writers like Louise O'Neill and Holly Bourne in portraying rape culture rather than simply focusing on an isolated incident or single monstrous individual… When Izzy finds within herself "that girl won't stand for it, that girl who won't sit quietly on the sidelines", it's genuinely inspiring and powerful.'

Irish Times

'Thought-provoking.'

Financial Times

'Perfect crossover… Its themes are dark, but its characters are bold and engaging.'

Heat

'One of those once-in-a-lifetime reads… There is relatability and new understanding found in every word in this beautiful, striking novel.'

Germ Magazine

'Izzy is an intriguing character… Readers will be shocked, angry and, hopefully, empowered by the novel's message.'

Booklist

'*The Sky Is Mine* is an exceptionally powerful and emotional read, exploring the themes of abuse and control in a realistic and thought-provoking way. I couldn't put it down.'

Eve Ainsworth, author of *Tender*

'In a strongly affirmative ending wrongs are righted… Older readers will respond to the message that speaking out against abuse and domestic violence is essential and that no one need suffer alone.'

School Librarian

'Unflinchingly honest, devastatingly raw and utterly compelling, this stunning YA debut is resplendent with heart, humour and so much hope. '

Simon James Green, author of *Noah Can't Even*

'*The Sky Is Mine* is a beautifully written, totally absorbing, utterly enraging and ultimately inspiring novel. I loved it.'

Keris Stainton, author of *My Heart Goes Bang*

'Amy Beashel's beautiful telling of Izzy's story is a call to young girls everywhere to stand up and make themselves heard.'

Anstey Harris, author of *The Truths and Triumphs of Grace Atherton*

'BRILLIANTLY written, fast-paced older YA, so strong on the pain and shame of female vulnerability and with a lead character, Izzy, who leaps out of the pages and makes you care deeply from the first page to the last.'

Perdita Cargill, author of the Waiting for Callback series

We Are All Constellations

AMY BEASHEL

ROCK THE BOAT

This book contains material which some readers may find distressing, including discussions of sexual assault (flashing), suicide, self-harm, alcoholism, aphobia, mood disorder and sexual content. We are grateful to Andi, Reno, Richard Dunhill, Elliot Jacobs, Alicia Milligan, Mia Schartau and Evie Smith for undertaking sensitivity reads.

A Rock the Boat Book

First published by Rock the Boat,
an imprint of Oneworld Publications, 2022

Paperback: ISBN 978-0-86154-065-5
eISBN 978-0-86154-066-2

Typeset by Tetragon, London
Printed and bound in Great Britain by Clays Ltd, Elcograf S.p.A.

Oneworld Publications
10 Bloomsbury Street, London, WC1B 3SR, England

Stay up to date with the latest books,
special offers, and exclusive content from
Rock the Boat with our newsletter

Sign up on our website
rocktheboatbooks.com

MIX
Paper from
responsible sources
FSC® C018072

For Monty.

You like to tell me the universe is
e   x   p   a   n   d   i   n   g.

Please know, my own universe is forever expanding from
simply knowing and loving
Y O U.

Kind.
Focused.
Sensitive.
Funny.

I can't wait to see what other stars will shine in your
constellation too.

X

One

Me? Scared?

No, no, no.

I mean, honestly, I just don't get it, why people freak when they're alone outside in the dark.

Because with a bit of stealth and a whole lot of moxie, it's fine.

Oh, and a smile too. I *always, always* smile.

Because this is peak life, right?

The queen-of-the-world buzz as I charge through town, weaving my way through the dazzle of lairy shirts and teetering heels spilling from the pubs at close to 11 p.m. The electric memory of Rollo's hands and mouth sending a heat that's almost fire across my skin. The roar of air in my lungs, as hard and frosty as the ground beneath my Doc Marten'd feet, which steer me from the street lights and the carnival of beer-drenched howls towards Good Hope Wood.

The treeline curls away from civilization back into itself like a black cat in the corner of a room. Separate. Content. Claws retracted but ready to spring and slash should anyone rattle its peace.

I quit running when I reach the trees, slowing to a pace Dad would rather I always stick to.

'Careful, Iris,' he says when I'm ironing a school shirt, or chopping onions, or standing on a train platform, just the wrong side of the yellow line.

'Careful.'

'Careful.'

'Careful.'

He'd stiffen and bug-eye if he saw me now, scampering across the fallen branches and crystallizing moss, an occasional chittering bat swooping in stealth-hunt above me.

He'd catch the way my head turns back to the lit path and assume the worst, that the boy I'm scanning for, running from, is the kind of bad boy in teen movies that are all angst and abhorrent behaviour.

But my life isn't that sort of story, and Rollo isn't that sort of guy.

He's not chased me for a start.

The path behind me is empty.

The wood ahead of me, though, is full.

Of trees, sure, but it's not only gnarled branches and parched leaves that whisper in the canopy. It's not only clamouring roots that burrow and slither through the ground. There are creature sounds too: scuttling, screeching, grunting. And creature smells: earthy and pungent and alive.

Stopping for just a moment, I inhale it.

All of it.

Though that's not what I'm here for.

What I *am* here for is a house buried in the depths of these woods. Not the sort of house you'd live in. From the photos I've seen on @MyEmptyHouses' account on Insta, the windows of this house are mostly cracked or missing, its carpets torn and stained. Everything about it suggests its occupants bolted some time ago.

~~People do that, don't they?~~
~~They make a home for you.~~
~~And then they disappear.~~

The bristling fingers of drooping branches whip my scalp as I run deeper into the woods, the dark stamping down on the moonlight. I pull my phone from my back pocket, ready to switch on the torch.

The screen is a swarm of alerts.

I swipe away any from Rollo. But my heart bruises at the thought of dismissing the ones from my best mate Tala. I open her voice note.

'What the fuck, Iris!' Her tone is a ruse. If this was the first time you heard her, that harsh opener with its blunt swear, you'd think she was tough, right? That she's the type who says what's what. The girl who'd hurl all kinds of bolshy comebacks if someone so much as dared to throw her the slightest shade.

In truth, with anyone that's not me or her parents, my best mate is practically mute.

In this voice note, however, she's unleashing a whole new Tala.

'You'd better listen to this message.' Her sigh alone is a flash of impatience. 'It's one thing ignoring Rollo, but it's another thing ignoring me.'

Jeez.

Rollo's spoken to her then? Relayed my sudden disappearance and his many unanswered calls? How long did it take for him to wake and notice I'd absconded? How many minutes until he pulled back the covers to fetch his phone from his desk drawer. He always makes a point of putting it there whenever we go upstairs.

'No distractions,' he said that first time, about four months ago, when his parents were at the cinema, and we had at least two hours of curtains-closed teasing seizing feeling.

Rollo's good like that. He's kind and careful and says things like, 'Are you sure you're OK with this, Iris?' and 'We can stop any time, yeah, just say.'

But then tonight he said things like, 'You know that gap year you're planning? I was thinking maybe I could come along for the ride?'

And despite the hum of a fresh orgasm that would normally have me buzzing with post-sex chat, I couldn't summon a single word in reply. Instead, I faked sleep until I could make a run for it.

'Where *are* you?' Tala's fury level on the voice note has quickly dissipated into concern. 'You want me to meet you at the bothy?'

I cut the message and start typing:

All good. Not at the bothy.

The three dots appear immediately.

FFS not another bando?

Tala might not share my passion for urban exploration, but she does at least know the lingo.

12

The house I'm now looking at is definitely a bando. As in *abandoned*. As in *forsaken*. As in the people who once loved this place have never returned to see what's become of everything they left behind.

Every inch of it is kind of broken.

Before I look around, I pull out a paper fortune teller from my bag. It's the kind everyone makes as kids, turning a flat square piece of paper into a three-dimensional soothsayer with pockets and flaps and eight fortunes written within its folds.

Only when Mum taught me how to make them, she didn't write eight fortunes. She wrote one.

You will be strong.

Over and over and over and over and over and over and over.

See? No matter which square I pick, I always end up with that one irrefutable destiny.

(Nice use of 'irrefutable', Iris.)

Before each outing, I make a new one from a map of my destination, always sure to write the same fortune on repeat. And then, once I'm at the location, I pose.

Fortune teller in one hand, phone in the other, I turn away from my reflection in the cracked and cobwebbed glass of the front door, raising my arm so the camera takes in as much of me and the abandoned house as possible. My smile is too toothy in the intrusive white of the flash.

And then it's not.

Hhhhhhhhhhhh.

My mouth shuts, clamping my breath behind my lips because wasn't that a heave of someone else's? Someone else's breath, I mean. Over there by what would once have been a fence.

13

Shit.

Keep your cool, Iris. I repeat, like one of my stepmum's yogic mantras.

All I can hear is the ragged thrum of my heart.

Keep your fucking cool.

I catch it, then, the glint of a man-creature's eyes.

As my thumb presses the lock key on my phone, I understand what people mean when they talk about being plunged into darkness. Because without that artificial light, I am drowning in black. Despite the momentary blindness, I don't shift my gaze.

Hhhhhhhhhhhh.

That sound like breath again.

I unclamp *my* lips and exhale. Watching. Willing what I thought was a face to be my brain playing tricks on me.

But when my eyes adjust to the darkness, they see specifics. A frayed woollen beanie. A long thick nose. Skin, partly bearded and white as bone.

He's about my dad's age, but their energy couldn't be more different.

Separated by just three rasping trees, we are locked. Wild animals standing our muddied, twisted ground, refusing to succumb to a blink even, as if just that tiny movement will make one of us prey.

Something squarks in the undergrowth.

You will be strong.

And I am.

I've seen the news. Read the statements written by mothers whose daughters have been raped or murdered. Watched Dad's face as he realizes no matter how much he tries to impose the

14

health and safety strategies from his office within his home, there is no guaranteed health and safety for girls. Not while there are men.

#NotAllMen

But some.

One.

#AllItTakesIsOne.

You will be strong.

The man-creature needs to see I am.

'Well?' I buck my head, like, *I'm ready for you*.

'Well, what?' His voice, rough as sandpaper, is neither aggressive nor kind.

From what I can see he's empty-handed. No rucksack. No camera. No sign, then, that he's an explorer like me.

So what is he?

That creeping snarl suggests maybe he's what Dad was afraid of all those times he told me to stop with the ridiculous night-time adventures. When he heaved a sigh and said something like, 'I'm worried, Iris. Are you actively looking for things that are dangerous or bad?'

The man-creature grows as he pulls back his shoulders. His coat gapes at the buttons with the effort, like there's suddenly too much of his body for the size of his clothes. 'You're just a kid.' He skulks forward, only an inch or so, but that inch is one less inch of space between us. 'Mummy not mind you being out this late?' His face twitches.

'My mother's dead,' I say.

Even here in the woods with this shabby man with his sneering lip, I muster the same matter-of-fact delivery I use every time someone asks about her. Usually, I shape this neutral tone to let people know that I've come to terms with my mother's death. I smile to reassure them it's OK to change the subject. That, like me, they are safe to move on.

With this man-creature, though, the fact is a different kind of statement.

It's: *I can cope with anything, mate.*

It's: *My mum died in a house fire on Christmas Day when I was ten. I know how to survive.*

His palm slips into his pocket, takes hold of something.

He laughs as he begins to pull it free.

The frozen air between us shatters and I run, the heat of my own exhale melting the numbness that had begun to settle in my cheeks. It's his laugh that chases me. Savage and nasty like bile he's hacking up from the back of his throat.

I thrash a path through the brown-black woods, my hands wildly jabbing the low-hanging branches, their bark scoring a map of this hot-pulsed pursuit into my skin. I am all lightning-fast feet and charged blood as I emerge from the trees on to the grassland that separates Good Hope Wood from the road, where a fox crosses then ducks beneath a fence that runs the perimeter of a new-build housing estate. A wild animal slinking between sleeping people's homes.

The man-creature has given up. At least that's what I hope as I look over my shoulder. The woods are an expanse of slate and russet shadow with no visible movement. Aside from my breathing, the world is now silent and still.

I keep moving.

Ten minutes later, I'm on our street. I press my thumb down

on the microphone button to record a slightly panting voice note to Tala, letting her know I'm home. 'All good,' I say, hitting send then—

Shit.

My ankle rolls over the curb and I stumble.

The shriek of tyres.

The outrage of panic-slammed brakes.

'JESUS!' A shout paired with the blare of a horn. 'You stepped into the road!' The driver shakes his fist at me.

'Sorry.' I smile. Not apologetically exactly but confidently, because Mum always told me a smile is what will see you through. I gesture at my ankle, turning my foot in small circles to make a point that my trip wasn't exactly voluntary.

No lasting pain. I am good to go.

But: 'Iris!' Our front door swings on its hinges as Dad runs down the drive, his eyes flitting from me to the car to me again.

Does he just lurk by the sitting-room window looking out for me?

'I'm fine.' I wave a dismissive hand in his direction as I hobble through our garden gate.

A couple of years ago, Dad and Rosa converted the garage into my new bedroom, so I have not only my very own bathroom but my very own door too. All glass and wide and sliding. Perfect for slipping out unnoticed – or back in.

Trouble is, Dad's never quite got a handle on the fact that private access is only really a benefit if your room remains private too. By the time I've faffed with the key, he's already sitting on my bed, his hurried route to my bedroom through the house evidently quicker than mine.

'Iris.' His shoulders rise as he deep-inhales the way Rosa insists will make him more chill. Despite his efforts, I can smell the panic in Dad's exhale as it fills the room. 'Tell me –' the vein on the left side of his forehead bulges bluish-green – 'the truth,' he says. 'Where on earth have you been?'

Two

I stand by my desk, running my finger down the dates on my puppy calendar, last year's Christmas gift from Tala, who knows I'd give anything for my own dog. Nothing as fancy as the fully coiffed Pomeranian holding a candy cane and sporting a matching striped bow tie for the month of December. Honestly, any old mutt would do.

My nail – grimy with woodland dirt – glides straight over the 17th and the 25th, right through to the end of the year.

Sweat seeps from my palms, which I clench into fists.

'With Rollo,' I say in answer to Dad's question. It's not a lie, but it's not exactly a truth either. Rather, it's a molten combination of the two.

'I was watching out for you.' His voice is a battle of accusation and fear. 'You looked scared.'

'I was almost hit by a car, Dad. Of course I looked scared.'

'Before then,' he says, his poker-straight back and tucked-in shirt a neat contrast to my crumpled duvet. 'You were running.'

I turn away, unfurl my fingers, stroke the thin-scored cuts that look like nothing but are quietly exploding. Every movement casual, I take the anti-bac gel from my desk drawer and enjoy its rubbed-in sting. 'I was running because I was late,' I say over the *click click click* as I pick the muck from beneath my nails. 'Scared for the same reason.' Back in my stride now, I'm able to face him. 'My curfew? There's a reason I call you the Stickler. I was trying to avoid *this*,' I point my finger back and forth between the two of us.

I'm sure from the way Dad nods – slow and pensive – that he senses the hike in my pulse.

But.

'OK,' he says, like he believes me, which, thankfully, is something he tends to do. He looks up, then, from his lap, which is where his eyes always go to when he's nervous. Maybe because his lap is somewhere broad and solid and safe? Almost exactly seven years ago, I crawled on to it when he sat me on the sofa and told me about the fire.

'I like Rollo,' he says now, literally twiddling his thumbs.

I know this already. For all his worry and naysay, Dad isn't one of those sitcom fathers who grill their daughters' boyfriends. And for all his stupid dad jokes, whenever Rollo's come to pick me up, Dad's never warned him to keep his hands to himself or quipped about having a gun.

'I don't like you being over there this late on a Sunday night.'

Here we go.

'But I *do* like that you're in a steady relationship.'

I don't mention that my steady relationship is over. That the first thing I did when Rollo suggested he join me urbexing around Europe next year is sneak from under the duvet and out the door. It was a dick move really. Not only for the hurt I caused Rollo but because Dad would be far more likely to get on board with my gap-year plans if he thought I wasn't heading to foreign lands alone.

'You *are* careful, aren't you, sunshine? You know. When you…'

I'm relieved when Dad's gaze drops again. I couldn't bear him looking at me when we talk, no matter how loosely, about *that*.

'Yes, Dad.' That's as much as he's going to get from me. And, to be fair, I think it's as much as he needs. Sex ed was mostly left to school and Rosa who, I know from overheard whispers, thinks there would be 'a benefit, Matt, from being more open'.

He stands up, pausing when he notices my dirtied Doc Martens by the back door. It's a running joke in my family that I like them box-fresh.

'You're sure you were at Rollo's, Iris?' His eyes lock on mine. 'You weren't off in some dodgy derelict factory for the sake of your blog?'

'It's not a *blog*, Dad, it's a feed.' I stand in front of him, blocking his view of my boots and pushing them behind the curtains as I draw them closed.

He holds his stare the way he always does when I haven't quite answered his question.

'I swear I was not off in some dodgy derelict factory.' More of that melded fact and fiction.

'Good.' Dad's happy to take my word for it. Isn't that easier than pressing for a thornier truth? 'Better that you're with Rollo than wandering around some dank building on your own.'

I nod as if I agree.

'I really don't understand it.' He's nothing if not predictable, because this is what Dad always says whenever the subject of urbex rears what he calls its 'perplexing head'.

'Maybe if you looked at my Insta without the filter of your health-and-safety-tinted glasses, you might see what I see.' I open my @DoratheUrbexplorer account on my phone and pass it to him.

For a minute or so he scrolls through my pictures. A window-smashed church. A shut-down holiday camp. A disused airfield. An ancient cinema ripe for kisses on the ripped seats of its dust-drenched back row.

'Nope, don't see it.' Dad hands back my phone. 'Just looks like misery to me.' He opens my bedroom door, and I hear Rosa softly berating Noah for studying so late after all their chat about burn-out. Noah will know better, of course. He always does. My stepbrother is so infuriatingly full of information, he's more often addressed – by me at least – as Know-All.

Dad glances back at me, taps his watch. 'Look, I think maybe we need to review your curfew.' I must pull a face then because he cocks his eyebrow. 'Don't be like that, Iris. You know we only ever try to be fair.'

✦

The man-creature's face flashes in my bathroom mirror as I brush my teeth, his thick and viscous laugh prickling my skin. When I snap off the light and blindly spit the toothpaste into the basin, my heart is a jackhammer punching against the dark.

Dad would be furious if he knew. A few years ago, when I first started properly exploring, he and Rosa called a family meeting, telling me they didn't think this new 'hobby' was appropriate. 'No scowling, Iris,' Dad told me. 'Is it so wrong that we don't want you getting hurt?'

I'm a big girl, I thought.

'Tell me honestly.' His voice was softer back then. 'You don't *want* to hurt yourself, do you?'

'No!' I'd snapped. Seriously, *as if.* Why would he even say that?

It's almost midnight by the time I climb into bed, where I rub my toes against the sheets to warm them, then flip the duvet up and under my feet to form a quilted cocoon. Snuggled, I flick through @MyEmptyHouses. My search for her post on the house in Good Hope Wood is accompanied by the rise and fall of Rosa and Noah's tender bickering.

While the words themselves are made indecipherable by the dividing wall, it doesn't take a genius to figure out that Rosa will be telling Know-All he's not helping himself – or his chances of a successful Oxford interview – by burning the candle at both ends. She will say this quietly and calmly because her quiet and calm nature is what makes my stepmother the Linchpin. Maybe it's all that bending and breathing she does on her rolled-out mat each morning. Maybe when she's holding that standing tree pose, it's not only her physical balance she's honing. I swear that woman never wobbles.

Footsteps make their way upstairs then the house falls silent.

There's nothing on @MyEmptyHouses about a creepy man-creature. I add a note in the comments, warning other explorers to take care, then click the link to a post on her website about the oddest items she's found in her five years of explorations. I look at each photo in turn. A pair of brand-new red stilettoes in a disused dentist's office. A frog specimen in a deserted uni building. A rabbit masquerade mask, leaning against a brightly wallpapered wall—

Wait.

What?

I zoom in on the rabbit mask. Its grey-brown tufted ears. Its empty eyes. Its black-nosed snout and its silver ribbon tie that's the exact same colour as the ribbons Mum once unspooled and braided through my hair. It's not only the ribbon that's familiar, though.

My ponytail – fading to violet from the vibrant purple I dyed it at the beginning of term – irritates my eyes as I lean over the side of my bed and reach under for my Box of Mum Things. I pull out the small black photograph album on which Mum silver-Sharpied our names in her loopy handwriting that always reminds me of those aeroplanes that write messages in the sky.

There are four photos. I only need one of them. It's of Mum and me when I was about five. We're with another woman and an auburn-haired girl I assume is the other woman's daughter. The two grown-ups are wearing masks.

Mum is a wolf.

Her friend is a rabbit.

And not just any rabbit but the exact same rabbit as the one in @MyEmptyHouses' photo, in which the mask sits on a mantelpiece, resting against what looks like bold-patterned wallpaper. It's not paper, though. It's paint. And I know this because I watched my mum's long fingers dip her brush in the palette of greens and browns and turn liquid into a wild forest on our drawing-room wall.

There's a link beneath @MyEmptyHouses' photo. When I click on it, it takes me to her original post from when she explored the place about a year ago.

Thing is, it's almost seven years since Mum died in the fire. I'm no maths genius but even I know the numbers don't add up. @MyEmptyHouses found the mask about six years after I was told that our house and all the things in it were burned to dust and gone.

The post is titled Rabbit House.

That's not what Mum and I called it.

To us it was Sunnyside.

It was home.

Three

It's a good thing it's Buddy, my favourite of all my canine clients, that I'm booked to walk this morning. His giant poodle pom-pom tail and enthusiastic pant make our 6.30 a.m. tramp about town kind of fun. My sleep-deprived mood is also helped by the ten quid I'll be pocketing. Each pound I earn takes me closer to those plans I've hatched in a notebook dedicated to my gap-year explorations. The thought of that Mediterranean sun softens the biting British cold.

I like this time of day, when the shops are closed, there are few people and the buildings themselves might talk to me. Some, with their small windows and medieval black-and-white exteriors, are reassuringly old, safe, permanent. While others, the ones with a blank facade and lifeless vast panels of glass, are more inclined to ignore whatever I might want to say.

I don't know what I want to say this morning.

Words like 'rabbit' and 'Sunnyside' and 'fire' and 'what the actual—' barged and barrelled their way into my brain last night, as earwormy as any of Taylor Swift's most annoying hits. As I walk, they're still going. Slippery and squirming from my head through my spine so my entire body's riddled with question marks.

'You OK, Iris?' As is his habit, Mr West is already standing on his front step, leaning against his cane, as Buddy and I make our way up the drive. 'You seem a tad out of sorts.'

'Pushed for time, that's all.' I shrug and hand over the lead. 'Tala's birthday!'

'Best get on then,' he says, his arthritic fingers ruffling Buddy's ears.

I hurry back home where I've left a bunch of handmade paper flowers for my best friend.

'Happy birthday!' I sing fifteen minutes later when Tala answers her front door.

She has no choice but to take the posy I shove a little too enthusiastically in her face. Despite the hours I spent following instructional videos on YouTube, the flowers look more withering weed than Britain in Bloom.

'Um, thanks?'

She ushers me inside as I garble on about how maaaaaybeeee I was a little ambitious gunning for a bouquet of eighteen roses as a nod to the traditional Filipino debut party Tala's mum had wanted to throw in celebration of her only child's imminent womanhood. Tala, usually so compliant, had refused.

'I know you said you'd rather stick eighteen thorns in your eyes than have eighteen boys presenting you with eighteen roses in exchange for a poxy dance, but I thought a paper version from me would be kind of cute.' It doesn't matter how many times I fail so dismally at craft, prior to every one of my creative endeavours, I'm cocksure I'll *finally* exhibit some of Mum's artistic genius. 'Given how they've turned out, you're probably relieved I didn't make it to eighteen!'

Tala raises the three would-be flowers higher and, for a moment, I think she might actually sniff them, her nostrils filling with the waft of my abundant use of glue. Instead, she takes a closer look at one of the petals, mouthing the words 'second' and 'chances' and 'remake' and 'world' printed on one of the leaves that were, before I cut and folded them, pages from her favourite book. '*I'll Give You the Sun*,' she whispers, and I swear to God she's now one hundred per cent crying.

I nod, my bobbing chin ruffling her centre parting as she throws herself at me for a hug. 'You might be shedding different kinds of tears if you saw how badly I butchered the novel.' Books are sacrosanct to Tala, who winces if someone so much as dares turn over a corner to mark their place.

'Forgiven,' she says into my collarbone. 'As friends go, you're my superlative.'

'Champorado, Iris?' Tala's mum calls from the kitchen, where, when we walk through from the hall, I see she's already dished me up a bowl of chocolate rice porridge and is now pouring me a glass of juice. She places both down on the table next to the small silver Christmas tree that's been a centrepiece since October.

'So long as there's a "ber" in the month, we're celebrating Christmas,' Tita Celestina said the first time I came to their house over seven years ago and she saw my jaw drop at the twinkling lights, multiple-baubled trees and three stockings hanging above the fire. It was September.

For now, mine and Tala's houses couldn't look more different. Hers is a festival of multicoloured ribbon and tinsel, while ours is a palette of magnolia and grey.

It was Rosa who suggested we postpone our celebrations. She and Dad got together as the first anniversary of Mum's death was approaching, and while it was only a month or so into their relationship, it was clear they were hoping we would spend the holidays together. But whenever anyone mentioned pantomimes, presents or trees, Dad would flinch.

'We could delay it,' she said. 'Just until Boxing Day, so Iris can commemorate her mum on the day she died.'

'What!?' Noah, who with his facts about black holes, beasts and bridges was already fast becoming Know-All, didn't look impressed. 'Not have Christmas on Christmas Day? But what would we do then?'

Rosa shot him a look that suggested maybe he could spend the day finding a smidge of empathy.

'I don't mind,' I said. 'I'll celebrate Mum on the seventeenth.' I stuffed a roast potato in my mouth like all of this was no big deal. The idea didn't come completely out of the blue. In fact, it came out of a conversation with Tala who, when I'd told her I'd been staying with Dad on the day of the fire, asked me what I remembered from the last time I'd seen my mum.

The question sparked a heart leap. There was a lot to remember. Too much. So I zoned in on the bit that shone brightest.

I remembered Mum's excitement. How she'd dashed inside for a wooden box that she passed to me through the wound-down car window.

'Pick,' she'd said then, arms fully stretched, hands holding out the paper fortune teller she'd made me a few weeks before.

I picked *pink*.

And I picked *two*.

She lifted the flap. 'You will be strong.' She'd reached inside the car, let the fortune teller fall into the box on my lap and stroked my hand. 'I love you, Iris. This separation isn't forever. But our love is, OK?'

That's what I wanted to remember. Not a fire or anything anything anything else.

So it was those words and that day that I chose to commemorate.

Each 17th December, Tala and I go to the bothy, where we light candles and hang flowers in Kilner jars from a tree. We eat cream cheese bagels because they were Mum's favourite, and sometimes a fat-bellied robin waits patiently on the ground beside us for crumbs. The following day, Rosa puts up our decorations.

'Always with the stories!' The drama with which Tita Celestina sweeps Tala's book from the table snaps me back into the present. 'Sit, sit!' She gestures at the chair while reminding her daughter of the importance of eighteenth birthdays in Filipino culture. 'You're a woman now, Tala.' She reads the blurb on the back of the novel before dropping it a tad dismissively on the kitchen island. 'Maybe that means you start your own romance rather than just reading about them!' Tita Celestina glows at the thought of it. 'Like Iris and her boyfriend KitKat.'

'KitKat?'

'KitKat?'

'It's *Rollo*, Mama.' Tala's talking to Tita Celestina but glaring at me, waiting for the whir that comes with her mum pressing the button on the coffee machine. 'All hail the Queen of

Romance,' she says, arching her perfectly manicured brow. And if it wasn't her birthday, I'd be asking my best mate why it is she's always so flummoxed by the Dumbbells when she's so able to summon ample sarcasm with me.

The Dumbbells, FYI, are what, back in Year Eight, Tala and I (perhaps childishly) called the girls at school who (perhaps dickishly) called themselves the Belles. As in the beautiful ones. As in the bitches who nicknamed Tala 'Redmond' after our physics teacher, Mrs Parks, delivered a ten-minute impromptu lecture on the world's quietest room at the Microsoft headquarters in Redmond, Washington.

'You going to tell me what happened last night or what?' Tala pulls a reindeer-decorated vase from a cupboard and begins arranging her paper flowers. I know this trick. She thinks by making herself look busy, she'll also look like she's less desperate for answers and that I, as a consequence, will be more likely to spill the truth.

A flash of the man-creature. I blink away all the possibilities of whatever it was he was about to pull from his pocket.

'Nothing to tell,' I say, trying but failing to style it out when my spoonful of breakfast burns my top lip, and I'm left with both porridge and drool on my chin.

'What a babe!' Tala wipes me clean with a sheet of kitchen roll. 'I can see why Rollo was so distraught when you left.' She scrunches the dirtied paper and gives me a look, like, *come on, Iris, please*.

'Well, if it isn't the birthday girl and the intrepid explorer!' Perfectly timed to save me from any further interrogation, Kristian, Tala's dad, walks into the kitchen in the same way he walks into any room – like he thinks that everyone in it is important. (Unlike *my* dad who walks into any room like he thinks that everyone in it is about to die.) 'Iris, girl, we need to sort your fringe!' Without even pausing for his morning coffee, Kristian grabs his scissors from the drawer. There are definite perks to your best mate's parents not only being super chill but also the town's best hairdressers.

Tala snatches her book, I snatch my phone, and we both sit in silence – reading, scrolling – while Kristian snips, and splinter hairs fall across my face.

An Insta alert tells me @SuCasaEsMiCasa has replied to the warning I posted last night.

Stupid bint. What do idiot girls expect going to these bandos alone?

I know that prick. He's been boasting on various urbex platforms about some epic Christmas party he's planning. This morning, his pathetically sexist comment is the only change on @MyEmptyHouses' website. Each of the times I've flicked through it, everything else has remained exactly the same. And yet my fingers can't help but refresh the page, and my eyes can't help but lock on to that image of the rabbit mask leaning against the hand-painted wall.

Last year.

@MyEmptyHouses was there last year.

I flit to the contact page and, in a brief email, ask @MyEmptyHouses would she, even though it kind of breaks the urbex code, just as a one-off, share its location. Or at least confirm it was close to Edglington, which was where Mum and I used to live.

Porridge churns in my belly.

Who knew oats could be so razored and raw.

Kristian brushes away the hairs from my face and the floor and disappears into the utility room, where he and Tita Celestina begin folding and bagging the gowns they've laundered to take back to the salon.

'Tal,' I say, rising from my chair. 'I found thi—'

But when she looks up at me, my best friend is crying. Not the glistening, sentimental tears of before but a rush of boggy wet that reddens her amber eyes. 'You found what?' she asks, wiping her nose on the sleeve of her grey-knit jumper.

'Doesn't matter.' I slide my phone into my back pocket. 'Just some stupid meme.' I nod at the closed book. 'Did someone die or what?'

She flattens her palm and uses it to push the novel away. 'No one died.' Her cry is more of a snivel now. 'They got together, fell in love, had sex, split up and got back together again. Same old same old story.'

'Is your mama on to something, Tal?' I push her hair away from her wet face. 'Now you're eighteen, is it time for you to find true lurve?'

She shakes her head.

'Well, what's got you so blue then?'

'You wouldn't get it.'

'I wouldn't get it? Why?'

She mumbles something indecipherable amid the clatter of glasses and bowls.

'What was that?'

'I said, "You only have one emotional setting."' The way Tala says it this time makes it dead clear. 'I'm sorry.' She softens. Everything about her droops as I follow her into the hall.

'One emotional setting?' I turn down my lips in mock sorrow. 'Bit harsh.'

'You think? It doesn't matter what happens to you: you fail a test, you end a relationship, the Dumbbells make some stupid remark. Whatever. You're so bloody…I dunno…stoic.' She passes me my purple puffer jacket that perfectly matches hers. 'Life must be so much less stressful when you can cope with whatever it throws at you.'

~~The acid snarls and scalds my stomach.~~

I shrug my shoulders, pull on my coat, kiss Tala on the cheek and smile.

Four

Last lesson before lunch, and the combo of a late night and early morning plus a stuffy English language classroom means I'm flagging. Not even the enthusiasm of everyone's favourite word geek, Mr Spence, is enough to hold my attention. But my droopy eyes snap open when a girl I vaguely recognize as a Year Eleven prefect waltzes through the door and announces in a soap-operatic tone that there's an administrative emergency in the staffroom.

'Seems we're finishing early.' Mr Spence looks genuinely gutted to be cutting our discussion on language as an indicator of personal and social identity short. 'Do feel free to continue the conversation until the bell.' He adjusts his black-framed glasses and gives us an optimistic nod of his neatly bearded chin as he exits the room.

'And don't forget revision plans.' Mr Spence has to shout over the noise that erupted in the nanosecond before he stuck his head back through the door. 'January might seem a long way off but it's nearly December and, believe you me, kids, with all that mocks prep to be getting on with, the next month is gonna fly.' His eyes land on me and his brow arches, like, *yes, you, Iris*. And I'm reminded of those occasional pep talks he likes to give me, using phrases like 'need to apply yourself' and 'just had a little more focus' and 'think about what university course will lead you into your chosen career'.

Chosen career? The only thing I want to choose is which abandoned chateau I'm going to visit first once I get the hell out of school.

There's a collective groan as Mr Spence leaves for the second and final time, and the class is faced with the realization of a Christmas holidays without much ho-ho-ho.

'Whatever,' I shrug, turning to Tala, who I know will be plotting a study timetable in her diary, pausing only to tell me things are getting serious now, and I need to stop winging it and instead start getting prepared.

Funny thing is, Tala's not. Planning, I mean. She's not even taken her diary from her bag. Rather, she's all eyes on Dougie, who's weaving his way between the desks and handing out flyers for a poetry night he's started up with some of his highfalutin mates in town. My bet is it's not just his Hawaiian shirt that's captured Tala's gaze. It's flamingo pink today. At least that's the predominant colour, which, by the time Dougie slides up next to Tala, isn't far off the shade of his suspiciously flushed skin.

'Hey.' Dougie's grin is magnetic. 'That poetry slam we talked about?' He tucks his shoulder-length curls behind his ears and hands her a flyer.

Tala takes the glossy paper.

'You should come,' Dougie says. 'I'm signing. You know…' He taps his right index finger to his chest, then presses a full palm to it twice before pointing that same finger at Tala. Her black hair falls in long curtains across her face as she dips her head, taking far longer than is necessary to read the details on the flyer.

I make the conscious decision to give them a little privacy. Not by giving them actual privacy, that would be madness. Rather, half listening, I open my email on my phone, repeatedly checking the inbox and junk. Nothing. I could just ask Dad about Sunnyside when I get home. There must be a rational explanation. I mean, he's the Stickler; there's *always* a rational explanation.

With Mum things were different. Things were untamed and lively and colourful. I know this because it says so in the journal Tala gave me to match her own. We were eleven, not long friends, but still, she'd dared to read me a poem she'd written about her cat.

'Tancred.' She showed me a photograph of a fat tabby. 'He was run over,' she said. 'But I wanted to remember other things about him too. Better things than the accident.' So Tala wrote about Tancred coming in through the cat flap with a greeting that sounded not like a fat tabby meowing but like a wiry human calling hello.

A few days later, when we were in French and supposed to be learning the days of the week (I was stuck on *mardi*), Tala slipped me something under the table. It was a notebook. *To remember the better things*, she'd written on the inside sleeve.

And I got it, why she wanted me to fill the pages with all the happy memories of Mum so I could carry those with me instead of the fact of the fire.

This rose-tinted take on life fitted with Dad's plan too. Because, seven months after Mum died, when we were about to leave our old town for our new town, he showed me the estate agent's pictures of our new home, empty of furniture and sadness. And he said that we'd be happy there, that things would be OK.

'The slam's next Tuesday. You can come too, if you like.' Dougie's looking at me now, though it's clear from his tone that I'm simply an accessory to Tala.

Usually I'd be nudging Tala's knee and elbow, like, *go on, girl, this clearly isn't only about poetry*, but the number of unread emails on my phone's home screen has just risen by one.

Shit.

'The first night's just a practice run really for a bigger date we're planning later this month.'

Dougie's voice fades to black.

@MyEmptyHouses has replied.

Hey @DoratheUrbexplorer, nice grid!

So... Rabbit House. I was there last year. GREAT location. All but one room almost perfectly intact. You know the kind of place where it feels like the people who lived there had just popped out to the shop for some Cheetos or something.

The kitchen looked like there'd been a fire. Nothing major. It's a safe bando. Structurally fine.

Found the mask in the bedside drawer. Put it back (obvs!!).

Rule #1: Take nothing but photos, leave nothing but footprints.

Rule #2: Don't disclose locations.

But yeah, Edglington. I'll give you that much. ✌

What had been a pummelling thud in my chest is now a swell of cramping heat and clamour in my head.

'Iris?' Tala's waving Dougie's flyer in my face. 'You OK?'

'Yep.' I take the flyer, staring at the sketch of a mouth and a microphone in an attempt to press the image of those typed words 'there'd been a fire. Nothing major' from my skull. Then, 'Yes,' I say, because 'yep' was too clipped or too curt or too unlike me. Because didn't Tala say, only this morning, that I am stoic and able to cope with whatever life throws at me?

Dougie's still hanging on for a response from Tala, when Evie Byrne, Queen of the Dumbbells, wisecracks about them being the perfect match.

'I mean, *he's* deaf, and *Redmond's* practically mute,' she squarks. Her eyes land on her crony Angeline, who obediently smirks at the jibe.

Tala's gaze drops straight to the floor.

Dougie, however, broadens and turns to Evie, their faces square on. 'Even if my hearing aids were off, your pathetic bullying would be abundantly clear.'

'Dougie sure knows how to handle the Dumbbells,' I say, once the girls with the venomous tongues have cleared, and Tala and I are heading to the canteen for lunch. 'Clapbacks like that are known to ignite a crush in a girl…'

Tala's brow furrows so deep you could almost wedge a pen in it. 'Don't.' She stands at the food counter, looking at the menu even though all either of us ever has is a baked potato. 'I've told you before,' she says as the dinner lady ladles on baked beans, 'I don't think of Dougie like that. And anyway –' she tips her head forward and lowers her voice – 'you know

I'm not sure how I feel about, you know…' She mouths the next word: '*sex*.'

'I'll tell you how you should feel about sex,' I say when we're sitting at a table and chugging on deliciously cold cans of Coke.

She scans the room as if scouting for eavesdroppers. 'Not *now*, Iris. Not *here*.'

But I can't help myself. 'I'm not saying I'm an expert or anything, but Rollo and I did get pretty good at—'

'Yeah, speaking of Rollo…'

I eye-roll my own school-girl error. 'Walked straight into that one.'

'And straight out of his bedroom, from what he told me.'

I pick at the grated cheese. 'He said he wanted to come with me. *On my gap year!*'

'And?'

'And it's too much, Tala. Too soon. Why would he want to go and explore abandoned chateaus when he's not even into urbex?'

She gives me this sarky shrug. 'I dunno, maybe because he's into *you*.'

'Next thing he'll be wanting to go Instagram Official.' I literally shiver at the thought of it. That sick feeling lurches even harder as my brain plays word association and takes me straight from Instagram to @MyEmptyHouses to Rabbit House.

'Tal,' I say, reaching into my bag for my phone to show her what I've discovered, but Dougie's sliding into the seat next to her, his tray laden with something that's not a baked potato, though what it actually *is* remains unclear. I tuck the phone and my secrets away for later.

40

'Well, that looks disgusting,' Tala says, and I almost choke on my Coke because when does Tala ever strike up a conversation?

'Maybe you should write a poem about it.' Dougie pokes his fork into the stodge that resembles a long-overused washing-up sponge. 'You did say how you were bored of poems banging on about love.'

When did Tala say that? Not that I'm her keeper or anything, but I generally know almost every word that spills from the girl's mouth.

Or at least I thought I did.

'I'd rather write it than eat it.' She grimaces as Dougie takes a bite of what may or may not be an omelette. 'Though I'm not sure I want that muck as my muse.'

'I'll leave you two to it.' I get to my feet. 'The library beckons.' Tala looks like I've just announced I'm off to Mars. 'My geography assignment's due right after lunch and I've not even started it yet.' She shakes her head. 'Birthday cake at the bothy later, though, yeah?'

'Sure.' Tala nods. 'I'll pick you up if you like?'

'Cool. Just remember what your mama said this morning?' I give her the wide-eye and dip my head towards Dougie. 'You're a woman now, yeah?'

She disappears behind her wall of hair. 'See you at five.'

Five

When my geography teacher, Mrs Doughty, spied the half-page effort from my hour in the library this afternoon, she delivered a speech about my lack of discipline when it comes to assignments. Her voice was so booming it silenced the previously chatty class.

'As much as I admire your explorations of our local landscapes, Iris, I do fear this extra-curricular passion of yours is becoming too much of a distraction.' To be fair, she wasn't wrong. Only today it wasn't images of the Lucchini Steelworks in Italy, or the Stora Enso Paper Mill in France that wound their way into my head but somewhere closer to home. It's still there now, as sharp as the pang in my lungs from the cold on the walk from school.

When I come into my room, the air is laden with the forced heat of radiators that Know-All cranks up high when no one else is home. He'll either be studying or hunched over his large table that houses all those Lego buildings he pains over. Hours spent sorting, sizing, stacking little blocks into churches, houses and shops. All that effort to make a whole other world. And yet he so rarely ventures out into the real one.

I go straight to the thermostat at the bottom of the stairs and turn it down before opening my window, because the air, otherwise, is too thick with the sweet balsamic scent of lavender. Like the pale walls, abstract art and neat plump cushions on the sofa, Rosa's electric aroma diffuser is a key element in her careful curation of calm.

Sunnyside was a rainbow jungle with frayed and crayon-stained carpets. Our drawings were Blu-Tacked to the walls.

I thought it was gone.

Dad *told* me Sunnyside was gone. He said there'd been a fire and Mum had died. Later, when I asked if we could go to the house to collect more of my things, his arms, which were wrapped around me, went from curled and bendy to straight and stiff. Like those slap bands my school friends and I would smack around our wrists in the playground, but in reverse.

We didn't go.

Dad and I never went to Sunnyside again.

Poof!

Just like that it disappeared.

And yet.

@MyEmptyHouses was at Sunnyside a year ago when she photographed a homemade mask and a hand-painted wall. Neither looks like they were so much as licked by fire.

When I pull yesterday's discarded T-shirt from the bedside table, where it landed after I yanked it off last night, the revealed clock says 4 p.m.

Time enough.

Sprawled out on the carpet, I imagine Rosa's face if she saw the horde of what I like to call 'miscellaneous items' beneath my bed. My curation's just different to hers, that's all. It's not like I don't know where everything is. See, right between the

43

box of Mum's ashes and the basket of *Dora the Explorer* merch I collected in a misplaced frenzy when I first came up with my Insta handle, is the Box of Mum Things. I slide it out and put it on my bed.

One by one, I remove the following:

A single silver key.

An angel Christmas-tree topper

A photograph album with four pictures.

1 Mum and me in the garden when I was a baby. Mum is holding me as she sits on the swing. Her smile is as big as the sky.

2 Mum with her own mother when she was a kid, perched on the stone doorstep of the rambling old farmhouse she and I later lived in. Sunnyside.

3 Mum and me on a beach next to a sandcastle half swallowed by the sea.

4 The Wolf-Mum and Rabbit-stranger with their daughters. On the back is a note written in felt-tip pen: S, I love this photo so much I had a copy made for both of us. B x

I hold the physical photo next to @MyEmptyHouses' photo, which I saved to my phone.

B?

Who is she?

What does she know about Sunnyside?

About that rabbit mask?

About Mum?

In the picture, the top half of their faces are concealed by the masks, but the love B and Mum have for each other is shiny in their eyes and scribbled in their smiles.

The last item in the box is the paper fortune teller Mum made me. I barely touch it these days. After too much handling when I was younger, the folds thinned and softened, and so I made copies instead, worried that under the pressure of my fingers, the original might collapse or tear.

I do look at it, though. Every week, on a Sunday night usually, when I take out the Box of Mum Things. Each of the objects inside is like a shell on a beach that preserves the sound of the sea. I hear her, see her, smell her and know that she loved me. That she – even now – makes me strong.

I put everything carefully back inside and slide it under my bed. I then head outside to the recycling, where I rummage through the paper-and-cardboard bin for a shoebox I saw Know-All chuck after he'd tried on the Adidas trainers Rosa bought him to mellow the formality of his university-interview suit.

'What the fuck!' A shout from the kitchen.

Know-All is trying to shunt an intruder cat from the countertop with the end of a broom.

He pokes again.

The animal responds with a hiss and a baring of teeth.

'You *know* we can't leave the utility door open.' Know-All's right, of course. After the mog snuck in a third time with the sole purpose of wreaking some kind of feline havoc, Dad flipped and his no-pets rule was even further set in stone.

'Mum's plant!' Know-All's practically shrieking as his nemesis paws Rosa's treasured flowerpot.

Ever since she and Dad moved in together only a few months after he and I left Edglington, it's been a long-running joke that my stepmum can't keep anything green alive. Until this year, that is. Her one healthy yucca takes pride of place on the kitchen windowsill.

'He's going to eat it!' The way Know-All's grimacing, you'd think we were at that gruesome point in the Attenborough show when the hatchling iguana's being chased by snakes.

I lift the cat off the work surface and chuck him outside. 'That,' I say, pointing at Know-All's fingers, which he's turned into shutters for his eyes because he couldn't bear to watch, 'is why you need to get out more. How you going to cope at uni if you can't handle one little pussy?'

Know-All's chin doubles as he retracts his head. 'Classy as ever, I see.'

'Nothing wrong with a bit of pussy,' I say. 'We've reclaimed it, don't you know?'

My stepbrother doesn't look so sure, but we talked about it at school. How words that were once so shocking can evolve and, in the right mouth in the right company, become something we're comfortable using. How time and context make them OK.

'If you ventured out to play a bit more, your vast knowledge might include such real-life nuggets.'

Back in my room, I put the shoebox on my desk and take out some scissors, paper and Sharpies.

I've been wondering if Tala's tears this morning were less because she was moved by the sentiment of the flowers and more that she was appalled by their poor execution. This is take two then. A second chance to show my friend just how wonderful I think she is.

The clock tells me I have forty minutes to get this job done before Tala arrives to take me to the bothy.

Unsurprisingly, it was Know-All who told me the bothy is a bothy. A few years back, during one of our more agreeable moments, he'd asked where I was off to and, for once, I saw fit to give him an answer.

'Here,' I said, pulling up the photo I'd taken there the previous week. It was spring, and in the picture, Tala was on the swing beneath a bloom of blossom on the tree.

'It's a bothy,' Know-All said with his usual you-must-be-stupid-if-you-don't-know-this tone. 'Basic accommodation. For gardeners or similar kinds of workers on an estate. They're often left unlocked for walkers or—'

'Are you ever *not* this boring?' I'll admit, it came off a little cruel, but you try living with the guy. Dad and Rosa thought us being the same age was a blessing, but the fact that there's only two months between us has always made Know-All's pedantry even more infuriating.

Tala's present complete, I pop into the kitchen for low-key party supplies and find Know-All, Dad and Rosa enjoying a cosy afternoon tea for three. Dad puts down the practice interview questions he'd found online to check where I am headed and with who.

'Whom,' Know-All corrects, and maybe I'm imagining

things, but it feels like there is a collective inhale, as if it's not just me who's biting my tongue.

'The bothy. With Tala.'

It might be a bando but, since he came to check it out for himself a few years ago, Dad's been pretty chill about the bothy. I swear though, when he sees me grab a box of matches from the shit-drawer, his face blanches to the palest shade of white on that paint chart Rosa agonized over when they decorated the hall.

'For Tala's birthday cake.' I waggle the solitary candle I've nabbed too.

He doesn't look convinced.

'Jesus, Dad. You don't have to wrap me in kid gloves, I'm sevente—'

'Cotton wool,' Know-All butts in.

'Huh?'

'Wrap you in cotton wool. Or handle you with you with kid gloves.' Could my stepbrother look any more superior? 'You were mixing your idioms.'

'Oh, fuc—'

'Iris!' Unsurprisingly, Dad's not keen on swearing. 'I'm not wrapping you in anything, I'm just thinking of your future. These places you go to. It's trespassing. What if you're arrested?'

'Unlikely, Matt.'

Dad turns to Know-All, who taps one of his A-level law books, which is, as usual, taking up far too much space on the table.

'Trespass itself is not a criminal offence.' Know-All takes a bite of his apple then deigns to elaborate. (Nice use of 'deigns',

48

Iris.) 'You can't actually be arrested for trespass. And trespassing alone would never result in a criminal record. It's only if Iris starts pinching things from the sites she visits that she'd have a problem. Then it's theft.' He takes another bite. How can the way someone eats an apple be *that* cocky? 'That said, we all know how desperate she is for cash for her gap year. Maybe theft *is* part of her bigger plan.'

'Just because *they* –' I cast a dejected look at Dad and Rosa – 'are very happy to plough thousands into *your* university fees but refuse to financially support *my* alternative learning experience, i.e. travel, doesn't mean I'd resort to crime. Why do you think I'm out walking dogs in the freezing cold all the time?'

He shrugs.

'It's called a sense of entrepreneurship, loser.'

'A step up from your usual sense of entitlement.'

'Seriously!' Rosa throws her hands up in the air, which is the closest she ever comes to losing her temper. 'Can you two not be together for more than a few seconds without bickering?'

I know it's peace she's after, but I'm not letting this slide. 'What is your obsession with the idea that everything goes my way?' I flare at Know-All. 'The fact that I have to walk dogs for money isn't the only thing that proves your theory nonsense. The obvious lack of my own dog is surely evidence that I don't always get what I want.'

'A dog is a big responsibility, sunshine.' Cue Dad's Stickler voice. Here we go, I've heard it all a million times before.

It's a relief, then, when Tala rings the doorbell, and I have an excuse to leave.

Dad follows me to the porch, waving to Tala, who shouts *hi* while dramatically miming how cold she is, before darting back to the warmth of her car.

'Iris?' Dad calls. 'Don't you have something you want to ask me before you go?'

I clench my hands around the shoebox so tight it's like my knuckle bones will burst through my skin.

Can he feel my confusion about Sunnyside vibrating between us?

Does he have answers he's able or willing to share?

I heard him one night in the weeks after Mum died, crying on the phone, telling whoever it was on the other end of the line that he didn't know what to do with all my questions. All my sadness. 'I can't bear it.' His voice was the sea in a storm. Wet and grey and unpredictable. 'To see Iris so unhappy. She wants to know things…but I can't…I don't… How could I?' He crashed. 'It's breaking my fucking heart.'

I was ten. The only body part I should have been breaking was an arm in a push-bike accident or an ankle on a trampoline. They would at least have been my own body parts. And the only reason for their snap would have been because I was having too much fun.

I didn't want to break Dad's heart, especially his 'fucking' one. He was so distraught with everything that had happened that he sounded not just woeful but really *really* angry too.

Anyway, we built a new life in a new town and we bought a new house, where we soon lived with Dad's new girlfriend and my new stepbrother. And everything now smells of lavender and, despite the bickering, we all try our best to get along.

All those years ago, he was determined to make my life so safe. So predictable. We both understood, then, that we would never really talk about Sunnyside. Or Mum.

And yet.

'Don't you have something you want to ask me, Iris?' he repeats.

I turn to Dad.

'Your curfew,' he says, tapping his watch. 'We were going to review it? Don't you want to know what time I expect you home?'

Of course.

The question – the one I really wanted answering – unspools from my tongue to the pavement as I run to the car.

Six

You'd think, from the number of times we've been to the bothy – almost once a week since we discovered it on our first unsupervised bike ride when we were thirteen – that Tala and I would know each tree, each stone by heart. But there's something different every time we come. Tonight, it's the oak with the swing. In the snatches of torchlight, its grasping branches look laden with hundreds of bruise-black shadows in place of leaves.

Inside, we stand our torches on their ends, casting yellow strips of light up the stone walls towards the low, panelled ceiling where delicate threads of spiderwebs are loaded with grungy clouds of clustered dust and long-dead flies.

Tala's already rolling the numbers in the padlock we keep on Tita Celestina's solid old suitcase that holds all our bothy supplies. She was going to ditch it after her annual visit to the Philippines last summer, when she realized a ninety-one-litre capacity wasn't enough for the pasalubong she needed to take out for her family and all the dried fish she needed to bring home for herself.

'Pasalubong,' Tala explained, 'is a big freakin' deal. Anyone returning to the Philippines does so armed with chocolate, clothes, toys, perfume. My family goes cray cray for things from abroad. And Mama loves to take them.'

'More and more of them!' Kristian rolled his eyes at the British treasures Tita Celestina had already begun stockpiling on their dining table several months ahead of her trip.

The rejected case was plenty big enough for our bothy essentials – blankets, magazines, snack bars, hand sanitizer, torches, notebook and pens – which are kept safe from the cold, the damp and the vermin that scurry across the bothy when we're not here.

Tala strikes a match and puts it to five tealights in jam jars, which she places in a neat line on the floor.

I lay down two thick picnic blankets. In the centre I place the fish and chips we picked up on the way, two cans of Coke and a raspberry oat slice from our favourite café, The Vault, with a single candle wedged into its almond-flaked top. After Maltesers, it's Tala's go-to treat.

Tala sits down next to me, spreads a tartan throw across our knees.

'Happy birthday!' I plonk the shoebox in her lap.

'More craft?'

'Oi! No need for that tone. You said you liked the roses.'

'I love them.' She uses the flashlight on her phone to read the label I stuck to the outside of this second gift. 'Tala's Best Bits?'

'Yeah. What does your name mean, Tala?'

She looks at me like I should be wearing a dunce hat instead of a beanie because we've been over this. How in Tagalog – the official language of the Philippines – Tala means bright star.

'Ipso facto, you shine!'

Tala removes the lid and takes out the pieces of paper I cut so carefully earlier. 'Winning a poetry comp when I was fourteen?'

53

She reads one of the little sheets, laughing at my stick-man interpretation of her holding a trophy and quill. She moves on to the next. 'Passing my driving test first time?' And then the next. 'Doing a handstand for thirty seconds straight.'

'I couldn't manage eighteen paper roses, but I could manage eighteen moments of your brilliant life. Obviously, you have way more successes, but my wrist was aching from all the poor drawing.'

'The drawing is *not* poor.' But then she sees the sketch I made of her reprimanding this kid in the park who thought it was funny to pull the legs off a spider. In the picture, the spider looks like a squashed blueberry and the boy looks like a potato. 'OK, a bit poor,' she concedes. But she's smiling. Like, really smiling.

'When the Dumbbells make you feel small, I want you to remember how much I love you.' I unwrap the fish and chips as she puts her best bits back in the box. 'I could have done another eighteen, and another. You really are amazing, Tal.' I know what's coming next. Our mutual appreciation has followed the same pattern since we were in Year Seven.

'No, *you're* amazing.'

The purple polyester of our matching winter puffers makes our hug a bit slippy, but it's just a good excuse to hold on tighter.

'You're amazinger.'

Tighter.

'You're the amazingest.'

Tight.

She pulls away from me and pokes her tiny wooden fork into a chip, which she dips in the ketchup she's squeezed from the too-small packet on the side of her plate. 'Without you, Iris, I'm just a subordinate clause.'

'Huh?'

'I need you. I don't make sense on my own.'

'That's the most romantic thing anyone has ever said to me.'

A moth throws itself repeatedly against the outside of the bothy window. I never understand why they put their fragile wings at such risk for a clearly unobtainable light.

She cuts off a bit of the battered fish and pops it in my mouth. 'I'm serious. You prop me up.'

A few minutes later, when our bellies are full but we've both agreed we probably have just enough room for pudding, I'm about to light her birthday candle and Tala coughs. Twice. I blow out the match and hold off on the whole 'Happy Birthday' song. I know this cough of hers; it's what she does when she's gearing up to say something.

'Iris,' she says.

'Yeeees.'

'Should we talk about Rollo?'

'KitKat, you mean?'

Tala shakes her head. 'Poor Mama.'

'Nothing poor about her, I think she was right.'

Tala looks utterly confused.

'What does the advert say you do with a KitKat?'

She shrugs.

'You have a break!'

'Lame, Iris.' She nods at the box of matches, like, *get lighting then.*

I take another one out and am about to strike it—

'So you're just on a break then?'

I fling the unlit match into the air in faux exasperation.

Rollo and I are *not* on a break. We are kaput. I told him as much this morning and then again this afternoon when he sent me yet another message asking if we could *please* just talk. I'd always thought the biggest bonus of our age gap was that Rollo was more mature than other guys I've been with. But today I realized how grateful I am for the fact he left school a couple of years back, which means his efforts of reconciliation are at least limited to the phone.

'Tala. Enough with the questions already. Do you want me to do this –' I point at the candle – 'or what?'

'What.' Like that was actually an option. 'You're the one who always tells me I need to be more outspoken,' she says when I exhale a testy sigh.

'As Mr Spence reminded us at the beginning of term, unlike a subordinate clause, a main clause is not dependent, it's complete in itself. It handles all the necessary information alone. I'm a main clause, Tal. I don't want to sound harsh, but I'm good enough on my own. I just don't need Rollo.'

'Sometimes I think you don't really need me either.' Her eyes are like Buddy the poodle's when I take away his ball. She lifts the raspberry oat slice from the plate, pulls out the never-lit candle and takes a bite.

'Oi, greedy!' I grab it from her before she scoffs the lot, and Tala laughs. Only it's not her usual laugh. The nub of joy in it is as small as the tiny, almost imperceptible tap of the match when it hit the flagstone floor.

I scroll through Spotify, looking for a particular track. 'It's your birthday, and you know what that means…'

She looks at me, like, *really, you want to conga? Now?*

I do. 'It's tradition!' One inherited from Tala's German father and Filipino mother, who discovered the conga when they met at a house party in Birmingham, New Year's Eve, 1999.

When I press play, though, Tala's not up on her feet like she normally would be, rather she's all head in her hands and tears.

'You know this is the third time you've cried today.'

'Sorry. It's just all of this…' She's flicking through her Box of Tala's Best Bits. 'I mean, it's such a lovely gesture, but…'

'But what?'

'But you,' she says. She puts the lid on the box like that's the end of it.

'*Me?*'

'Like Mama said, I'm supposed to be a woman now, whatever that means. But seriously, Iris, I wasn't joking when I said I'm a subordinate clause. I can't even summon the guts to put my hand up in class. We both know you do most of the talking for me.'

I could point out that actually Tala was pretty chatty with Dougie earlier but, as it's her birthday, I bite my tongue. 'I don't mind.' I sit back down next to her, elbow-nudge her side. 'That's what best friends are for.'

'Is it, though? Because you don't seem to need me the way I need you. You're so together. So sorted. Honestly, Iris, I swear you could pull off a conga even if you were the only one in the room.'

'Together? *Moi?*' I press my hands to my chest and

feign disbelief. I mean, she's probably right, but it wouldn't hurt to let Tala think I'm not as capable as I seem. Who knows, it might even help to have a second opinion. 'I'll have you know I've been in complete inner turmoil since Sunday.'

She sits bolt upright and goes hard on the eye to eye. 'I *knew* there was more to this thing with you and Rollo.'

'Not that.' I pass her my phone.

Tala studies @MyEmptyHouses' photo as I tell her about the masks Mum used to make in her workshop in the attic. How one day she'd be an owl, a few weeks later, she'd appear as a wolf, a deer, a swan…

'It's one of hers,' I say, zooming in on the rabbit, telling her how @MyEmptyHouses confirmed she took the picture at Sunnyside about a year ago.

'But Sunnyside was—'

'Burned to the ground?'

'There must be some mistake,' she says. 'You've asked your dad, right?'

I shrug and scrunch my face up into what can only be an, *erm, no*.

A beat later: 'Will you come with me? To Sunnyside?' This was *not* part of the plan. I hadn't even decided for sure that I was going to Sunnyside. And if I *do* go, well, bothy aside, I always prefer visiting bandos alone.

Sunnyside is *not* a bando.

No? Well, what is it then?

It's home.

'When?' Tala asks, licking the gem-bright bumps of raspberry from her fingers.

'Tomorrow.' The word makes the decision so done and dusted. 'I know you're not one for skipping school, but how about it?' I sweep the last almond flake from the plate with my thumb and offer it up by way of a bribe.

Tala doesn't often say no, but I can see from the way she's biting her lip, resisting the morsels, that she's totally torn.

'It's just…' She doesn't look at me, her attention is instead on the fish-and-chip wrapper that she's screwing into a ball. 'I don't want you running with the wrong idea and going off on one about me fulfilling Mama's romantic wishes because – as I keep saying – it really isn't like that with me and Dougie—'

'Dougie and me.'

I know, I know, this pretentiousness is more Know-All's style, but the English-language A level I only took so I'd have a class with Tala has really brought out the grammatical pedant in me.

'He's asked if I fancy working on some poetry stuff together tomorrow afternoon.'

Work on some poetry stuff together? I mean, *come on*, how can this possibly not lead to anywhere but lingering kisses by a babbling brook or whispering sweet nothings in a field of windswept corn?

'These slams he's doing in town sound really interesting…'

If you say so, Tal.

'It's just I've been writing again and…' Her voice drifts as she opens the calendar on her phone. 'Any other day, Iris, and I'll come. How about Saturday?'

'Let's just see, eh.' Is it wrong that I'm relieved she can't make it? 'It was just an idea. I might not even go.'

'You don't mind?'

'Course not.' Anything that helps my best mate overcome her relationship rut is one hundred per cent cool with me. 'Swing?' I ask. If she won't conga, the least she can do is help me soar. We made the swing ourselves from rope and wood, and when Know-All spotted it in the photo and said it was childish, I was sure then that he really didn't know everything because there is nothing wiser than reaching for the sky.

'In the dark?'

'Just quickly?' I'm already standing, pulling on my gloves. 'I'll push.'

Outside, the unkempt grass crunches with hard frost at its bottom; its wet tips lick long slicks on my jeans.

Tala's about to take a seat when something moves at the base of the tree.

A high-pitched birdsong trembles and we stop, dead still. 'Listen.'

'The robin?' Tala whispers, and I shrug. Because there is one that lives here. With its soft puffs of red feathers, it's a light-footed wisp of a creature who, in the daytime, flits, sweet and curious, about the branches, braving close encounters if there's even a slight chance of gathering food.

But isn't it a bit late? A bit dark?

Rosa, in her efforts to be at one with nature, has been reading about the common British garden and told us a few weeks ago that robins are often the first to sing in the morning and the last to sing at night.

'They stay in the same place all year round and sing to defend their territory.' Of course, Know-All just had to chip in.

'Not just their territory, Noah. They sing to defend their babies in the nest too.'

When Rosa said that, I thought of a slumber party Mum and I had in the living room one night. She inflated helium balloons which floated away from us to the ceiling. Chairs, sheets and cushions balanced and towered to make a sleeping den on the floor. Someone rang the doorbell but rather than answer it, Mum turned up the volume on Abba.

'That should see them off!' she laughed, pulling me from the sofa so I would dance with her. Her magic could make Sunnyside a haven.

I'll go.

Tomorrow.

It's decided.

What harm can come of going somewhere so safe? So home?

Tala and I are statues now beneath the never-ending sky, lit by the bloom of silver-white from the moon.

The robin, though, moves. On skinny legs, it skits to the seat of the swing.

Its quivering chirps are the only sound in the world.

Until—

A violent thwacking of wings above us.

The thick black bodies of crows.

They flap viciously against the branches, whipping any last remaining leaves so they fall around us like nature's reminder that nothing sticks.

Everything comes apart.

There's a reason why, when they're gathered, these creatures are called a murder.

The robin has gone.

I clap my hands together repeatedly until the crows scatter across the moonlit sky like black-feathered graffiti.

Seven

My gloveless hands might be rapidly freezing from chilled red to the numb and bloodless yellow they turn in extreme cold, but my cheeks flush warm and prickly with the sun. I grip the handlebars tighter, rounding the corners with a familiar confidence of where they will lead me. From the moment I hoiked my bike off the train and on to the platform at Edglington, everything felt so different to my usual explorations. Normally it's all about discovering something new.

This isn't new.

Not the weathered and graffitied bus stop. Not the official sign for nearby Wrekin nor the unofficial sign for homemade cake. Not the church steeple I mistook for a rocket. Not the post box the same red as the blood from my seven-year-old bashed-up knee. Not the thatched cottage where I spied a witch in the crooked window. Not the village hall hung with bunting or balloons for a party. Not the fence I jumped nor the green I cartwheeled across nor the gnarled tree stump on the riverbank, where I threw stones and sticks into the water. I know its rush across the rocks. Its smell too: mud and moss and Marmite on my fingers when we'd scoot here for a picnic in the summer, and I'd dip in my toes.

None of this is new.

Not the hills, nor the woods, nor the farm with its racket of squawking hens and jumbo machines, its waft of manure, which is pungent but comforting because it means I'm almost…what?

Home.

The seashore crunch of gravel as I turn from the road into the drive is not new either. The splintering wooden gate to the garden will squeak as I open it. And stick too. I'll have to wiggle it an inch or so up over the flagstones, which are uneven because of the crocodiles that writhe beneath.

'Jump the cracks,' Mum would say.

She says it now in a voice as winsome as birdsong.

'Here, I'll hold your hand.'

Of course, there is no voice. There is no hand.

There is no Mum.

But still.

I can taste the sticky mustard smoke of her cigarettes, how it mingled with her perfume, which was clean and pink and summery, even in winter when the cloud would come down so low some mornings we could walk inside its white.

Today, though, this not-new world is green.

Sunnyside.

I run my finger in the circled groove we made in the house sign with a penknife one summer's afternoon. My lips were tacky with raspberries and lemonade. The ants that crawled across my bare feet were as black as my nails, which were long and crusty with dirt. Mum was sweating with the effort, her fringe slicked, and the sun in her squinting mischievous eyes as she told me her father would not be happy if he could see what we were doing to his precious sign.

He was dead by then, as was my grandmother.

'They live on in the house, though,' Mum said.

There is more memory in each of these straight-lined rays of sunshine Mum and I carved into this sign than I could ever write in a notebook.

I—

She—

We lived here.

We *lived* here.

In this house that I was told had burned to the ground.

Maybe not those words exactly, but something that made me think the bricks, carpet, wood, pipes, tiles, curtains, sofas, beds, plates, pictures on walls, clothes in cupboards, papers in drawers, teddies on beanbags, jewellery in boxes, masks in bedside tables, everything and all of it was melted or scorched to ash.

But it stands.

At least on the outside.

Everything and all of it stands.

Vibrations in my pocket.

Tala: Tried calling. Went to vm. Where are you?

Tala: Mssg me.

Tala: Iris?

Tala: Pls

'Just wanted to check you're OK?' Tala's voice when I call is quiet, not that trembling shyness that stops her talking in class. Her pitch today is higher. Sharper. Shocked.

'You know me, Tal. Forever stoic.' As I look again at the sign, though, someone needs to remind my heart.

'It's just Shreya, you know, the girl from my English lit group?'

'She's not joined the Dumbbells, has she? I swear if those bitches recruit anyone else to start picki—'

'No, Iris. It's nothing to do with the Dumbbells. Some guy flashed her.'

'Flashed her?'

'Yeah. On her way to school. Near Good Hope Wood.'

The man-creature's guttural laugh runs goosebumps across my skin.

'And you're not here, and I started to panic because I know you walk the dogs at all times of the day and night, and what if he does it aga—'

'I'm cool, Tal.' I gulp a lungful of cold clean air. 'I'm at Sunnyside. No flashers here. I'm fine. Promise.' I have to promise too, that I'll tell her everything about today. 'Every single detail,' I say, wondering how I'll possibly remember all of this once I'm home.

The bell on my bike dings a pathetic warning as I hang up and lean it behind the bushes that run alongside the boundary wall. Hand in pocket, I walk to the front door, fingers grasping at the silver key from the Box of Mum Things. Like everything else, I'd kept it for nostalgic not practical reasons. I never thought it might actually let me in anywhere.

That it might actually let me in here.

My breath steams clouds on the glass panels of the door as I press my face to it.

Inside, it's the same but different.

Small but definite changes.

The woodwork, while still white, isn't peeling.

There are coats and bags and shoes, but they're all stored neatly on hooks and shelves rather than heaped on the floor.

I take a step back and my breathy mist fades.

What else will or won't match the image of 'home' I have in my head?

My hand with the key and the too-shiny lock is the ugly stepsister with her foot and Cinderella's shoe. No matter how much I shove and twist and wrangle, it won't fit.

Some explorers might smash windows or crowbar the door. But locked-up buildings are like locked-in secrets, sometimes it's better to leave them be.

I could check other windows, other doors.

@MyEmptyHouses found her way in, after all.

I head round the back into the garden, where visiting adults would always say how quiet life is in the countryside away from the grumble of cars and people crumpled into too-small spaces in town.

Rubbish.

It was never quiet.

Because what about the animals? The woodland ground-bound creatures that scurry through bushes. And then the birds too, in their hundreds, thousands even, forever hooting, whistling, chirping. Even the trees were noisy. *Suthering*, Mum called it. 'It's like whispering,' she told me. 'How their leaves and branches use the wind to talk.'

The grass is shorter, neater than it ever was when we were here, when it sometimes grew so long that it tickled the tops of my calves. Otherwise, the garden's the same. A large expanse of lawn with a greenhouse running down one side and a potting shed at its end.

The potting shed. Rot-softened wood and breeze-rattled windows. Soiled crates stacked precariously by the door.

My heart slumps into my stomach and my stomach slumps into my pelvis. What I mean is, everything sinks.

If the house and garden memories are a curved ray of sunshine, the potting shed is something else.

~~Go on.~~

~~Look.~~

I can't.

I—

The fortune teller: fresh and predictable.

You will be strong.

I slip my fingers inside the tiny pockets, and it works. It reminds me where and what I am.

In a regular bando, I'd be setting up a shot. But this isn't a regular bando. This isn't abandoned.

Sunnyside is full and cared for.

Wings disturb the trees, which disturb the branches, which disturb the swing.

The swing.

There were very late nights or very early mornings when Mum coaxed me from my bed, still in my pyjamas, and pushed me so I could reach for the firework of stars.

I sit now, fortune teller on my lap, and slowly begin to rock.

The cold clean air rushes against me.

Her hands press on my back. 'Iris,' she suthers.

Smiling.

Laughing.

Crows caw in the skies above.

The slam of a car door, though, is louder than a murder.

Black wings scatter and scarper.

Heart roaring at the hint of a stranger, I do the same.

Eight

I jump mid-air from the swing and run for cover.

Back door: locked.

Windows: locked.

Greenhouse: locked.

Only the potting shed is open.

I can't.

There is nowhere else.

It used to be that the potting shed *was* its smell. Rotten eggs and damp gloves. Sometimes there'd be coffee too. ~~Coffee, or something stronger?~~ That's what I remember most about this wooden shack at the end of our garden.

~~That's what you remember most? Really?~~

~~Not the dark at its back?~~

No, the light at its front.

~~Not the unmotherly moans?~~

No, her fingers in pots.

~~Not the waiting for her to…~~

…sow and prune and deadhead. Yes, that's what I remember. Mum tending to the plants. To the flowers. To life. That's what I see as I rush into the cluttered space with its too-closed-in air that smells not quite of rotten eggs or damp gloves but of the ghosts of them, swooping up and around the rafters, down to the tiny, now-dried-grey balls of soil I must have missed when I swept the discarded bulbs from the floor.

I shake away the memory. It's not the in-here past but the out-there now that counts.

And out there now, this second, there's a girl – a girl, phew! – maybe about my age, coming round the side of the house. I see her as I crane my neck across the shelf to look through the south-facing windows of the shed.

She doesn't walk like an intruder. Rather, in her skin tight running pants, she struts. Every stride of her legs has purpose. The way she places her feet, it's like she intends to be in that exact spot, like she feels the ground throughout her entire body. She has what Rosa would call 'poise'.

She stops. 'Hello?' Her voice has less certainty than her limbs.

The swing, still swinging, catches her eye, and she walks again, confusion knitted into her brow, which furrows further still when she bends to pick something up from the lawn. She crouches to examine it, and a pair of neat red braids waterfalled with multicoloured bows graze her shoulders as she carefully pushes her fingers inside the folds I made in the map this morning. She moves them back and forth, looking from the fortune teller to the house to the garden as if unsure where her fate will be revealed.

'Hello?'

I pull my head back from the glass so I can only just see her as she reaches into her oversized pocket, which is luminous yellow – a contrast to the rest of her coat, which is grey.

Who is she? What is she doing here? What does she know about the fire? About Mum?

In her hand now, is that her phone?

I can't let her call someone because that someone might then call my dad.

Shit. Could she already know Dad? But if she did that would mean *he* already knows about Sunnyside, how it's still standing apparently unscathed by flames. And he can't know that. Can he?

The second her thumb slides across the screen, I burst through the potting-shed door on to the grass.

The girl's wide mouth is open and screaming.

My hands shoot in the air like I'm some douchebag in a dodgy cop show. 'It's cool.'

At least she's no longer yelling.

'I… I used to…' But I can't say what I want to say, which is that I used to live here. That this used to be my home. So, 'I'm an explorer,' I say instead.

Even though it's true, in the sudden silence, I hear how crazy this sounds.

The look – rattled and pale – on her face suggests she thinks so too. She blinks three short, sharp blinks and pulls her shoulders back. It works some kind of miracle, because where a moment ago she looked a bit freaked, now the girl stood in front of me looks fierce.

'An explorer?' She slides her phone back into her pocket. 'You know this is the Midlands not the Antarctic? What even is there to explore?'

I shrug. 'Not much, if I'm honest.'

~~Which you're not.~~

'Well, duh.' She holds out the fortune teller. 'This yours?'

Our fingertips touch when I take it.

'I swear, it's not as odd as it sounds.'

'No?' I'm not sure if it's her tone, or the way she checks her watch like I'm keeping her from something hugely important, but her vibe is pretty snippy.

'You heard of urbex?'

She shakes her head, but only just, that square jawline of hers barely moving.

'Urban exploration? Looking round empty buildings and stuff.'

'You're stumped here then, mate, because this place isn't urban or empty. No wonder you look so disappointed.' The frostiness of her expression melts as she smiles this smile that's a Tic Tac. White and fresh and cool. Sort of sweet. And sort of moreish. 'Órla.' It's not only our fingers that touch this time but our palms too.

'Iris.' My voice isn't quite itself. A bit cracked, like the one time I regretted not taking Tala's advice to prep for exams and bottled it in my GSCE French oral.

'I've gotta say, Iris.' Órla's still handshaking, not quite ready to let go. 'You should be very happy it's me and not Mam who caught you doing your *exploration*.'

'Your mum? Do you…' There are too many reeling questions about this girl, the house, and Dad, even, to know where best to begin. Her eyes keep hold of me until I land on, 'Do you guys live here?'

'God, no.' Another quick glance at the time. 'Mam's an estate agent. She just keeps an eye on it for the owners. Well, pays *me*—'

'The owners?' Trying to sound, look casual, I take a seat on the swing. 'Who are they?'

'Don't ask me, mate.' She starts towards the house. 'I'm just the lackey who freezes my tits off twice a week, checking there's been no funny business.' Her body, when she spins round to face me, has so much more grace than her chat. 'What am I going to write in my report today then, eh?'

'I dunno, maybe a sentence or two about how you rescued a damsel in distress by letting her pop in to use the loo?' I give her my best save-me look while silently asking whatever invisible gods might be listening to please let me inside the house.

'Never one to turn down a damsel.' Órla beckons me with one elongated finger and waves her key.

Nine

My heart, like time and everything else in the universe, slows as Órla unlocks the door.

'You all right?' Her tone's suddenly kind of nervy.

And when I catch a glimpse of myself in the mirror on the wall by the coat hooks where my lilac mac hangs by the waxy Barbour Mum wore because it smelled of her own mum, I can see why.

I look sick, all the colour drained from my face. And though it's not exactly baking in here, a slick of sweat seeps from beneath my beanie down my brow.

'Yeah.' I shake my head, like it's one of those old Etch A Sketch toys and by shaking it, whatever I've seen here will disappear. 'Must be the change in temperature or something.'

'Maybe.' Órla small-shrugs, like, *whatever*. 'The loo's at the back, off the dining room.' My face must be a question mark. 'You said you needed a wee?'

I can't speak.

Can't move.

'Go on then.' She nudges me with her elbow, the way Tala might when she clocks I've zoned out in class.

My steps down the hallway are rapid then practically a stumble when I reach the door to the drawing room, where

75

Mum's woodland mural brightens up the fireplace. The far wall is covered with a different, less fancy kind of art.

'My father will be turning in his grave,' Mum said as she Blu Tack'd my biro'd depiction of her in the garden in the alcove above the dresser. 'I never understood why this room was called a drawing room if we weren't allowed to draw in it.' She rolled her eyes. 'He said it stems from "withdrawing", that people – men, most likely – withdrew into here if they wanted more privacy. But who wants to withdraw, Iris? Much better to throw yourself all in.' She kneeled back down on the floor, where I'd been creating my art. 'We'll make it a gallery, shall we? A proper *drawing* room?' She handed me another sheet of paper and a red felt-tip pen.

There's a house, a horse, a rocket, a dress, a magpie sitting in a tree. There's an eye, a sun, a robot, a rabbit wearing a top hat inside a TV.

What the fuck?

All of this should be gone.

Burned to dust.

I reach out to a painting of a jellyfish, my finger tracing the outline of a bean-shaped body as wobbly as my legs. *Iris*, it says at the bottom, *age 7½*.

'Wrong room, mate.'

Before Órla has a chance to do anything but poke her head through the door, I mutter something about no sense of direction and make my way back to the hall.

'Through there.' She points to the dining room, swings around the newel post and takes the stairs two steps at a time. 'I'll just have a quick shifty up here.'

With Órla out of sight, it's not the dining but the sitting room I go to. Three rainbow cushions sit on the L-shaped sofa. Everything is plumped and dusted.

Scurryfunged.

'It's that mad rush of tidying you do before visitors arrive,' Mum called to me from her bedroom one afternoon when Dad was on his way to see me. I was gathering hula hoops, feathers and teddies from the floor, shoving them into the cupboard beneath the stairs. Like then, the snug today offers the most presentable version of our life together. Mum's magic lingers but the evidence here has mostly been packed away. Where there was a French flag from our Parisian lunch, there is now a framed poster of the Shropshire Hills. Where there was a carpet of sequins tipped on to the floor for an impromptu disco, there is now what looks like an Ikea rug. The walls are still green, but the shade is a touch lighter. The finish a ton better. The cracks in the skirting boards have been filled.

Despite the changes, the gap between Mum and me is narrower here than it's been in years, like she could walk in at any moment and tell me the sun is shining so why don't we go outside for some Vitamin D. 'It's tip-top for your mood!'

'Tip-top,' I whisper now, exaggerating the hard 'p's like she did to give the two words the joy of a circus.

The floorboards creak in the guest-bedroom-cum-playroom above.

How long do I have?

I want to touch everything.

Every single trinket and book.

'Out with the old,' Mum said early one morning, pointing at the gaps on the bookshelves from where she'd been 'sorting'. Her hair smelled of smoke and there was grass between her toes. 'It's like your gums.' I ran my tongue into the hole where I'd lost a baby tooth the week before. 'Sometimes you need to make way for the new.'

When we left the bookshop later that day, our rucksacks sagged like weary children on our backs. I complained my wrists hurt from the weight of what she called 'coffee-table books' that she'd stuffed into plastic bags when the rucksacks were full.

At home, there wasn't enough room on the shelves, and we no longer had a coffee table.

I head back to the hall.

'Better?' Órla and I meet at the bottom of the stairs.

'Is it always like this?'

'Like what?' Her wide eyes flit across the space like I've seen something she hasn't.

'Like the people who lived here never went away?'

'S'pose.' She shrugs. 'I've not really paid much attention. I just check for leaks or signs of a break-in.' She presses the home button on her phone to flash up the clock. 'Ready?'

'You know, it might not be the Antarctic, but it *is* freezing out there.' I nod at the door. 'We could just hang out here for a bit? Enjoy the warm? Look around?'

'Look around?' Her eyes narrow in what I'm guessing is suspicion. 'Why?'

And I guess, to most people, wanting to wander around a stranger's house might seem kind of odd, but I just need this girl to think Sunnyside's no different for me than any other bando. 'Better question is *why not*?'

Órla rolls her eyes. 'Because it's kind of boring.'

'You think other people's lives are boring?'

'Probably not actually, compared to my own.' There's a flicker of intrigue in her smile. 'Ten minutes, Marco Polo.'

'Ten minutes? I'd normally be in a place like this at least a couple of hours.'

'You clearly have a lot more free time than me.' As if primed to ensure she doesn't go thinking her time's her own, Órla's phone starts ringing in her bag. 'Go on then! Just don't take anything!' Her mock-teacherly tone turns into a sigh as she skulks to the kitchen to answer the call.

'When do I ever let you down?' I hear her say. 'I promise. I'll be there soon.'

Her words fade as I climb the stairs slowly like I used to, avoiding the squeaking floorboards in case Mum was sleeping. Hovering outside her room now, I press my head to the door as if—

As if what exactly? As if I might hear her breathing? Snoring? ~~Crying?~~

Whatever fantasy my brain concocted in the seconds it took me to get here unravels the moment I enter Mum's room. She is not on the bed. She is not at the dressing table. She is not at the window waving at a younger version of me outside on the swing. And she hasn't been for years.

The smell of Mum – the washing powder, the spritz of perfume after a cigarette, the oily citrus residue that would cling to her skin after she peeled an orange with the rind remaining in one glorious long piece – has been replaced with the whiff of furniture polish, air freshener and bleach.

The things we spray to stamp out the smells of people's real and messy lives.

Ten

If she knew the truth, I'm not sure Órla would actually accuse me of stealing. I mean, sure, she did tell me I wasn't to take anything, but every single item in that house – even the swanky new kitchen, the only room that wasn't a pretty close match to how my ten-year-old self left it – is surely already mine? But how to relay that fact without spiralling into the whole fucked-up story? So, no, better to keep the rabbit mask I took from Mum's bedside drawer in the bottom of my rucksack, where I snuck it while Órla was still on the phone to someone. Someone who, from Órla's end of the conversation, had sounded like they weren't best pleased she was off adventuring with me.

The tyres of her car snarl into the gravel as we pull out of the driveway, and my bike – shoe-horned into the boot – shunts against the door. The bell vibrates a weak protest at the speed.

'Not that I'm complaining because I'm very grateful for the ride to the station and everything, but...' I hunker down, double-checking I've zipped up my bag. Zipped up my memories. Zipped up my questions about Sunnyside, the fire and Mum. 'Who are we rushing off for anyway? That heated discussion back there a booty call from your boyfriend, was it?'

'I don't *do* boyfriends.' Órla's eyes, when she glances across at me, are Joker-level intense. My gaze fixes on her left arm, where a drift of rainbow-jewelled bracelets gleam against her pale-as-a-page flesh, visible now since she removed her coat when she got in the car.

'Don't blame you.' My finger hovers above the WhatsApp icon on my phone. A number four sits in a tiny red circle in its top-right corner as a reminder of the unread pleas from Rollo. Not that I ever even called him my boyfriend, but he'd obviously made the leap. I caught the first line of the last message as the alert flashed up on the screen.

I don't know what happened with us

Us? When did he and I become an *us*?

'Sadly, I've not done girlfriends for a while either.' Órla's bottom lip slides into a mock pout. 'You'll have time for that later, Órla,' she says, impersonating a Liverpudlian accent.

'Naysaying parent?' I gear myself up for a hard-relate.

'Naysaying coach,' Órla says, batting away any further questions with offers of a drink or snack from the tote she tells me to unwedge from behind my seat.

'This bag is a full-on tuck shop!'

'If the tuck shop was run by Gwyneth Paltrow.' The force with which Órla rolls her eyes surely can't be safe while driving.

She has a point, though. I was expecting a treat, but the bag, clinking with an armour of enamel badges, is busting with goodness. Apples. Tubs of dried fruit and nuts. Mini packets of wholegrain crackers. Individual portions of cheese.

I take an orange juice – not from concentrate. 'Guess there's no chance of a hot chocolate with all the trimmings from the Starbucks drive-thru?'

'One day.' Órla's voice is far too wistful. Then, 'Shit!' My head almost hits the dash as she slams on the brakes. 'Feckin' eejit!' She waves a fist at the dude who pulled out in front of us on the roundabout. 'Jeeeeeeesus, some people.' She takes her eyes off the road for a second to check on me. 'Bollocks! Sorry! You OK?'

I am *not* OK. I mean, physically, yeah, I'm all good, but aesthetically, I look like I've both dribbled and pissed myself. Basically, I'm drowned in juice.

'There's only one thing for it,' Órla says, checking her mirrors before executing a perfect turn in the road. 'You're not going to the station. *You –*' she grins as she heads in the opposite direction – 'are coming home with *me.*'

※

When we walk into Órla's house, she immediately drags me up the stairs, past walls lined with photo after photo of her wearing next to nothing, and holding medals and trophies galore.

'Er, what's all this?' I stop halfway up. There she is, fierce and limber in a leotard, leaping and bending with a hoop, a ribbon, a ball. 'You're a gymnast?' I point at the framed newspaper clipping of her holding what I read is a British Championships gold. 'Oh my God. They call you the Golden Princess!'

'Among other things.' Her eyes, I notice, are fixed on a shot in which she's stood in line with four other girls dressed in the same black and purple leotards and topped with the same tightly drawn buns.

And there they are again, those three sharp blinks and the pulled-back shoulders I'd seen outside Sunnyside. A brief smile, then, before she turns and strides away.

I follow Órla to her room, where she removes a stack of clothes from her wardrobe. Everything is neatly folded or hung in colour order from dark to light. 'Here, pick one. You can't go home like *that*.' She nods at my drenched jumper.

A pink T-shirt unravels as I lift it from the top of the pile.

'Not my best work.' Órla winces slightly as a roughly embroidered speedometer is revealed on its front. 'I hadn't been sewing long.' She tugs at a loose green thread. 'It was my coming-out outfit.'

I feel her eyes on me as I look closer. The measurements aren't rising miles per hour, but rather show an increase in 'gay', ranging from 'straight as a line' through to 'curious' to 'Yup. 100% queer'. The pointer is pointing as far round to the right side of the circle as it could possibly go, where two hundred miles per hour on a car would be.

'I don't actually wear it. The needlework's too shit, and the orientation labels are a bit reductive too. But it served its purpose.' She takes it from me and holds it against her chest. I try not to stare. 'Mam got the message that I wouldn't be living life on the *straight* and narrow.' She sighs. 'At least not as far as relationships are concerned.'

The next top I pick up is pale blue. It's all right but very plain. I place it on the bed next to the coming-out T-shirt, which Órla has begun refolding. I don't know what it is about them, but her hands, the way they move, are kind of enchanting.

'Maybe if you don't wear it, I should borrow that one?' I run a finger across the pointer and shrug.

'Sure.' Órla smiles. 'While you get changed, I'll go eat something before training. *That's* why I was rushing you earlier. As Mam reminded me for the millionth time when she called, I needed to come back here to *refuel.*' She says 'refuel' in the same way Know-All says 'urbex', like it's so incredibly irritating and passé.

The bloom of bracelets clatters in protest as she slips them over her slender fingers and drops them on to her bedside table.

Silence follows.

And then I'm left alone in her room.

To explore.

There's as much bling in Órla's bedroom as there was painted on the ceiling of a ballroom at an abandoned country hotel I explored last month. Shelves of perfectly spaced trophies and matching-framed certificates. The girl's a superhero. In some of the pictures that line the wall behind her bed, Órla spirals a silk ribbon as empowering as a cape. The leaps are so high she's practically flying. Graceful and dauntless. Focused and free.

There's just one tiny corner of the room that's not an homage to her gymnastic triumphs. A small desk holds neatly arranged piles of fabric offcuts, images torn from magazines and, right in the centre, three printed A4 sheets: *The Fundamental Pisces Traits Explained*. Someone has circled the words artistic and creative in thick red pen. Tape, scissors and a rainbow of cotton reels hang on a pegboard on the wall.

The front door opens then closes, and a voice – loud, smiling and Irish – calls hello.

When I come downstairs a few minutes later, I walk towards the kitchen, towards the soft rolling chatter, towards a red-headed woman in a camel-coloured coat with her back to me, removing all the bows then unwinding the braids from Órla's hair. Though she has to pull the strands tight as she coils them into a bun, there's a tenderness in the way her mum – I assume this is Órla's mum – touches her daughter.

'Will you want a banana?' Before Órla has time to answer, her mum grabs one from the bowl on the island, peels it and hands it over, ordering her to, 'Eat up now. Quickly, if you're to take your friend to the station. Have you been staying hydrated?' She goes to the sink and fills a tumbler.

'Any chance I could have one of those?'

Órla's mum is smiling as she turns, but when she sees me that smile is suddenly tangled with something that looks like disbelief.

Or fear.

Eleven

'Sarah?' she says, but then jolts her head, like, *you can't be*. 'Iris?'

I want a rewind. To the 'Sarah'.

Mum's name.

Sarah.

Sarah.

Sarah.

We barely speak it at home.

There's that saying, isn't there, that a person's not really dead until their name's no longer spoken. And as well as that saying, there's that feeling of hearing someone say Mum's name with love when I'm used to hearing it said with regret.

Órla's mum's electric-blue high heels bite into the ceramic tiles as she walks towards me.

'You *are* Iris? You *are* Sarah's daughter?'

I look from her to Órla, whose face is scrunched in utter bewilderment, and nod.

'I'm Bronagh.' Her Irish lilt has the warmth of a pebble in your palm after it's laid in the sun. 'My God, youse are so much like her at seventeen.'

There was that comment once from Dad about me inheriting Mum's height, but aside from that, no one's ever mentioned any real resemblance. And I certainly haven't seen it. In the few photographs I have, I can't spot any similarity. I've held the pictures next to me by the mirror. Searched for twinned noses. Twinned eyes. Twinned chins. If I hadn't dyed it purple, there'd be our dark hair maybe, but otherwise nothing.

'How did you…?' Bronagh's question drifts, and in her ellipsis I hear the same tangled knot of confusion as in my head, which is a thick web of *how* and *why* and *what* and *where* and *who*. Because *who* is she?

Only I can't get the words – the words that are just one syllable but so fat with impossibility – from my brain to my mouth. My lips are clamped because if I unleash my tongue it will be too hot with the liquid tumult that's been brewing in my belly since I first pulled up at Sunnyside this morning.

~~WHAT THE FUCK?~~

'I met her outside Sunnyside.' There's a solidarity in how Órla comes to stand by me and takes my arm. It steadies the flow.

'So you know all about your house then?' Bronagh's smile is a bloom of recognition and relief.

And I'd smile too, because that's what I do.

But I can't.

'I've been keeping tabs on the place,' she says, fetching the glass of water I'd asked for and handing it to me like a glass of water is everything I need. 'Your dad asked me to. After that series of break-ins last year? Sure, you will have heard about those?' Her eyes are swimmy but full of optimistic expectation. 'Nothing was really taken. It was as if they were just there to have a look around, which makes no sense to me at all, but…'

My brain can't get beyond *your dad asked me to*.

Dad *asked* her to look after Sunnyside?

So he really does know the entire house wasn't destroyed in a fire?

The tumult expands in my stomach like it's no longer liquid but gas. A helium balloon pressing against my insides and lifting me up so I float above Bronagh and Órla and myself.

From up here, we look normal.

Almost.

Almost normal.

'I was best friends with your mam,' Bronagh says.

From above, I watch how I nod, like those little dogs Tita Celestina has in her car, their heads bobbing up and down because of the motion, not because they actually understand.

'Though we didn't see each other for quite a while before the end. For years, though, God, we were thick as thieves. Look!' She pulls a photograph from under a Birmingham Sea Life magnet on the fridge and passes it to me.

The balloon bursts, and I drop back into myself.

The picture is of a wolf and a rabbit and their daughters.

'OMG. Iris! This is you!' Órla's looking over my shoulder.

When I tell her yes, the helium must seep from my stomach up into my throat because my voice is pitched so high it's unreal. I try to explain that the copy I have of this photo is one of the few things I have of Mum's, but the words are a stutter.

'She was so happy.' Bronagh pales further, which you'd think would be impossible, but her hundreds of freckles are richer now against her china skin. 'To look at her there, you'd never think she'd…' Her long, ringed fingers press her chest as if to contain whatever might otherwise burst through.

'She'd what?'

Bronagh's eyes close for just longer than a blink. 'The way she died.'

'But the fire was an accident.' The exact words Dad used when he first told me.

'The fire was an accident, Iris.'

No need for questions, then, because even amid all the snarling uncertainty that comes with being a half-orphan when you're ten, your dad still knows everything and will only ever tell you the truth.

Sunnyside, though? Where was the truth in the perfectly intact drawing room, bedroom and sitting room? Where was the truth in the shoes on the shelves and the coats on the pegs? Where was the truth in the clothes in the wardrobes and the pictures on the walls?

I can't breathe.

'Your mam…' Bronagh swallows the words she was about to say, but whatever they were are so bulged with meaning that, even left unsaid, they saturate the air between us. 'I'm gonnae drive you home,' she says. 'You need to talk to your dad.'

Twelve

'There *was* a fire.' Dad's hands are on my arms, and I want to shake them – him – off. But who knows what would happen if I moved? Because I am thunder and lightning concealed in flesh and hair and eyes and teeth and skin. 'There *was* a fire,' he repeats. Though no matter how many times he says them, those four words are not an explanation.

I haven't said anything.

Not a peep since I came through the door, where Dad had likely been waiting since he answered Bronagh's whispered call about forty-five minutes ago.

Maybe I should have let Bronagh come in. She offered to as we were manoeuvring my bike from the boot of her car. If I'd said yes, perhaps her presence would have been the kick in the gut Dad needs to spit out the truth.

Instead, I just thanked her for the ride and the stories she'd told me about Mum, which were tales of dancing and laughing and chasing boys and dreams and all the kinds of anecdotes I hadn't realized I ached for. The only other person in my life who really knew Mum is Dad, who, on the rare occasions he speaks about her, lowers his voice like people do when they're nervous of waking a sleeping baby.

So Bronagh is gone, and now it's me and Dad and Rosa.

We are in the kitchen, where the too-bright lights expose the lines scoured into his face.

Rosa, ever the Linchpin, gives him one slow nod, like, *you must continue.*

So, what, Rosa's in on this mystery too? What is it with all these adults and their shared rotten secrets? And how dare my stepmother just sit there emanating that permanent yogic in-through-the-nose-out-through-the-mouth calm?

'I think we should sit down,' she says, and one minute we're standing and the next we're sitting, and yet I don't remember moving at all.

'There *was* a fire.' Dad's hands are shaking and his face is crumpling.

Unsure he can take any more, I quash the thunderous monster in my gut, ignore its bucking need to scream at Dad's endless repetition.

'It was contained to the kitchen,' he says. 'But when the fire brigade got there, they found Sarah dead in the other room.'

'Was it the smoke then?' Which is still all kinds of grisly but doesn't explain him not telling me about Sunnysi—

'Not the smoke.' Dad's fingers stretch for mine across the table. 'There's no easy way to say this, Iris.' He inhales a breath deeper even than Rosa's. 'Your mum took her own life.'

Thirteen

It makes no sense.

It makes no sense.

It makes no sense.

Your

mum

took

her

own

life.

Even when I break it down, the sentence is a mismatch of words that can no way belong with each other.

mum

own

her

your

life

took

When I look at Dad, his lips and his tongue are moving like he's still talking. 'This isn't how we wanted you to find out. And I'm so so sorry. We want to explain.'

Can't possibly—

What does he—

93

Why would she—

Who would even—

'Iris? I know this is hard, but you must listen. Please, listen to me.'

'Why would you say that?'

'Pardon?' Dad's milky eyes are honed in on my mouth like it's not working. Like it's not doing what I'm trying to make it do.

'Why would you say that?'

'I can't hear you, Iris.' The screech of his chair against the floor as he stands echoes the hot howl in my heart.

When he kneels in front of me, I want to remind my dad how much tears can hurt the people who watch them fall. I mean, that's why I stopped shedding them, right? Because I saw what they did to people.

To him.

And now his are killing me.

'Give her some space.' Rosa coaxes him back round to his side of the table. 'I'll make tea.'

'Tea?'

So my mouth *is* working then.

Why would anyone want tea?

How could anyone do something so ordinary as boil a kettle or grab milk from the fridge when the air is thick with something that feels like but isn't fire.

It was never fire.

Rosa stops with the water and the tea bags and sits down next to me, gives Dad some signal I can't quite fathom. His lips start moving but, no, I'm sorry, I can't listen because—

What if it's true?

Lalalalalalalalalalalalalalalalalalalalalalalalalalalalala.

'It doesn't mean she didn't love you, sunshine. She loved you so—'

Why can I still hear him?

Lalalalalalalalalalalalalalalalalalalalalalalalalalalalala-lala.

'…much. She really did. She wasn't well. We—'

Louder, Iris, louder.

Lalalalalalalalalalalalalalalalalalalalalalalalalalala-lalalalalalalala.

'…didn't realize at the time, but it's an illness, Iris. It's no one's—'

Why isn't this working?

Lalalalalalalalalalalalalalalalalala-lalalalalalalalala.

'…fault. We know this is a shock and we will answer all of your questions.'

But I know what happens when I ask questions.

'I can't bear it,' he said on the phone all those years ago. 'It's breaking my fucking heart.'

If I am made of thunder and lightning, Dad is made of desperate pleas. 'Iris.'

I can't break him.

Not again.

He's all I have left.

You will be strong.

'I'm OK,' I smile. 'I mean, yeah, it's a surprise but—'

Swallow the shock, Iris.

'Mum's been dead for years.'

I stand. Flick the switch on the kettle. Grab the milk from the fridge.

Ordinary *is* possible.

'How it happened doesn't change anything. Not really.'

'Let me.' As she pours the water, Rosa's voice is as perfectly balanced as her body when she's in some convoluted yoga pose. 'You remember, love, how your dad said sometimes your mum was too sick to look after you?'

Sure, they'd mentioned that occasionally she needed a break.

But Mum was happy.

Mum was kind.

Mum loved me.

~~Mums who are happy and kind and love you don't…~~

'Yes!' Am I too quick? Too firm? 'I remember.' Slower, this time. Softer.

Rosa passes Dad a tissue from the shit-drawer. He wipes his cheeks. Blows his nose.

His arms around me, then, are tentative and make me think of that book I saw on Rosa's side of the bed a few weeks ago. *How to Hug a Porcupine.* Is that how they think of me? As prickly and tricky to hold. He recoils and sits back down.

'When I first got the call…' Dad looks from Rosa, who's placing three steaming cups on the table, to me. 'I really did think Sarah had died in the fire. It wasn't a lie. Not then.' His tone is bruised, tender. 'But when the facts changed, the story didn't. You were ten. How could I tell you that new version? How could I say that your mum—'

'Committed suicide?'

Rosa's inhale is ever so slightly shorter, sharper than usual. 'We try not to put it like that,' she says. And maybe the face I'm working so hard to keep neutral is rattled because my stepmother lays her hand gently over mine on the table. 'The only things you can commit are crimes or sins. Suicide is neither.'

Thanks for the clarification, Rosa.

I snatch my hand away from hers.

As we sat and watched the sky one night, Mum told me that we are all made of stardust, but she was wrong. Because I am made of millions of bullets each etched with three letters that spell one word:

'How?'

'Pills,' Dad says.

Then, 'Why?'

'She wasn't well,' Rosa says.

'She wasn't well? Like, what? Cancer or something?'

'Mentally.' Dad says the word like he's been rehearsing it.

'Mentally? She was *mental*?'

'She was ill.' Dad's at it again with all this repetition.

Rosa straightens in her chair. 'We need to be careful how we talk about it, that's all. The words we use are important.'

Who the fuck is this woman to tell me how to talk about my mum?

Is it true, though? Are words what's important or do actions count for more?

Because Mum used words to tell me she loved me but then she did *that*.

You will be strong.

And I am strong. I am. But the thunder monster wrestles stronger in my belly.

'As far as your dad knows, Sarah was never diagnosed. But from what you told hi—'

The veins in the back of Dad's hands bulge as he squeezes Rosa's fingers. She stops talking.

All of us do.

Because what is there to say?

Fourteen

'I can't believe this place belongs to you!' Tala, who was here after I got back from my 7 a.m. walk with Wookie the pug, is looking at photos Dad sent me of Sunnyside on my phone. 'My uncle doesn't even own a house and he's forty-four!' She takes one of Rosa's homemade mince pies I snuck from the kitchen and shuffles along the mattress to make room for two.

'Alexa, what's the time?'

'The time is eight fifteen a.m.'

Twenty-five minutes until we have to leave for school. I've not even had a shower.

'From what your dad says, Tal, I think your uncle not being on the property ladder is mostly down to him being a big man-baby who likes to live at home where he's waited on by his mum.'

'True,' Tala says. And I'm about to thank God that at least I'll never be at risk of developing those kinds of co-dependency mummy issues when my phone pings with a message from an altogether different type of problematic male.

Know-All: A girl in my law class set this up after what happened to Shreya. You should join.

99

The link he's sent takes me to a WhatsApp group called 'Home Safe'. The description suggests we girls need to work together, share where we are going, the idea being that if one of us is walking home alone and another member happens to be nearby, we can walk together. At the very least, we can confirm we've arrived – unharassed – at our destination.

'You seen this?' I forward the link to Tal. 'Like any of that lot would actually have rushed into a rescue mission if I'd messaged them telling them some dude was leering at me in Good Hope Wood on Sunday night? Bunch of—'

'You were in the woods? After you left Rollo?'

I shrug, like, *yeah, what of it?*

'And there was a man there?'

'It was cool, Tal.' And it was, it is. I mean, sure that rough laugh echoed in my head whenever I took an alley or turned a corner as I walked Buddy on Monday and again when I was out with Wookie today, but that's just life. The situation in the woods was totally within my control. As soon as I thought things were turning sticky, I ran.

Other sticky situations aren't so easy to escape.

'And this thing with your mum, that cool too, is it?'

'I said so, didn't I?' It's true. As Wookie snuffled the pavements for kebab and Maccy D titbits, I'd called my best mate and told her exactly that. 'I want you to know that I'm cool with what I'm about to tell you,' I said before filling her in on all the domestic and death shit that went down yesterday.

My instinct had been to keep schtum. Because maybe Dad was on to something when he'd kept it a secret. Who needs to know *that* about my mum? But I get the sense that Rosa and

Tita Celestina's habit of swapping recipes probably extends to them swapping gossip too.

I hadn't banked on all of Tala's questions.

The only one *I'd* asked when Dad and Rosa repeated I could ask them anything was *why*. And they didn't have an answer. Or, more specifically, the only answer they had was poor.

'She was ill, Iris.'

'You *are* all right, aren't you?' Tala's voice now is cracked. Her eyes are glassy. I swear that girl's propensity for crying is borderline nuts. Though Rosa would obviously have me use a different adjective.

'Am I all right? Course I'm all right. I'm seventeen and own a four-bedroom farmhouse with a huge garden that even includes a swing.'

'You sound like an estate agent.'

'And you sound like Rosa!'

'But your mum,' she says, leaning her head on my shoulder. 'Are you—?'

'Alexa, play Lady Gaga.'

I get up and walk to the bathroom as 'Poker Face' fills the room.

✳

'How's the delectable Dougie?' I ask ten minutes later as I emerge, blotched and sweaty faced, from my en suite.

Tala glances up from her book and double takes. 'You're a lobster! You *do* know a shower's supposed to be refreshing? I don't get why you don't turn down the heat.'

~~She's obviously not felt the delicious relief of the burn.~~

I pick up Órla's T-shirt from the pile of clothes on the floor and sniff the armpits.

'That new?' Tala squints to read the text on the tee.

'Borrowed.' My cheeks burn with something more than the heat of the shower. 'You know – Órla? Who I met yesterday?'

'Yeah, you might have mentioned her one or two or, I dunno, twenty times.' Tala's eyes round like there's deep meaning in her observation.

'She was cool, that's all.' And that *is* all, right? I mean, sure, my nerve endings blaze whenever Órla pops into my head, but that's just because it's a relief not to be thinking about Mum. 'So… Dougie.'

Tala rolls her eyes.

'Get many sonnets written yesterday afternoon?'

'No sonnets, Iris.' Her voice carries the same monotone note the Dumbbells use to convey their boredom with anything outside their razor-sharp contoured circle. 'I went to a poetry thing with him last night actually.' She keeps her eyes on her book like this isn't breaking news.

'Er, you did *what* now?' Without me? Tala went somewhere without me? 'And?'

Her gaze drifts across the page.

'Ugh. Like blood from a stone!' I pull my jumper down over Órla's sartorial masterpiece before taking centre stage on my rug. 'There once was a girl called Tala. Who liked…eating… Maltesers and…masala?'

Tala gives in to my demand for attention and drops the book.

'She went to a slam…where they only had…had…ham?' Shit, the last line of a limerick is always a killer.

Quick scan of rhyme.com on my phone and I'm sorted. I inhale, pull my shoulders right back like Órla did when we met in the garden at Sunnyside, then raise an imaginary mic in my hand. 'There once was a girl called Tala. Who liked eating Maltesers and masala. She went to a slam. Where they only had ham. And that messed with the feels of amyg-daaaar-la.' I bow. 'Dibs on poetic licence for my pronunciation of amygdala.'

'Ms Reid did always say you needed to work on the finer details in biology.' Tala's laugh slides into a sigh.

'Er. And what was that about?'

She jerks away from my drippy hair as I flop down next to her on the bed.

'Come on. What's up?'

'The slam.' She picks at the loose thread of cotton on the cuff of her cardigan. 'Dougie was right, it was really cool.'

Pick.

'He and his mate Jenna signed.'

Pick.

'It was amazing to watch. Really clever and funny.'

Pick.

'And the poets. I don't know how to describe it. It's like their words actually took up space, you know?'

Pick.

'Dougie thinks my poems are as good as anyone's there.'

'And that's a reason to sigh why?'

Tala's small enough already, but she's shrinking to even tinier proportions. 'I could never do that.'

I hate to say it, because I'm normally all for crushing negative thinking, but – honestly – she's probably right. I mean, the

Dumbbells didn't nickname Tala after the world's quietest room for nothing. I'd never say it to her face or anything, but sometimes even mean things are true.

I wriggle my arm around her shoulder and, despite my sopping hair, she nestles in for a hug.

A few minutes later, I twist up on to my knees and take her by both arms. 'I've got it!' I'm bouncing like Buddy with the brilliance of my plan. 'I'll perform for you!'

Tala pulls her chin into her neck, like, *I don't get it*.

'Dougie says your poems need to be heard, but he didn't say *you* have to be the one to perform them. And you've got to admit, while the limerick itself was kind of sketchy, my performance was Eilish-level cool.'

Her arched eyebrow might suggest she thinks I'm being cocky but, when Tala speaks, her voice is chock-full of delight. 'You were pretty awesome.'

'You're awesomer.'

'You're the awesomest.'

But before Tala can hand me the notepad of her best literary works for a first rehearsal, our lightning-bolt moment is rudely interrupted by Dad knocking on, then poking his head round, the door.

'Here again, Tala?' There's no reproach in his tone. If anything, he sounds relieved when he says how Tal and I never part for more than eight hours max. His voice is less jovial, more pitiful, when he turns and asks if I'm OK.

What is it with everyone forgetting just how capable I am in a crisis?

Not that any of this is a crisis.

But.

First Dad. Now Tala. Then right on cue, my phone flashes with an alert.

Rollo: Pls Iris. Can you reply to just one of my messages?
I just want to know your ok.

If I wasn't concerned it would give Rollo the wrong impression, I'd reply stating the simple difference between 'your' and 'you're'.

'I'm fine,' I tell Dad. 'Tala and I are just plotting a poetic takeover. Hey, we could hold a Christmas slam here? You wouldn't mind, would you? Just fifty or so of our closest wordsmiths gathering in the front room?'

Dad's eyes flit as he tries to figure out if there's any seriousness to my idea.

'Chill, Pops! Just teasing.'

His face blooms with relief.

'Keep her in check, please.' Dad smiles conspiratorially at Tala. 'She says she's joking, but we all know how good Iris can be at clandestine plots.'

~~Truth is, apples never fall far from the tree.~~

Fifteen

Aside from the walk with Buddy, which was an hour of pure poodle pleasure, each of the three days since I went to Sunnyside has gone pretty much the same.

And it's exhausting.

With the exception of 'Are you OK?', no one's actually asking me questions. Not with words anyway.

Their eyes, though. And their constant head tilts, like Dad and Rosa are waiting for me to either buckle or burst. Then there's their non-stop knocks on my bedroom door, followed by a gently spoken offer to talk. The monitoring's got so intense that tonight the unthinkable has happened and I'm heading upstairs to Know-All's room for some peace.

'Hey.'

The way he uprights and narrows at the sound of me, I'm not sure my stepbrother is game for being my haven. Contrary to his blatant wish that I get the hell out of here, I step further into his room with its flashes of orange on the feature wall and matching shelves running between his built-in desk and bed. Who's he trying to kid? The three grey walls are so much more him. That and his modelling table, which takes up such an absurd amount of floor space it stops anyone who comes in his room from doing anything remotely fun. Not that anyone but Dad or Rosa ever normally comes in. Or that Know-All ever wants to do anything fun.

'What is it you like so much about Lego anyway?'

He flips over an index card from the deck on the table. *Jesus.* Must the dude cram every single second with revision?

He doesn't say anything. Doesn't even look at me until I pick up one of the green columns that make up part of the set of Central Perk. It's ironic really, that for his birthday Know-All asked for the café from *Friends* when he doesn't have any.

Still he says nothing.

I watch him, how his eyes move methodically from the instructions to the pieces, how his hands do exactly as they're told.

'No wonder you and Dad get on so well. You're as much of a stickler as he is.' I place the column back on the table. 'Only a true stickler wouldn't keep such colossal secrets from his daughter.'

Like the orange juice when Órla slammed on the brakes, my words sploshed out. And, quite clearly, we're drenched in them.

Know-All has stiffened over his miniature armchair, as if the nobbles that click the two bricks together have stuck his body in position too.

What in stepfamily hell ever possessed me to come up here? I know none of us has been behaving normally, but seriously. There I was doing my utmost not to talk about Mum with Dad or Rosa, and then less than a minute with Know-All – my least likely confidante – out pops an obvious allusion to my dad's hitherto hidden fondness for huge, fucking lies.

~~Well, well, well.~~

~~Somebody's mad.~~

I'm *not* mad.

'I'm sorry,' I tell Know-All, which might be a first. But I *am* sorry for that look that fell across his face just now. I've been trying to avoid that look for years. Because back when Mum died, it wasn't only Dad's heart that I was breaking. When they saw me – the half-orphan – I wrecked everyone else's hearts too.

Mothers on the school run, the same ones who'd raised their collective brow when Mum had shimmied into the school twenty-five minutes late, dressed for a West End singalong production of *Mama Mia* rather than a West Midlands Year One nativity, those same mothers reached out their fleshy arms and tried to hold me. It was easier, perhaps, to clutch me to their bosoms than to look at me and confront the mum-shaped wound written across my face. And easier for me too not to look at them, to avoid the pity-shaped tears in their eyes as they thought about their own children and all that *there but for the grace of God…*

I'm halfway out of the door when Know-All coughs a cough that's not a tickle in his throat but a readying. His stance too. It's him bracing himself to speak an awkward truth. 'Iris, I know things are really hard for you right now, but go easy on Mum and Matt, yeah?'

Isn't that exactly what I've been doing?

Haven't I kept quiet?

Kept smiling.

~~Kept seething.~~

Kept strong.

He lays down his tools. 'I mean it. Mum's been stressed recen—'

'Stressed? When is the Linchpin ever stressed?'

His voice drops to a low rumble. 'When she's worrying about your dad, when he's worrying about you, which is pretty much most of the time.'

~~FUCK'S.~~

~~SAKE.~~

'They don't have to worry about me. I'm fine.'

'So you keep saying.' And, *God*, the way he looks at me.

'Whatever.' It's not my canniest comeback.

'No, not *whatever*.' His tone bloats with impatience. He picks up a flat beige tile and attaches it to the brown one.

'What exactly is your problem, Know-All?' I take a definite step forward into his room. Right into it. Broad-shouldered. Feet apart.

And I stare.

He breathes in through his nose just like I've heard Rosa tell him to when he's freaking out over exam papers.

'My problem is that Mum's been quietly worrying about you and your family's secrets for years.'

And that's when it hits me. How stupid I've been. How it can't be just Dad and Rosa who've known the truth. How all these other people must have been in on it too. Know-All. The school-run mothers who were probably never thinking *there but for the grace of God* because, surely, even without the grace of God, their children would never, ever be like me. Because they didn't have the kind of mothers who…

'I didn't *ask* Rosa to worry.' I don't mean to sound so tightly wound. So petty. But it's hard to control my voice when every inside part of me feels like it's about to burst through my too-taut skin.

'I know you didn't,' Know-All says, only not in that smug way he normally claims to know everything.

Flustered, he drops the Lego chair. Brown and beige bricks and tiles scatter as they hit the table. He doesn't huff or puff or swear, just turns the instruction pamphlet back a few pages to start the process again.

'Does it not drive you mad when it breaks like that?'

He shakes his head. 'That's the good thing about making things in miniature.' The arsenal of index cards topples to the carpet as he pushes everything aside to make more room for the build. 'When your world's this small, the problems are small too. And the smaller the problems, the easier they are to fix. At least you'd hope so,' he says, bending over to gather the drift of cards on the floor.

Sixteen

'That's better.' Dad flicks every light switch as we walk through Sunnyside, like he really believes it's that easy to banish the dark.

When I told them I wanted to come back, he'd offered to keep me company. I said no at first, but the hurt on Dad's face was salt in the wound Know-All carved into my heart when he revealed that Dad and Rosa are in a constant state of angst because of me.

'You might need someone there,' Rosa suggested. I didn't tell her I'd hoped that someone could be Órla. That I was going to suggest I kill two birds with one stone: returning her T-shirt while simultaneously revisiting my childhood home.

'Let your dad go with you,' Rosa said. 'Being back at Sunnyside could be a bit…' As always, she was looking for the right word. The word she came up with was 'strange'. She and Dad both then ignored my insistence that I'm very well versed in visiting *strange* buildings alone.

Rosa had a point, though, I suppose. I mean, the shock of seeing Sunnyside last week could have been awful. But while I would totally have held it together even if I had been on my own, I reckon Órla being there the first time did sway my mood further towards the right side of OK.

Anyway, I'm used to Sunnyside being strange. It always was. Or at least my friends, the few who came over, said so when they saw the old shop mannequin we sometimes dressed for dinner sat at the dining table. Or as they watched Mum's brilliant multitasking: she could cook while dancing under the thirteen disco balls that threw metallic diamonds of light across the length of the kitchen floor.

Those quirks have gone now. Since what he thinks was a break-in, but what I know was @MyEmptyHouses' exploration a year ago, Dad's been sorting the house. Getting it in 'tip-top shape' was how he put it in the car on the way over.

Tip-top.

The phrase belonged to Mum, not Dad, whose demeanour's generally too sober for onomatopoeia. Is it even onomatopoeia? Autological, maybe. What I mean is, saying it used to make me feel it, so…

'Did you ever live here?' It feels like something I should know. But I can't remember much from when I was really little. And I can't imagine that he and Mum were ever a fit.

I hadn't meant to ask Dad any questions. Really, I just want him gone. He's supposed to be hammering at the fence panel he was keen to fix before he gets Bronagh to 'take a look at the place', which makes no sense because hasn't Bronagh or, more precisely, Órla, been *taking a look* at Sunnyside twice weekly for a while?

But the way Dad moves through the hallway to the toolbox he put down by the front door is so familiar, like it's not just Mum's ghosts that might haunt this place but his too. His former selves, like the one he showed me in a photo last night:

a picture of him wearing a fox mask Mum had made for him 'back in the day'.

'I kept it,' he said, handing me the mask like it was evidence. Of what, I'm not entirely sure.

It's funny, because the Mum I knew was so different to the Dad I know that I can't imagine them as people who would give each other anything. Only Dad didn't look like the same man in that photo. Not just because he was younger. He was topless too. His sinewy bicep flexed as he poured a shot of amber liquid into his mouth that was broad and open with a hedonistic smile.

(Nice use of 'hedonistic,' Iris.)

'I was here for a while, yes, when you were little.' Dad runs his finger for dust along the top of a framed painting of an elderly lady sitting primly on a chair while a man I assume is her husband is hunched over a newspaper. Mum said it was called 'My Parents', and for years I thought it really was my nana and granddad. I could never have pictured my own parents like that. So quiet. So content. So together. 'You were only one when I left. You wouldn't remember.'

I don't.

I don't remember.

We discussed this theory once, with Ms Reid in biology, that a human body replaces its cells every seven years, in which case Dad would be twice transformed since that photo. And me? I would be a different girl – almost woman – to the one who knew my mum.

But Ms Reid said the theory wasn't quite right anyway, that there are some neurons, the ones in our cerebral cortex apparently, which never change, and cells in our hearts which are replaced at a reducing rate as we age.

I tell Dad he can head outside. The way his shoulders drop is a giveaway, even though he's working hard not to look relieved.

Google tells me the cerebral cortex is linked with processes like thought, consciousness, emotion, language, reasoning and memory.

Memory.

The bit of my body in charge of all this shit is one of the few bits of my body that is supposed to be permanent. And sure.

But I can't remember a dad who could be carefree.

And yet he could.

And I can't remember a mum who would—

And yet she did.

*

They say time flies when you're having fun, but when you're searching your dead mother's house, time moves as fast as that NASA probe that touched the sun. But while the spacecraft was torch-proof, my hopes of finding answers are more easily scorched.

Despite all the cushions I've pulled from the beds and sofas. Despite all the books I've taken from the shelves. Despite every single piece of paper I've slipped from drawers and weighted down with Mum's clutch of painted stones: nothing.

'Iris, what have you done?'

This mess is Dad's worst nightmare. Because it's not just in Mum's bedroom, where Dad has sat me down on the chair at the dressing table, that looks like it's been burgled. There's the litter of coats, their pockets turned inside out, and bags, their zips gaping, on the landing carpet too.

Dad snatches at my fingers before they can rattle the dressing-table drawer. 'Stop.' His eyes are as dark and wide as the wardrobe, with its doors swinging on their hinges, its contents puked on the floor.

'It must be here!' I push against his hands. They're on my arms now, keeping me seated, keeping me still, keeping me from my search, which is vital if I'm ever to know the *why*.

'What? What must be here?' His head swivels, side to side, up and down.

'The note.' Fury rumbles in my gut because hasn't he kept enough from me already, must he also keep me from this? 'There's always a note.'

'Iris.' The way Dad says my name is the same slow, broken way he said it when I was ten and the two syllables rutted a fault line running right through my middle. 'There wasn't a note. I checked too. As soon as I knew how she'd died, I came and searched everywhere.' Something about me must mellow because he loosens his grip and scans the room. 'Though I have to say, I didn't make quite as much mess as you.'

He's trying to lighten the mood.

It's what we do, isn't it? We make each other better. We urge each other to smile.

'I'm sorry there isn't an answer, sunshine.'

An hour or so later, I've rehung clothes, refilled cupboards, everything's in its proper neat and tidy place. To look at it, you'd think it was all OK.

115

'We need to be heading off soon,' Dad says when he finds me in my old room, under my old duvet, feeling too big, too grown for my old bed.

This morning, I suggested, totally casually, that seeing as she lives so close to Sunnyside, we should pop in on Bronagh. I wanted to thank her, I said, for looking after the house. And I had a T-shirt to return to her daughter, I told Dad, deliberately saying 'her daughter' because my skin flushes with a whispering heat whenever I so much as think of Órla's name.

It's already 2.30.

Rolling on to my side, I slide my hand under the pillow like I do when I'm going to sleep.

There's a thin crackle of paper.

Paper?

My heart rustles as I scramble for it.

It's too thick to be a note. And when I withdraw it from beneath the pink covers, it's too bright. Too festive. A present concealed in homemade wrapping paper. Cream with green-pencilled Christmas trees. The drawings are scrawled, chaotic even. But in their messiness, the trees are real too. I recognize the style instantly.

'Merry Christmas, Iris' Mum had written in gold marker. The letters wrap around one single cloud hovering above the trees.

Inside is a plain white T-shirt and a pack of seven fabric crayons. And a note.

Not the note I was looking for but, still, a note.

Fill it with rainbows
X

116

'Iris,' Mum always liked to remind me, 'means Goddess of Rainbows. And it's so true,' she sang once as she made bacon sandwiches in a ball gown, because *Strictly Come Dancing* had inspired a kitchen waltz. 'You bring me so much colour and light.'

I know she told me this because I wrote it in the Better Things notebook Tala gave me.

When did Mum hide the gift? Did she expect to see me open it? Had she imagined us drawing the rainbows together?

The T-shirt is too small. Like everything else in this room, it belongs to another (mothered) girl from another (mothered) time. I slip it into my bag and head downstairs.

'I told Bronagh we'd be there by three,' Dad reminds me as we climb into the car a few minutes later.

When we pull up outside her house, Órla appears in the window as if I'm not the only one who's been looking forward to this reunion. My heart, which should be broken by Sunnyside, pounds a beat that's surely incongruous for a girl who's just been searching for a note from her dead mum.

Seventeen

'Hey,' Órla and I say in unison.

'Here, will I take your coat?' Bronagh asks, and I'm conscious, then, of the checked shirt I chose to put on this morning, the questions that had rushed through my head as I toyed with leaving two or three of the top buttons undone. After much doing and undoing in front of the mirror, I'd eventually plumped for three. Too many, maybe. When I shrug my puffer from my shoulders, there's a lot of gaping, a slither of bra and a flash of amusement from Órla as I fuss with the fabric like a Victorian lady in some ditch attempt to protect my modesty.

'Youse can head into the lounge for a wee bit while your dad and I get a cup of coffee.' Bronagh nods her head towards the sitting room which, since I was here last week, has undergone a festive transformation.

'Watch where you stop!' Órla says as I pause to take it all in. I follow the line of her finger, which points at a sprig of mistletoe pinned to the top of the doorway above me. Her mouth curls into a smile as she puts her hands on my hips to move me gently aside so she can pass.

'Have you been outside today? It's freezing!' Sure, I'm babbling. But maybe if I focus on the glacial temperature, I won't feel so hot.

'Mate,' Órla says, making her way to the tree in the corner. 'Are you seriously small-talking me? I mean, surely we have more interesting things to discuss than the weather?'

She has a point. There is a lot I've wanted to discuss with Órla. Like her incredible gymnastic achievements, whether fear was the only thing she felt when I ran out from the potting shed at Sunnyside, if she's ever, you know, met a girl who hadn't previously thought she was anything but straight but somehow changed her mind?

The words had come so easily when I'd rehearsed them in my bathroom. They made me sound inquisitive but chill. Now, though, I can't summon the moxie to be so bold. 'What kind of thing do you want to talk about then?'

'We could start with why on earth Mam keeps this shit!' Órla is on her knees, holding up a reindeer with a red pom-pom nose, googly eyes and antlers twisted from pipe cleaners. Until she plucked him from his prime position, Rudolph was the only homemade decoration on an otherwise perfectly co-ordinated, interiors-magazine-worthy tree.

She knee-walks closer, closer, closer, until she's perched in front of me, more dazzling than any of the ornaments in her cobalt-blue jumpsuit blazoned with golden stars. 'Every year Mam insists this –' she presses Rudolph into my palm '– is the *pièce de résistance*.' Now she's in touching distance, I can see the constellations on Órla's jumpsuit have been stitched by hand. 'You can't tell me it doesn't need binning. I've offered to make her something else. There's a ton of amazing ideas that would work so much better with our scheme. But she's having none of it.'

Sure, the reindeer is battered and kind of crap. But I get why Bronagh keeps it.

To hold on.

'I like him.' I'm towering over Órla, who lifts a hand up to me, like, *pull*. It's warm when I take it. Soft. And my own hand is shaking, then, as I hang the reindeer back on the branch. It twirls and reveals its backside, where three small letters are scrawled in blurred red ink. 'Ó.M.G.?'

'That's me.' She drops into a deep and dramatic curtsey. 'Órla Mary Gamble. An exclamation since the day I was born!' Her arm brushes against me as she rises and reaches across to take two gold-foil-wrapped teddy bears from a bowl artfully arranged between candles on the sideboard. 'The irony is, she'll hang my old tat on there, but these fancy chocolates are "too naff" to hang on her tree! Want one?'

'Obvs.'

We're unwrapping the chocolates when the door to the living room swings open. I'm expecting Dad or Bronagh, who've been engaged in whispered conversations in the kitchen, but in walks a tracksuited woman with an impeccable blonde bob. She wags a bony finger cartoonishly in Órla's face.

Órla swallows, quick-licks a smudge of chocolate from her lips.

'All those Christmas treats will add up, you know.' The woman's Liverpudlian tone is lighter than her eyes, which narrow as that finger draws an invisible line from Órla's mouth to the fist she's clenched around the scrunched-up chocolate wrapper.

'Um, Iris, this is my coach, Catherine.' If a moment ago she was an exclamation, right now Órla's a low-level hum.

As if only just noticing there's someone else in the room, Catherine turns her gaze to me, those blue eyes scanning the length of my body.

'Nice to meet you.' It's my best voice. The one I normally save for meeting the parents.

She nods, as if words are a waste of her time. Reverting to Órla then. 'You don't exactly look ready.'

Órla's hands flit to her jumpsuit, pulling apart the top two poppers. Underneath is that black and purple leotard she'd worn in all those photos on the stairs.

The chocolate wrapper, released from Órla's unfurled palm, falls with a silent bang to the floor.

'I'm always ready,' she says, smiling, though it's not until Catherine leaves the room that the smile moves beyond Órla's stiff cheeks into her eyes. 'Looks like that's me gone then. An extra training session,' she explains and pokes out her bottom lip in a pseudo pout.

'You can't get out of it?'

'You're kidding, mate?' She opens her calendar on her phone. 'Every day's accounted for when you're headed for Olympic gold.' It's not that she sounds unhappy, just a little rehearsed. 'It'll be worth the sacrifices when I'm on the podium, right?'

'Absolutely! I barely have enough focus to finish one whole day at school, let alone the determination it must take to get on a GB squad. The minute Dad and I are out the door, he'll cite you as a shining example of how my prospects might be improved with a different attitude.'

She shrugs. 'Maybe it's not our attitude that's different but our fortune.'

121

'Fortune?' I think of the 'Pisces Explained' print-out she had on her desk when I was looking round her room a few days ago. She's not going to go all astrological on me, is she? Start asking my sign?

Órla's square jaw juts a little as she bites on her bottom lip. 'Yeah, fortune; it's what's in those origami things you hold in your photos, right?' A flush of pink colours her cheeks. 'I may have seen them when I hypothetically stalked you on Insta.'

Aha. I'm not the only one who's been doing some research. Thank God for YouTube and the videos people have posted of Órla's comps.

It's funny how hard your heart can thump when only an hour or so ago it had turned to stone.

'It was cool seeing you, Iris.'

'Oh, before you go…' I reach into my rucksack.

'You could have kept it.' Órla doesn't need to step closer to take her T-shirt, but she does. 'I thought it suited you.' Her head tilts slightly like she's asked me a question. And the smile lines around her emerald-bright eyes disappear.

Is she asking where I am on the scale she embroidered?

I've wondered too. In the late nights since Tuesday when I've not been able to sleep for all the *why*s and *how*s and *what the actual fuck*, I've urged my clamouring thoughts to move beyond Sunnyside and Mum.

And each time, they moved to Órla. And when my mind moved to Órla, my hands moved to my waistband, to my knickers, to the place that has always been pleasure.

But no matter how much I try to move away from them, Sunnyside and Mum lurk.

And who wants to think about their mum when they're thinking about, well, *that*?

And with everything that's going on, should I even be thinking about *that*?

Should my hands even wander?

Is it sick to make my body a refuge?

To hanker for some kind of release?

'Órla, Catherine's waiting for youse in her car,' Bronagh calls from the hall. 'You need to get to gym.'

'What I really need, Iris –' Órla leans in closer '– is to give you my number.' Despite how hushed it is, her whisper is pulsing sparks on my skin.

Eighteen

'Sarah always liked milky coffee until lunch.' Every time she speaks, Bronagh leans towards me on the sofa. She and Dad came into the lounge after Órla left for training. And while the room's still shimmering with fairy lights, it feels different now. It's lost some of its sheen. 'Then she'd switch to black Earl Grey for the afternoon.'

I didn't know that.

'And sparkling. Anything sparkling. Cans of pop. Prosecco. She was always up for a party. Always the first one to—'

'What happened?'

If Bronagh is toppled by my tone, she doesn't show it.

'With Mum, I mean?' Because Prosecco and pop and parties sounds fun and everything, but didn't Bronagh say they weren't close by the time Mum died? 'What happened? Did she change?'

'Iris.' Dad's eyes narrow, and he places his cup down on the table. His back straightens. He's brewing an apology on my behalf.

'It's OK.' Bronagh looks at me, her smile not completely disappeared. 'I loved Sarah,' she says, closer now than ever. 'But, honestly, she wasn't always the easiest person to be friends with.' Her hand is on my arm, her fingers gently squeezing.

'You lived with her, Iris. I think you probably know what I mean.'

~~I know.~~

I daren't move in case I nod.

'My dad got sick, and I'd been heading back and forth to Ireland for a few years, which meant – what with all the ferrying Órla about for gym – I didn't have the energy I'd had for Sarah before.' A tear rolls down her cheek and over her chin, disappears into the thick rib of her maroon jumper. 'And, honestly, I felt let down. All those long phone calls at all hours of the day and night. All the times I'd rushed over to console her in person. I promise, I never begrudged it. But when Dad was ill and I was the one who needed a bit of support, Sarah wasn't there for me. Like always, she just had so much going on.' Bronagh's voice, usually such a song, is flat now. 'As terrible as it feels to say it, sometimes your mam was…'

She takes a sip of her coffee as she picks her words. It's a common theme, isn't it, this attempt at precision when describing Mum. 'Sarah was a lot, that's all. Always in her head, and sometimes she couldn't get out of it. There was an evening she called. I'd not long returned home from tending to Dad when Pete – Órla's father – said I couldn't keep putting myself through it. I didn't talk to her. I had to think of me.'

There's a fussing in my belly. Anger, maybe, but churned in with something else.

'We should probably be going, right, Dad?' I stand. Too quickly, I know, for it to seem anywhere near as casual as I'd intended.

125

'When you leave someone like that,' Bronagh says, 'even if you're right to put yourself first, well, it can be hard to live with.' The air between us thickens.

'Right.' I'm not sure if Dad's responding to me or Bronagh, though he's already grabbed his coat and is clearly heading for the door.

Bronagh follows us. 'You can call me any time, Iris.' She pulls a piece of paper and a pen from a drawer in the hallway cabinet and writes down her number. 'It's important for you to understand who Sarah was. The whole of her.' A flash, livid as lightning, passes between her and Dad. 'For you to know the truth.'

'Thanks,' Dad says. Though he doesn't sound grateful for anything with his clipped goodbye and his hand on my back urging me towards the car.

My phone, when I check it as we're pulling away from Bronagh's, is littered with WhatsApps from Tala. There's also a string of messages from the Home Safe group I didn't leave for fear of looking like the lone dick who wasn't on board with female solidarity, or safety in numbers, or whatever else the girls are hoping to achieve. I *am* on board with all that. I just don't like that lot thinking they've a right to my whereabouts is all.

Freya is home safe from her shopping trip to Birmingham.
Aisha is home safe from Charlie's.
Chloe is home safe from the pool.

What would I write, even? Iris is home safe from the house where her mum decided the world wasn't enough?

'Why did *you* leave?' We're almost home when I break the silence. 'Sunnyside, I mean.' Though what I actually mean is, *Why did you leave my mum?*

Dad's always super focused when he's driving, but right now his fixation on the road ahead is intense even for him. 'It was complicated, sunshine.' His eyes move only to check the mirrors.

I heave a breath huge enough that Dad understands *It was complicated, sunshine* isn't a whole enough answer.

'Sarah, she was…' He flicks the indicator, turns right, stops at the red light, which switches to amber then green. 'She could be…full on.'

The word I would use is 'exuberant'.

(Nice use of 'exuberant', Iris.)

'Did you love her?'

'I did, yes.' His smile when he finally looks at me is sad.

'But you left anyway.'

He pulls in to our driveway, nodding this small, heavy nod like his head, or what's inside it, is jammed, and I think that's conversation over. But then, 'Sometimes, Iris, even when you love someone, leaving is still the best thing you can do.'

Day had turned into night during the journey home. From the warmth of the car, we see Rosa in the yellow-lit window pulling the curtains to keep out the dark.

'I appreciate it can't be easy. To hear negative things about your mum.' A patter of rain falls against the windscreen. Even though we're no longer moving, Dad turns the knob for the wipers. 'It could be hard with Sarah.' He pauses in between every sentence, like he's clawing for palatable truths. 'It wasn't

127

always obvious to know what to do.' The blades swoosh across the glass, rhythmic, incessant, determined to stave off the rain. 'That Christmas Day, for example.' Dad sits facing forward, eyes on the front wall of the house, and chews his lip as he turns off the engine. The wipers stop, and the rain, heavier now, waterfalls to the bonnet then disappears. 'Sarah asked me to take you to Sunnyside for breakfast.'

'What?' I don't remember everything about that morning, but I *do* remember we didn't go to see Mum. 'She'd asked us to go over?'

And we didn't?

Like when she phoned Bronagh, who didn't take the call.

'I wanted you to have a happy Christmas. Your happiness has always come fir—'

'First.' As I nod, a soft huff of something I don't want to be feeling puffs from my nose. 'I know, Dad. I *know* you want me to be happy.'

'She was slurring her words when she phoned me. She sounded drunk.' Dad is half in shadow, half in the orange glow from the street lamp. 'I didn't want you to see her like that. It wouldn't have been nice for you.'

~~I'll tell you what wasn't nice for Mum: thinking that we'd all abandoned her, that when she obviously needed us, we made a conscious decision not to go.~~

Nineteen

The school canteen, with its bright lights and noisy gossip, is even harsher than usual. I'd rather the shadowy corners of an abandoned building and the challenge of finding my way in.

Weirdly, though, I'm not buzzed with the idea of doing it alone.

'Please, Tal. It's safe, I promise. Just an old Italian restaurant. You know the one that's been shut for, like, forever. It's not even as if we'd have to go to the middle of nowhere. It's bang in the centre of town.'

'Iris.' Tala puts her knife and fork down on the table with a clatter that turns too many heads in her direction. Her head drops and her eyes fall into their usual hiding place behind her hair. 'Don't you think it's a bit silly –' she's whispering now – 'to go anywhere like that at the moment? With this guy on the prowl?'

'You mean, the one I already escaped?' His lingering laugh, though. His ill-boding sneer. How the more I think about it, I don't think it was a blade in his pocket. 'I don't see why I should miss out when that creep's the one in the wrong.'

Tala shrugs. 'I just don't want you getting hurt, that's all.'

'So come with me.'

'Iris, I know you don't think so, but there are, occasionally, more important things than urbex.'

'What, like this?' I examine the revision timetable she made for me. 'I've stuck to it since you gave it to me on Monday.' When I say stuck to it, what I actually mean is, I've had the relevant textbooks out on my desk while composing, editing, then never actually sending messages to Órla. Instead, I've just scrawled her name repeatedly like some pathetic cliché. 'You honestly think I should spend my Friday night getting to grips with water and carbon cycles?'

'Your geography A-level result will thank you for it.'

'And my boredom level will condemn me to hell. C'mon, Tal.' I slide the timetable into the back pocket of my bag. 'We can resume our revision tomorrow…'

'I've scheduled English lang, French lit and psychology for tomorrow. I need to hone my German oral presentation tonight.'

'Surely you can nail the oral in your free period after lunch. And I'm walking Buddy at six, so it'll be at least seven thirty before you and I head out?' The later the better if we want to avoid getting caught. Though I don't mention that obviously.

'I guess.' She picks at the nail of her ring finger with her thumb. 'If you really need me to.'

'Brilliant.' I'm pulling up the article I read about the shut-down restaurant when—

'It's just, in that free period this afternoon, Dougie and I were going to go through my poems to see which ones might work for the slam.' Tala doesn't phrase it like a question, but there's a request in her softly delivered statement for sure.

130

'Oh.' A small lump of potato sticks in my throat. 'If I'm the one doing the performance, should we not pick those together?' I glug some Coke.

'I already asked you, but you didn't seem interested.' She's still quiet, but the softness has hardened into something new.

'When?' I wrack my brain but can't recall her saying anything about choosing poems.

'Saturday. I sent you a WhatsApp. Well, five, actually. Asked which one you'd be happiest reading.' She stirs the gloopy cheese into the beans. 'You didn't reply.'

Shit.

'Crap, Tal. Was it in the afternoon?' She nods. 'I was at Sunnyside and then with Bronagh and Órla, you know the girl I met at—'

'Yes, I know Órla.' *Jeez*, did Tala just roll her eyes? 'You've mentioned her, like, a million times. At least five hundred thousand of those were on Monday when you repeatedly told me she'd given you her number.'

I swear it's the swig of Coke that sends fizzy jets across my skin.

'There were all those alerts from the Home Safe group over the weekend. Then you must have sent something else and I didn't scroll back through your previous messages. I'm sorry.' The kids in the queue for canteen slop gawp at my too-loud sing-song apology, and Tala sinks into her chair.

'You understand, right?' I ask a few minutes later as we walk down the school corridor about to go our separate ways for class. 'About the missed message? Saturday was kind of intense.'

131

Tala stops dead still.

'Watch it!' Know-All, of all people, stumbles into her.

Despite myself, I help him gather the textbooks he dropped in the collision. 'Dick,' I spit as he skulks off down the corridor.

Tala takes the cuffs of my coat sleeves in her hands. 'Are you OK, Iris?'

'Sure.'

She doesn't look convinced. 'Only you seem a bit…'

I cock my head and let the pause ride. 'A bit…?'

'I dunno, angry? And a bit…' Here we go again. 'Distracted,' she finally says.

I could tell her. About what Dad said in the car on the way back from Órla's. That Mum wanted us to go for breakfast on Christmas Day and, when we didn't, she…

But if I tried – to tell her, that is – it might not be words that vent from my mouth but a scream.

'I think I might like Órla,' I say instead.

Tala's brow is totally, *well, duh!*

'You're not, you know, surprised by the fact that she's…' It's *my* turn to clamour for words. 'You know? A girl.'

'Well, it would explain why you did a runner from Rollo.'

'I liked Rollo. I *really* liked Rollo. It's not that I don't like boys, I just…'

'Like girls too?'

'I guess.' We continue walking.

'Typical!' Tala shakes her head, laughing. 'That you're open to anyone, and I can't find a single so—'

'Open to anyone?' My mouth drops and my voice pitches higher as I feign shock and turn to face her. 'Tala Fischer, are you suggesting I'm greedy just because I happen to like a girl now too?'

'I didn't mean it like that I—'

'I know you didn't.' I loop my arm through hers. 'I'm teasing. And anyway, there are more important things to get worked up about. Like your assumption that you can't find anyone is a classic case of speaking too soon.' I nudge her in the ribs as Dougie walks out of the boys' toilets.

No word of a lie, his pupils literally dilate when he spots her. 'Tala! Madame Cuthbert's not going to be *très content de toi*!'

'*Pourquoi pas?*' Tala says.

Damn, this is the closest I've ever seen her to flirting, and I don't understand a word. 'English, please, people.'

Tala smirks, like, *I told you so*, because at the end of Year Eleven she banged on and on about what a good idea it would be for me to take French A level if I was planning on one day exploring France. Whatever, though, right. I'll just pick it up when I'm there.

'Madame Cuthbert won't be happy because –' Dougie waves some papers in my face before refocusing all his attention on Tala – 'I couldn't stop reading your poems last night. Got so caught up in them, I didn't have time to finish the chapters of *L'Étranger*. I've printed them off so we can mark them up later, yeah?'

'Looks like I'm not the only one to be distracted by the kindling of luuuuuurve,' I tease after Dougie's said his see-you-laters and disappeared into the crowd. Who knows, maybe it's a good thing I didn't read Tala's messages, because now she and Dougie have a few more hours to get all poetic. Or whatever other euphemism we're using these days for getting down. 'You do your thing with Dougie, yeah.' How else will she ever get over this barrier she's put up against sex and/or love?

Given I have no such barriers, several hours later, on my way to fetch Buddy for his afternoon walk, I send Órla a text.

Fancy a taste of urbex?

By the time I knock on Mr West's door, she still hasn't replied.

'For heaven's sake!' The vaguely recognizable man who opens Mr West's door is far less pleased than Buddy to see me. 'You're the dog-walker, aren't you?'

I nod as I pat Buddy's huge bouffant. I swear, there isn't a single time I've seen him that he hasn't made me smile.

'You're on my list of people to call,' the man says, one hand holding Buddy by his collar, the other rubbing his brow. 'You'll have to come in a second.' He moves back into the hallway. 'It's a bloody long list.' He sighs as he closes the door. 'Dad had a fall a few days ago.'

'Mr West? Is he OK?'

'He'll be fine.' His voice is somewhere between anguish and exasperation. 'I'm Adam, by the way.'

'Iris.' As I crouch down, the poodle's black mop-head ears soft-flop on to my face and his duster-brush tail sweeps maniacally across the floor.

Adam takes the lead from where it hangs on the coat hooks and rolls it into a neat loop. He's very particular about the way he places it inside Buddy's empty water bowl, which is on top of the dog crate. Also stacked are Buddy's neatly folded blankets, his Tupperware'd food and his favourite ball which, way beyond Adam's obvious desire for order, is attached to a manky matted rope.

'Buddy going somewhere?'

I don't know this dude, but the combo of his flushed cheeks and darting eyes make his discomfort an easy read.

When he finally speaks, I swear he says something about the rescue centre.

'What?' I stand so I can hear better and Buddy lunges, his paws press heavy against my chest.

'Dad'll improve with some physio, but it's unlikely he'll ever be as mobile as before so…'

'So…?'

'He won't be able to walk Buddy, and he can't afford to pay you to do it every day, so…'

What? Does he think by not finishing his sentences, I'll get the thorny gist, and he won't have to articulate Buddy's sad fate aloud.

'So…?'

'So Buddy is going to the rescue centre.' There. He said it.

Buddy's claws scrape the laminate with impatience to get outside.

'And Mr West agreed to this?' I don't mean to come across accusatory, like Know-All when he's playing at being a lawyer in some pseudo family row. But a few weeks back, I spied Mr West and Buddy sitting together on the sofa and finally understood the actual integrity of the cliché *man's best friend*. 'They need each other.'

'Dad agreed it was for the best.'

Buddy cranes his neck, mouths that manky ball and drops it at my feet. This is what he does when he wants to play. When he's happy he wags his tail. When he senses danger, he bares his teeth. When he's hungry, he sits by the back-left cupboard of the kitchen, where Mr West keeps his food.

I think of Mr West in a hospital bed unable to make his needs this clear.

His son hands me thirty quid, tells me he's sorry not to be able to give me more notice, but, given the circumstances, 'I'm sure you'll understand.' And before I have the chance to tell him, *I'm not sure I do actually*, Adam West closes the door.

✦

'I *don't* understand,' I spit, half an hour later as I stomp into our kitchen, red hot with the charge of my walk home in my stupid too-thick purple puffer.

Dad, on the phone, clocks my fury and holds up one waggy finger to tell me he'll just be a minute. His brow crinkles as he rounds his eyes, like, *chill*.

'I see what you mean.' He raises his voice over my slamming and rattling as I set the oven to warm a mince pie. 'So it's best for us to hold off doing anything until after Christmas?'

~~Why do today what you can put off until the future, eh, Dad? And who cares who gets fucked up along the way?~~

'They're separating Mr West and Buddy.' The words thump out of my mouth and into the kitchen the moment Dad finishes his call. 'Dumping Buddy in a rescue centre just when Mr West will need him most.'

~~Obviously~~ Dad tells me I need to calm down.

'I'm sure they didn't come to the decision easily,' he says once I've told him the full story. He winks and snatches the last bit of mince pie from my plate as if all of this can be swiped away with his clownish habit of stealing my snacks.

'You think it's OK then?'

'What I think is that sometimes people have to make difficult choices.' He holds up two more mince pies – this pathetic look on his face – puts them in the oven, then smiles, like everything is so easily resolved. 'Having a dog is a huge responsibility.' Here we go. Cue a lecture on why Dad'll never allow us to get a pet. 'Mr West won't be able to look after Buddy, not in the way Buddy needs to live a happy, healthy life.'

'And it doesn't matter that Mr West is going to feel like crap after his fall, and his favourite creature in the world won't be there to comfort him?'

'Mr West will have his son. And Buddy will have a new family who are more able to give him the care he needs.'

In Dad's eyes everything's sorted. I don't bother mentioning how when I left, and Buddy realized he wouldn't get his walk, I could hear his whining, even after Mr West's son had shut the front door.

'That was Bronagh on the phone, by the way,' Dad says as I take one of the freshly warmed pies and sit down at the table.

The name Bronagh knots with the name Órla and ties my tongue. I just about manage a 'Hmm?'

'About Sunnyside.' Dad sits opposite me. 'I wanted to chat with you about it. I was thinking you'd probably want to sell?'

'Sell?' Shock unravels the knot and the word spews out of me.

'She says buyers stop looking this close to Christmas. That we're better launching in the new ye—'

'Sell?' I repeat, because, what the fuck, did he just not hear me?

'Yes.' And I swear his eyes are too bright, like selling Sunnyside is his best idea yet.

'But I've only just got it back.' My mind flashes to the box of ashes that sits next to the Box of Mum Things. How everything tangible I have of Mum's fits under my bed. How Tala and I turned the bothy into somewhere I could think of her on her anniversary because there wasn't a grave or a bench, even. There wasn't *anywhere* I could go.

Until Sunnyside.

And he's suggesting I sell it?

'I thought…' Concern makes slugs of the veins on his temples and neck. 'I thought with what happened there that you wouldn't want to…'

What happened there.

It's not a memory, is it, if I wasn't there to witness it. If I didn't even know it happened until last week. But my head has built a picture; piece by jagged piece, it's made an ugly jigsaw of that Christmas morning with my mum and those pills.

It's not like I didn't think about it when I was at Sunnyside. That when I was in the sitting room, where Dad said they found her, I didn't imagine Mum on the sofa. What she might have been wearing, or the sickly swollen yellow of her skin. It's not that I didn't hold and smell the cushion, wondering if her head had laid on it. Or look at the ceiling and try to conjure the last thing she saw.

Those things did happen. But other things happened too.

Like when I touched the things she touched and all my whole-body aching was smeared with something like joy. Joy being too big, too happy a word really, but whatever the word is, it brought me closer to her than I've been in seven years.

'I've been doing some work on it,' Dad says. 'To make it nice for you, obviously, but also to make it ready for sale. I thought you'd find such a big property a burden, sunshine. Especially one of that age.'

The kitchen isn't a battleground. I hear what Dad's saying and see the sense in it. But my heart numbs as he runs through all the handyman jobs he's done there. Every little task he details adds another inch to the invisible line he's drawing between us on the floor.

'You have a lot to think about,' is how he finishes the conversation.

I nod because he's right and smile because he's nervous.

Dad kisses me on the crown of my head. As he leaves the room, I feel the buzz of my phone in my pocket.

Órla: Tell me where and when to meet you. I'm in.

Twenty

'Obviously, I didn't get the memo about the dress code.' Órla raises her arms, turns her palms skyward and pulls a face. '*You're* like something out of *The Matrix*, and *I'm* like bloody Poppy from *Trolls*.'

'That coat *is* kind of a rainbow and the hairband…' I don't even know where to start with the broad pelican-print fabric twisted into a chunky knot on her crown.

'Oi! I made this!' She pats the top of her head in what I think is mock self-consciousness.

'I love it. All of it. Even the boots,' I say, only now taking in the tiny little flowers she's painted on the toes of her shoes. 'It's all just a little…' I tread carefully. 'Conspicuous?'

'I guess I do stand out in the dark.'

It's true. Only a rookie would rely on the night-time, back-street murk to give her cover. Windows from the adjacent flats overlook the courtyard where we're stood contemplating how best to scale a bin.

'Perhaps I should have been a little more prescriptive.'

But Órla shakes her head. 'Honestly, mate, prescriptive is the last thing I need.'

I put a finger to my lips to signal quiet.

'That bag is a Tardis,' she whispers as I pull out gloves, head torch, wipes and – *that's what I was after* – a silicon respirator I place over the lower half of her face.

'In case of dust,' I explain, grabbing a bandana and tying it so it covers my mouth.

I hoick myself up, no grace in either the hefty swing of my legs or the bovine grunts as my chest hits the top of the wheelie bin. I heave my knees beneath me. There are many reasons I usually do this alone and the view Órla must currently have of my upended denim-clad butt is one of them.

The window is, as I thought when I did a recce on one of my walks with Buddy, wedged in its swollen frame but easily openable with my library card. Tala would be fuming at the sacrilege. It's the only time mine gets any use.

'Ready?'

Órla, still on the ground but with her arms held high for me to take them, looks anything but.

Somehow – with a disconcerting amount of groaning – I haul her up on to the bin, where she lands with a *whoomp* on top of me, squishing the McDonalds' bag I'd balanced on my lap. The burgers are likely ruined, though this tragedy is softened by how close our faces are. Even with the silicon respirator between us, I can imagine her breath and how it might tickle my nose.

'With all those back-flipping, high-flying, mat-tumbling moves of yours, I thought you'd find getting in here a piece of piss.'

'It's hardly the same,' Órla says once she's removed the mask and taken the torch I offered the second we were safely inside. 'A gym is well lit and has a sprung floor for a start. This place has a very different, much spookier vibe.'

Here we go. Spooky is why Tala rarely comes with me. 'It's like a horror film,' my best mate says if I take her anywhere but the bothy. And it's game over before the exploration even starts.

'Shiiiiiiiiiit.' Órla casts her torchlight into the furthest corners of Matteo's, which was, and still looks like, an Italian restaurant. Nothing eerie about it. Not to me. Sure, there's a little mould on the walls and the scent is more malodorous than margherita. (Nice use of 'malodorous', Iris.) But it's kind of romantic how the tables are still laid with green and white tablecloths, plates are set with cutlery and red napkins are folded into crowns. I'm not sure it's romance on Órla's mind, though, when she grabs me, pulling me close and huddling into my side, her breath hot on my neck as she whispers, 'You think there's ghosts?'

'No.' My heart twitches with disappointment. 'But it's cool, we don't have to stay if it's too much.' It's the stock answer I give Tala whenever she's freaked. There's nothing worse than exploring with someone who fails to see the beauty in these places because their vision's too drenched in fear.

'Go?' Órla practically blinds me with the torchlight she blasts in my face. 'Why would we go?'

'You're not scared?'

'Scared?' She turns the torch on herself. 'If you'd faced coach on a Sunday afternoon after an entire weekend of disappointing ribbon snakes and botched hoop catches, you'd know there are far more terrifying things than ghouls! Bring on the phantoms!' she laughs as she steps forward, undeterred by the dark.

A coffee machine sits ready to bubble and grind on the bar, where bottles of unopened wine stand tall among glasses and an optimistic corkscrew. There are menus, promo leaflets, receipts and a drift of mail by the door. In the kitchen are washed pans, half-used jars of herbs and spices, a folder of recipes all stained despite their plastic sleeves.

'Mate, look.' Órla's rifling through the various papers and books on the bar. 'All these reservations in the diary.' She flicks the pages. 'How long's it been shut?'

'Four, five years maybe.' I overheard something recently on the local radio station Dad likes listening to in the car. A piece on high business rates sounding the death knell of the independent high street. The phrase *death knell* had stuck in my head.

'You think people turned up wanting their carbonara or whatever, and the Italians had just scarpered?' Her narrowed eyes catch mine as she flips the book shut. 'I bet the manager was a Sagittarius.' She fake shivers. 'They're the worst. Flighty as hell.'

I hate the fact that I even know this about her, because all that star sign stuff is claptrap, but Mum was a Sagittarius.

There's a precision to the way Órla struts into the kitchen, the same specificity to her stride as I saw in her competition videos that I may have watched once or twice or even twenty-seven times a day on YouTube.

'There's actual food in the cupboards,' she says. 'You'd think they'd've sorted all that. You know, got their shit in order before they left. But it looks like they just bolted without thinking of all this crap they were leaving behind.'

I'd told Órla when we first climbed through the window that she could remove her mask because Matteo's looked safe enough. There was just a regular layer of dust. But her take on the people who once worked in this place hangs in the air, making it claggy and difficult to breathe.

This is not the mood I'm after.

'We should eat,' I say, bright and breezy. 'Before those squashed burgers get too cold.' *Eau de boeuf* puffs from the crinkled top of the paper bag as I plonk it on a table. 'You might want these.' I pass Órla the anti-bac wipes, which she runs over her chair before sitting down.

'Is there anything you *don't* have in that bag?'

I'm switching on a couple of battery-operated tea lights and, honestly, tonight, I'm even impressing myself.

'Wine, *signorina*?' I grab a bottle from the shelf behind the counter, hold it like a baby I'm entering into a beauty contest.

'Driving, remember? Anyway, drinking dulls the senses.' Órla opens the burger box, takes a good whiff. 'And I'd rather mine were fully alert.' Be still my ramped-up heart as she looks up at me through her lashes. 'It's been a while…' And I swear she's hinting at the possibility of some kind of liaison, but, 'McDonalds is on coach's "No List"! Don't think I've had one for years.'

'So am I about to witness a rebellion?' In an act of pure encouragement, I take an animalistic bite.

Shouts from the street seep through the tiny cracks in the windows and Órla's head whips, like an owl's, checking the shadowy corners for signs of imminent threat.

'They're outside.'

Her chest deflates as she releases her held breath. 'Forget the burger, me just being here is a rebellion.'

'Oh God. Have you absconded?!' A smear of ketchup drips like cartoon blood from my sleeve from when I wiped my mouth with the back of my hand. 'Your mum *does* know you're with me?'

'I'll cover for you with Catherine.' It's not just Bronagh's *voice* that Órla impersonates. 'But just so youse are clear, it's a one-off, pet.' Órla mimics Bronagh tilting her head too. That sympathetic chin-dip I've seen in countless mothers when they talk to or about me and my 'situation'. 'A friendly face might be what Iris needs right now.'

My nails press, keen and sharp, into palms. 'So this is a pity visit?'

'Oh, get over yourself!' Órla shakes her head, laughing. 'This is about me having a night *off schedule* and us having a bit of fun.'

Her lips part, and, within a few no-talking minutes, the burger and fries are gone. 'Fuck me, that was good.'

'I think I might be a bad influence!' My eyes fix on her fingers, which she's licking clean of salt and grease with her tongue. She glances up at me while she's eating.

'I have this theory.'

'Oh no!' Because if Órla's theories are anything like Know-All's, we might be here a while.

But Órla quirks her brow, like, *hear me out, yeah?* 'On our own, we're one thing, like this certain version of ourselves with these traits we think are the essence of us. But then when we meet someone, when two people come together…I dunno, they make something new.'

'Is that what we're doing tonight then? Morphing your old burger-shunning self into a beef-devouring glutton.'

'Nice use of "glutton", Iris, but that's no—'

'Wait. What?' The accusation in my tone punctures Órla's easy smile. It deflates into bruised concern. 'What did you say?'

'You mean my theory?'

'No, after that.'

'Nice use of "glutton", Iris. Why? What did I...'

'Nice use of "adore", Iris,' Mum said one morning at breakfast when I told her how much I *adored* pain au chocolat.

Words were Mum's thing. I may only have been ten when she died, but even by four or five, she'd already instilled the value and thrill of them. 'Good pronunciation of *shock-oh-la* too.' Her mood was as sweet and warm as the pastry. 'We should go to Par-ee,' she sang. And even though my geography skills were lagging behind my linguistic achievements, I knew she was injecting a very un-English twist into her intonation of the city, which she told me was filled with exquisite architecture, exquisite clothes and even more exquisite cuisine.

I repeated the word 'exquisite' into my orange juice as she promised me a boat down a river, a climb up a tower and a train that would shuttle us from one country to another beneath the sea.

There was no trip to Pa-ree. Or Paris. But, a day or so later, there *was* a living room decorated in French flags, and onion soup for dinner. There was a wine glass filled with Ribena, and whitish gooey cheese to spread on hunks torn from a stick of crusty bread that, when she pulled it from the hamper, was as long as my leg.

'What do you think?' Mum's eyes flitted between me and our Parisian picnic-style supper.

'Egg-skwiz-it,' I said, and she beamed.

'You caught me off guard…' I try to explain to Órla.

'Iris?' The room's not so cold really, but I'm grateful for the warmth of Órla's hand.

'Mum used to say that. About the words, I mean. "Nice use of such and such, Iris."'

'Same!' I swear Órla sparkles, like, *this is a sign*. 'Mam does it too.'

And for a moment, I think maybe there's an element of truth with the *this is a sign* thing, but then it hits me. 'It must have been something Mum and Bronagh did with each other. When they were younger maybe.'

When they were friends.

'I'm sorry,' Órla says, and I know where this is headed. 'About your mam.'

This is the point where I normally tell people I'm over it. That I was a kid when it happened and, sure, it's sad, but, honestly, I promise, I'm OK.

But.

'I miss her.'

My shameful sorrow stinks. More than the fetid smell of the room, even. And it must get inside Órla's mouth and nose because, for a minute or so, she doesn't say anything, just stares at the table, still holding my hand.

Finally, she breaks the silence, 'My nan – on Mam's side – she believed everyone's soul returns as a bird. She swore on her life my granddad came back as a seagull. Reckoned he never missed a single holiday with us after he died.' I'm expecting piss-take in Órla's eyes when she looks up at me, but what actually lies there is hope. 'Honest! She could pick him out from a flock whenever we were at the seaside. Nan's a parrot that lives at our local indie coffee shop now. Doesn't stop squawking judgements on customers who come in for a flat white. She never could abide anyone who didn't appreciate the value of a good old cup of tea.' Órla's fingers drift from mine as she leans back in her chair. 'I like it. It means when people die, they never really leave us.'

The idea is serene, peaceful, though the uglier truth of how Dad shunned Mum's invitation on Christmas morning cuts its way through the quiet image, as loud and violent as the cawing murder of crows driving away the robin at Sunnyside.

'But what if the person who died felt like we wanted them to leave? Would they still come back?'

She doesn't answer, doesn't really speak even as I spend the next half an hour truth-spewing about Dad's secret-keeping, Mum-rejecting ways. Was Órla right then? In that theory of hers. In her company, do I become someone new?

It's only when I pull the fortune teller I made for the restaurant from my bag, put my fingers within its folds and ask her to pick that she breaks her silence. 'That one,' she says, pointing at one square and then another. I lift the flap and read her that irrefutable destiny.

You will be strong.

She smiles, even when I show her how Mum gave me no other option.

'It's funny, that word.' She's climbed back out of the restaurant window and is sitting waiting for me on top of the bin. 'Strong.' It's just one syllable, but its punch lands heavy against my chest. 'People say it about it me.' She swings her legs round and jumps to the ground below. 'You know, because of my training?'

'You do look fit.' If Órla is aware of the two ways in which my observation is intended, she doesn't show it. Her eyes are suddenly dreamy, her attention no longer on me.

'But despite the timetable, it's not really in my nature to stick to a schedule.' She stuffs her hands in those giant yellow pockets. 'Us Pisces tend to be more ephemeral creatures, you know?'

I drop down beside her. 'Maybe it's not your star sign that shapes you then?' Our feet walk in perfect step with each other as we make our way back to her car. 'Surely you don't actually think your life is written in the stars?'

She stops. 'And that's crazier, is it, than you thinking yours is written on a scrap of paper?'

Twenty-One

'It'll have to be a jungle wee,' I tell Órla, pointing across to one of the narrow paths that wind between the shops in the older part of town. 'And when I say jungle wee, what I mean is alleyway. Urbexer's prerogative,' I add when she shakes her head. 'If you're going to be @DoratheUrbexplorer's sidekick, you'll have to get used to squatting wherever you can.'

'Hey! I'm nobody's sidekick,' she balks. 'And anyway, it's not just a wee.' The rise of pink in Órla's cheeks is visible in the street lights.

'You think your coach has hard-wired your digestive system to oust the burger asap?'

'It's not a poo if that's what you're thinking!' Órla shoves the paper bag of burger wrappers in a nearby bin. 'I think I've got my period. I don't suppose you have anything in your Tardis bag for that?'

I offer up a napkin, pretty sure from the glare Órla fires that it definitely will not do.

✦

Twenty-five minutes later, we're sliding the back door to my bedroom and I'm directing Órla to the en suite – where there's a basket of the world's finest sanitary products – while promising the healing powers of a cup of Rosa's Womankind tea.

'I'll be back in a min,' I say to the closing bathroom door before hurrying down to the kitchen, where Dad is banging on about the garden centre his colleague recommended for his perfect *real* tree.

Rosa looks up at me from her seat at the kitchen table and mouths, '*You OK?*'

I nod and press the button for the kettle. 'Drink?'

But neither she nor Dad is listening.

'Your artificial one's been great, but you have to admit, the branches are all bent in on each other.' Dad pulls this face like an imperfect tree is as difficult to deal with as an imperfect daughter. 'Half the fake pine needles have gone.'

Rosa might not say anything, but she is definitely one of those people who gives meaning to the phrase 'silence speaks volumes'.

Dad, seemingly oblivious to the significance of his wife's quiet, prattles on.

'C'mon, love, we've talked about getting a real tree for years. And given we won't put it up until the eighteenth, we can definitely keep it sprightly till Christmas Day!' He shoves his phone, which I'm guessing displays the garden centre website, in her face. 'And any reservations you've had have surely been allayed by your recent botanical success.' He pulls the thriving yucca from its sacred position on the windowsill and presents it to Rosa as if it holds all the glory of an Olympic flame.

From what I've seen, yoga is comprised of slow and considered movements, but the way Rosa's up and out of her chair and sprinting for her yucca rings of Usain Bolt. She swiftly returns the plant to its rightful place.

'I know it's not the best of trees, Matt. But I've had it for years.' Even over the roar of the boiling kettle, I can hear my stepmum's tone is chock-full of nostalgia.

'Exactly!' Dad's, meanwhile, is chock-full of contempt. 'It's knackered.' He lays his hands on the table, like, *case closed*, and my heart and belly are rolling with the gall of his easy dismissal of his wife's decrepit but beautiful tree. 'Let's bin it.'

Is flawed and a little broken really so impossible for him to bear?

I swear I feel the whip of their heads turning as I slap two mugs down on the counter.

'Yeah, just bin it!' It's me talking, but I don't recognize my voice. Not just the volume of it, which is big and bolshy and bold, but the scrape and scorn and scratch of it. 'Why on earth would you keep something that's a little bit damaged, eh? I mean, God forbid you try to fix it. Far better to put it out of sight and replace it with something all shiny and new.'

Dad stands, then, his arms spread, and his hands turned upwards, his eyes wide, like, *Iris, please*. He moves to hug me.

'No.' It's the only word I can say now because 'no' is small and there's not much room on my tongue, which is thick and heavy with something bigger than a two-letter word. Something heftier than the stupid fucking artificial Christmas tree that I don't like much anyway because everyone knows real trees have that delicious smell. But that's not the point. The point is, Dad's just playing to form. Because isn't it easier to get rid

152

of a problem rather than deal with it? To put a broken tree in a skip. To separate a frail old man from his dog. To sell a house that's witnessed tragedy.

'Iris,' he pleads, ignoring Know-All, who's just walked into the room. This is exactly what Dad can't handle. This rage and chaos shooting from me is exactly what my father's done his utmost to avoid.

I fix my mouth shut and the storm rumbles down my throat into my gut, gravity fighting thunder, as the gale of wrath and exasperation ignites my legs and feet with fire.

I want to kick him.

Stony and furious, I settle with stomping my foot.

Know-All buries his mouth in his palm and fake coughs, 'Toddler.'

'Iris,' Dad repeats, all soft and gentle, because isn't it true that he would never knowingly hurt a fly? 'What's come over you?'

'What do you fucking think has come over me?'

'Iris.'

I slap Rosa's hand away as she reaches for me. 'Don't even.' It's scrappy, my voice. Scorched with mean. I swipe at my long-held sweltry tears and fix my stare hard on my stepmother's face, which is going guns to hold on to her usual linchpin calm.

'Light the log burner, Matt,' she says.

'But—'

Rosa makes a stop sign with her hand to halt her husband's rebuttal of her instruction.

Dad goes.

'I heard you from my bedroom. Is all this –' Know-All caricatures a crying face – 'really over a tree?'

'Noah.' Rosa rests a hand on her son's shoulder. 'Be kind. *Please.*'

'Sure,' he says, but the moment she turns her back, my stepbrother looks at the box of tea on the side and smirks. 'Might want to up the dosage of your *women*'s tea if this is what happens when you get your period. Though, PMT has been accepted as a reason for diminished responsibility in several British legal ca—'

'Ó.M.G.!'

The route between the table and my bedroom isn't long but is frenzied and forever when you're gulping for air and hoping you haven't blown it.

'Iris?' Rosa calls from the kitchen, but her words won't quite reach my ears because all my senses are on Órla. Or the absence of Órla, who is definitely, one hundred per cent, gone.

Twenty-Two

'Shit!'

What did I expect? If Know-All heard that drama from up in his room then of course Órla will have heard it from mine. It's no wonder she disappeared. I told her I was fetching tea. And not just any tea, but a tea that would instil balance. If she hadn't left, she would have drowned in the fucking irony.

'Knock, knock,' Rosa says a few minutes later, not actually knocking because her hands, when she walks into my room, are full with cups of that bloody herbal tea. 'You were making these?' Her voice has an edge of pride to it, like, *finally, you share my faith in the healing power of herbs.*

'Too late.' If my crying before was fast and furious, now it's sloppy and sad.

Thing is, I don't *do* crying.

You will be strong.

And I am.

And yet.

I don't do stepmums either, at least not stepmums with sympathetic faces, open arms and an invitation to breathe.

I *have* ~~had~~ a mother.

And to accept anything else would be…

~~What?~~

Betrayal.

And yet.

I don't bat Rosa away when she puts the mugs on the bedside table and reaches again for my hand. Rather, I let her lead me to the bed, where she sits down beside me, closer than usual, and tells me it's OK not to be OK.

It's hardly original, but I don't roll my eyes or tint them with scorn.

'Tala gone home?'

I shrug, not bothering to explain that it wasn't Tala I was making the stupid drink for. It's ridiculous but, if I tried the truth, I know I'd stumble just saying Órla's name. 'You might as well have it.'

'We could probably both do with some calming,' she says.

'From what I remember, it was only me who just went batshit over a tree.'

'You know, Iris, when Noah's dad left, all my friends kept telling me how incredibly I'd adjusted.' Rosa takes some of her own deep-breath medicine as she pulls ever so gently away. 'I was thirty-two, a grown woman with a decent job and a beautiful son. And I swore I wouldn't be downtrodden by a philandering ex-husband, who was never good enough for me anyway.'

She wrangles a tin of lip balm from her pocket, pops the lid off and uses a finger to dab the paste across her lips. 'I sorted a mortgage on a new house, cut and dyed my hair, and signed up to yoga classes in a bid to make myself physically and spiritually well.' The vanilla balm smells so good. 'I did everything right. And everyone was so impressed by how I'd held myself together.

How, despite everything, I was absolutely fine. They told me how magnificent I was. And I believed them, Iris. I was sure I was magnificent too.' Her fingers fiddle with the loose threads on the cuff of her cardigan. 'Then one day I totally lost it over a busy lizzie.'

'A what?'

'It's a plant people give kids to ignite an interest in gardening. They're supposed to be dead easy.'

I try not to laugh, because I can guess where this is headed. We all know that – one precious yucca aside – Rosa's a serial plant killer.

'It didn't flower and I was furious. I'd done everything I should have done by that bloody plant. I'd cared for it, watered it and it still couldn't give me the one thing I wanted. So I smashed the pot and screamed blue fucking murder!'

'Rosa!' I'm no prude, but seriously, my linchpin stepmother is not the kind of woman to swear.

'I know, fucking shocking, isn't it?'

And with all her peace, serenity and yogic breathing, it kind of is.

'But it wasn't just about the busy lizzie, Iris, and I'd bet my entire collection of Christmas baubles that, for you, it's not just about my old tree.'

We sit in silence and sip our tea.

'I'm doing some yoga tomorrow, if you fancy it?' From the buoyant sparkle in her eyes, I'm guessing Rosa's not kidding.

'Maybe we could all give it a go.' Dad's leaning, in what I reckon is an attempt to look casual, against my door frame. His face is older than I ever imagine it, with deep lines around his weak smile and an expression that's a jumble of unease, apology and hope.

Whenever I've mocked Tala's magnificent propensity for crying, she's always been quick to point out the healing benefits of a good old blub. How it releases actual feel-good chemicals that ease both physical and emotional pain. So, having just bawled, when I see Dad, I'm not expecting that seismic temper to re-rupture. I thought perhaps I'd quelled the violent bloom of anger in my gut.

He's trying, I can see, to be close to me without being overbearing. To talk to me without asking too much.

It *is* too much, though.

All of it.

What he did to me by keeping his secrets.

What he did to Mum by keeping me away.

And all the time playing this role of the Stickler, who'd never think of breaking any rules.

Only rules aren't just about wearing PPE or using a proper tool for a job.

There are other kinds of rules.

'You know yoga's what brought Rosa and me together,' he says, and I can see how he's debating whether he should remain on the border or take a step into my room.

Maybe he hears the firework explosions in my head or smells the sulphuric stench of rolling magma in my heart. Whatever, he stays where he is.

I gulp the Womankind and ache for the balance it promises.

Rosa, usually so astute, starts laughing. 'Slight exaggeration, Matt. You came to just enough sessions to invite me for a post-class coffee, where you convinced me you were a yogi, and that together we'd soon be doing the flying bow!' She cocks her brow. 'Reality check: once you'd lured me in under the false pretence of your meditative potential, I never saw you go down in a chaturanga again!'

I sip, then gulp, then neck the fucking tea.

My stepmum might be all giggles but none of this is funny. Because doesn't their meet-cute sum Dad up.

'He's a fraud.' I stand to make myself as big as possible. 'Isn't that basically what he's done to all of us? Convince us he's one thing and then blindside us with the reality of being something else.'

'Iris,' Rosa says. 'Come on now, lovely. That's not fair.'

'You think?' Everything's volcanic energy now. The tension. The silence. The truth. All of it unspoken but rumbling in the room. 'We think we know him, but just as he made you believe he was the kind of man who would bend himself backwards into a bridge, he made me believe he was the good guy. And sure, I thought he was prissy and annoying, but at least I knew I could trust him because Sticklers aren't dangerous. Sticklers extinguish fires. They don't start them.'

'Iris, please.' Even if I wasn't eyeballing Dad, I'd know from that feeble crack in his voice that his eyes are pricked with tears.

'You know who saw him best?' I'm roiling now. 'Mum.' As I spit her name, a blaze of gall and spite and loathing emanates from my skin. 'She was on to something with the fox mask, wasn't she? She saw just how sly you could be.'

'He never set out to lie.' Rosa's voice is the sea on last year's Greek holiday.

Warm.

Calm.

Deep.

'He thought if you continued believing the story about the fire, it would be easier for you to bear.'

I want to charge in and kick up some fucking waves.

I ignore her, look only at Dad. 'You say you didn't tell me because you were trying to protect me. But you were protecting yourself. You broke Mum when you took me to live with you. Then trampled all over her broken pieces when you refused to let me see her on Christmas Day.'

'Iris,' Rosa says. 'It's not like th—'

But Dad shakes his head. 'Rosa, no.' It's a surprise we can understand his words for his sobbing.

'So it's all right for you to cry, is it?'

If before I wanted to be giant, now I want to be small. To be ten years old and not told that I should be happy but allowed instead to fall apart because my mum is dead and isn't that reason enough to cry?

'I'm sor—'

'Leave. Me. Alone.' Each word is long and unbending. 'You're good at that, right?' I refuse to look anywhere but right at him when I hiss, 'Wasn't it exactly that ability you have of cutting people out that killed my mum?'

Twenty-Three

'Palitaw anyone?' Rosa's already cracking open the cake tin Tala gave her when she arrived to pick me up a few minutes ago. Never mind that we've not long finished our excruciating Saturday morning family brunch, or that she and Dad have come to an abrupt halt in their vinyasa flow.

'Mmmmm,' Dad says, leaning against the banister and taking a bite of one of the sweet rice cakes Tita Celestina has cooked up as part of her and Rosa's *cultural culinary exchange*. 'Have one, Iris. They might even be better than Rosa's famous mince pies.'

'You ready?' I blank Dad, grab my coat from the understairs cupboard, and look directly at Tala, whose eyes glare with something like, *what on earth's going on, Iris?* 'The bothy?' I say, eager to get away, because the reason she's come over is nothing to do with me ignoring Dad and everything to do with me commemorating Mum.

'It's only six days until the seventeenth,' Tala said yesterday. 'We need to plan.' Given we do the same thing – light candles, remember Mum's best bits – every year, Tala's sense of urgency was a little unnecessary in my opinion, but I'm happy to play along now if it means we can get the hell out of here.

But Tala's turned to Rosa, who's asked her something about the poetry slam, and before I know it, my stepmum is telling my best mate that she knows a few moves that could do wonders for her confidence on the night.

'Come,' Rosa says, taking Tala by the elbow to the two yoga mats rolled out on the living-room floor. Tala removes her puffer then jumper and starts laughing as Rosa lays her hands on her arms and begins contorting her into what she blissfully calls 'the eagle pose'. Dad copies. The three of them stand there, one-footed and totally wrapped up in themselves, Tala and Dad looking pained while Rosa, still and serene, tells them – in a voice pinched from one of those meditation podcasts she gobbles up most evenings – that their twisting is acting as an opening.

'You need to focus on the difficulty of it,' she says. 'And by acknowledging the hard stuff, you might transform. Come on, Iris, you too.'

I don't want to transform.

That's why I messaged Órla in the early hours of the morning and told her I didn't think we should see each other any more.

What was it she said in Matteo's? That on our own, we're one thing, but in meeting someone else, together, we become something new. But the new something I became in Órla's company – spewing all that stuff about missing Mum and resenting Dad – was a monster, a growling torrent who couldn't keep schtum.

Dad topples, laughing, while Rosa explains to Tala how to unwind herself, chuckling with preposterous joy as she watches her from behind and tells Tala she can see her wings.

'You see them, Iris?'

I shrug. All I see are Tala's protruding shoulder blades.

Is this my problem?

Is my failure to see beyond the obvious why I can't conjure Tala's wings? Why I can't picture my best friend as a soaring, courageous bird?

✳

'Spill it.' To her credit, Tala lasted the whole fifteen-minute car journey to the bothy before asking why I'm not speaking to Dad. But now we're here, it's not only the fire she wants to get going. 'Come on,' she says, hands filled with kindling. 'Talk'.

'I'm fine.' I busy myself with rummaging through the suitcase, with laying out blankets, with opening two cans of Coke and a packet of Maltesers to share. 'If your poems are as good as your fires, we're going to storm that slam,' I say as Tala flumps down next to me with a notebook and pen. 'You going to show me, or what?'

'OK,' she says, only her voice when she says it is the same voice she uses in class when she has absolutely no other option but to say something out loud. It's a mutter, an embarrassment of letters barely forming words.

'Whassup? Isn't Dougie hailing you as the new Emily Dickinson?' I put my hand out for the printed A4 sheets she's just pulled from her bag. 'It's only *me* reading them! You know, your number-one fan!'

'I just don't want you to…'

Even when I take hold of the paper, she still won't let it go. 'To what?'

'Judge.' This time, it's not a mutter. It's clear and specific and as sharp as a guillotine, slicing the air between us into what feels like a before and after.

'When have I ever judged?'

'The Stickler? The Linchpin? Know-All?'

'One-phrasing people? They're nicknames, that's all.'

She shrugs and lets go of the paper, which I unfold to reveal the poem's title written in large, bold capitals across the top of the page:

I'M ACE

'Loving the confidence, Tal! And you are, you know! You *are* ace.' I wait for it. For Tala to say, 'You're acer,' but she doesn't. Rather she sits, not exactly *not* looking at me, but definitely not looking at me in a way that suggests she's in the mood for the mutual adoration that's been the seven-year key to our patter. 'You're the acest,' I say anyway.

'Maybe not in the way you think, though.' She taps the paper. 'It doesn't scan so well on the page. It's meant to be read out loud so I could—'

'I'm sure I'll get the gist.'

''K.' She folds her arms, curling in on herself a little. It's a good job I've offered to perform for her given she's so prone to wanting to disappear.

I move my lips as I read, imagining how it will feel to stand in front of an audience. To do this thing for Tala. To bring her words to life:

Ace as in excellent, a master and such.
Ace as in a score with no opponent's touch.
Where the touch leads from
hands on hips
or fingers on face
or lips on lips
and whoa,

       stop,
       please…
       I'm ace.

Ace as in no thank you, that's not for me, please.
Ace is…
no, not-a-phase,
no, not-a-tease.
Ace as in
yes-let's-be-companions,
yes-let's-be-friends.
Ace as in yes, yes, yes,
I'm too ace to pretend
any longer that my body's on fire
with anything close to your sexual desire.
It's more like indifference,
like, if there was a take-it-or-leave-it,
I'd give it a miss and you'd better believe that
this isn't a phase or a fault in my making.
It's just I don't like sex the way that you don't like…
baking.

'You're ace?' It's less statement this time, more question.

'Yes,' Tala says.

'But you've never even done it.' I pull at the zip of my puffer. 'Sex, I mean.'

'No,' she says.

'So how do you…' It's so hot in here. 'Are you at least going to, you know, try?'

'I dunno, Iris.' The paper scores a line into my forefinger as she snatches it back. I stuff the thin wound into my mouth to suck it better. 'Forget it.' Tala scrunches the poem and makes to throw it on the fire.

'Tala Fischer, don't you dare!' I take her hands in mine, unfurling her right fist. The poem-ball drops to the stone floor. 'It's cool.' I bring her in for a hug. 'I'm just surprised that's all. I thought—'

'Why?' Tala's movements as she pulls herself away from me and bends to pick up the poem are very particular. Slow and deliberate, as if she's stiffening into the fight or flight mode we learned about in biology.

'Why what?'

'Why are you surprised?' It's not that Tala's loud or abrupt even, but there's a challenge in her tone and in the way she pulls the opposite corners of the paper so its creases are stretched and her crumpled truth is exposed once more.

Outside, cloud must have swamped the winter sun because the bothy darkens.

'I just can't imagine not being curious, that's all. So you don't think you'll ever…'

'No!' Her eyes flash with irritation. But Tala's voice, when she speaks again a few seconds later, is mellow. 'This is who I am.' Her words, though quiet, are brimful with acceptance. 'It's unlikely but not impossible, I guess, that at some point I could change my mind. *You* never used to like girls, but look at you now, going gaga over your gymnast.'

I haven't told Tala about finishing things with Órla. Not that we even had *things*. Just one evening I'd imagined bustling with promise but which, in reality, went from heavy conversation to period drama to family fallout. And *poof!* Just like that, she – and any chance of romance – was gone.

I smile and puff a little indiscriminate noise from my nose. I know what Tala will say if I show her the messages I sent. That first one that suggested the timing wasn't right for me to think about anything but family shit right now. The second one that silver-lining'd how Órla (and her coach) will thank me for not tempting her to skip any more training in favour of burgers. Órla can think of me, then, when she's up on the podium, the national anthem blasting, receiving her Olympic gold.

If Tala read those messages, she'd see something more than what they say. She'd see links. To Rollo. To Felix. To Jasper. To Jack. To all those good, kind boys she says I've walked – or in Rollo's case *run* – away from. She reckons I have a habit of ditching a good, kind someone before that good, kind someone has the chance to ditch me.

I wish she'd never taken A-level psychology.

'How do you know, though? That you're ace?' I ask her now, balancing the Maltesers in two pyramid piles, one for her, one for me, one for her, one for me.

'I guess the same way you know you're not.'

167

One for her. One for me.

She picks the Malteser from the top of her pile and begins nibbling off the chocolate coating. 'It's not always easy confiding in you, Iris.'

'Why?' That word on its own always sounds so critical.

'You tell me.' She might be smiling, but there's nothing about that smile that reaches her eyes. 'It's not as if *you* ever really confide in *me*.'

My throat closes. Even if I wanted to spill out all my secrets, the words couldn't squeeze their way through.

Tala shuts her eyes for a few seconds. When she opens them, it's like she's realized she might as well take the conversation back to her. 'I have tried to talk to you.' The small, sphere-ish middle of her mutilated Malteser begins to melt as she pops it on to her stuck-out tongue. 'But you don't listen,' she says, once she's done. 'You just make a joke of it, or act like it's simply a case of biding my time.'

'When have I ever made a joke of it?'

'Er, Haribo?'

And it's not the heat from the fire that's turning my cheeks red now, but shame.

A few summers ago, we took a school trip to France, and there was an incident with Jameson in the women's toilets on the Portsmouth to Caen ferry. Tala swore Jameson's face when she went down on him with a mouth still zinging from the sweet and sours she'd necked on the coach looked like he'd contracted something.

I've always assumed – and yes, jibed – that's why she's not dared go near a boy since.

'I told you I hated it, that I had no interest in doing that, or anything like it again. But you kept going on about me giving it another shot. With another boy. Or—'

'Because it won't always be like that, Ta—'

'Can you hear yourself?' she snaps, stands, the toe of her shoe catching her pyramid, which comes apart, sending the balls of chocolate in different directions across the blanket and on to the floor 'You're so sure you have people nailed.'

On all fours, I scramble for her Maltesers.

Neither of us says anything. All I can hear is the roar of the fire, and the roof and window shuddering under the sudden downpour of rain.

I put the grubby chocolates back into the empty packet, pluck one from the top of my pile and hold it out to Tala in the palm of my hand. As she takes it, a gust of wind blows the bothy door open.

'The seventeenth then?' Tala breaks her silence. Through the crack, I see the robin land on the step. 'Would you like to do anything different this year to remember your mum?'

Twenty-Four

'Iris!' Bronagh's voice matches the buzzy jollity of the hive of carol singers huddled outside the station toilets going full pelt on 'Rockin' Around the Christmas Tree' like they've been hard-lining yule logs and rum balls since 7 a.m. 'I'm so glad youse asked to meet up.' She wraps me in a giant hug which, with that long grey furry coat she's sporting, makes me feel like there's a yeti swallowing me whole. 'I still can't get over how much youse look like Sarah. It's your eyes, maybe.' She studies me with such intensity, I don't know where to look. 'Or your mouth.'

Is that it? My eyes? My mouth? Or is there more of me that carries echoes of my mother. Not just my appearance, but something deeper, something in the way I riled Tala. How she was so sure I'd judge her in the same way she seems to think Know-All, Linchpin and Stickler are judgements on Noah, Rosa and Dad.

'Mr Taylor's a busybody,' Mum said when the neighbouring farmer had come to ask if she was aware of the guidelines regarding lighting fires in your garden.

'That woman is a jobsworth,' she spat when the librarian insisted she couldn't take out *Wuthering Heights*, *Tess of the d'Urbervilles* and *Rebecca* until she'd returned and paid the fine for the ten books she already had on loan.

'That teacher's a supercilious twit,' she mumbled as I climbed into the car after the head had swept her away for a 'quiet word', leaving me with her PA for yet another game of noughts and crosses. I was over it by then; we'd been playing since all the other kids were picked up and taken home from school over an hour earlier.

'You like hot chocolate?' Bronagh's pleased when I nod that I do. 'Will we go to Birdies then? Your mam always loved a hot chocolate with all the marshmallows and squirty cream.'

Maybe it's the lack of space inside Bronagh's car, but the missingness of Mum is so much fleshier here. Or perhaps it's hearing about her. These little details creating a bigger picture, which in turn creates a bigger hole.

The details are why I came, though. Why I messaged Bronagh when Tala dropped me home after the bothy yesterday, and asked if she wouldn't mind meeting up and answering some questions about Mum.

A few minutes later, we're in the kind of cute independent coffee shop that only really exists in movies. The back wall is concealed with fully stacked bookshelves Tala would die for. Two wooden letter boards preside over the counter – one offers the menu, the other details the many ways in which Birdies wants to boost the mood of its local community. Their next effort, in three days' time, is a singalong screening of *Scrooge*. The *pièce de résistance* is a giant birdcage in a corner by the window, where a parrot is perched on a swing, his beady eyes on the man in front of us who is ordering a flat white to go.

'Bad boy! Bad boy!'

'Take a seat,' Bronagh tells me, tilting her head towards the empty table by the judgy bird.

'Good girl! Good girl!' the parrot squawks as I sit down.

'Good girl! Good girl!' she repeats when Bronagh joins me with not just hot chocolates but a slab of cookie too.

Bronagh catches me staring. 'Thought we could go halves.'

And while I promised myself I absolutely would not make this visit anything about Órla, my heart can't help but pang at the thought that with all those restrictions her coach puts on her diet, Órla probably never gets to share treats like this with her mum.

'I think she likes you,' Bronagh says, sending my panging heart waltzing because it's clearly not only me whose brain can't help tracking back to the unfulfilled possibility of Órla and me as something more than *just friends*.

'Has she said something?' My attention is resolutely fixed on how many tiny pink and white marshmallows I can scoop on to my spoon as I imagine Órla, whose reply when I'd messaged her had been pretty, perhaps even *too*, chill – You have a lot going on, Iris. It's cool – crying on her mother's shoulder.

'You could say that!' Bronagh laughs. '*Good girl! Good girl!*' Her head bobbles as she does a poor impression of the parrot, and my panging, waltzing heart slumps into my belly, where it clags like the marshmallows and cream. 'I'm fairly sure that bird is my mother. After she moved back to Belfast when I was twenty, she always swore she'd never live anywhere but Ireland, but there's something about those beady black eyes.'

Right on cue, the parrot cocks her head and glares at Bronagh. '*Hola!*'

'Mam loved a holiday in Spain.' Bronagh shrugs, like, *that proves it*. 'I went there with *your* mam once.'

'You did?'

'Sure I did, the summer before she went to uni.' Her deep inhale is different to Rosa's. While my stepmother's breath appears restorative, Bronagh's is resigned. 'It was the summer before the first time I lost her.'

'Lost her?'

'Yeah.' She licks a large cookie crumb from her lip and looks past me through the floor-to-ceiling window to the busying street outside, obscured slightly by the steam of hot breath and coffee. 'Sarah went AWOL on me more than once, but that first time was more my doing than hers. I should'ae done better by her but…'

It's funny how many times people's sentences drift when they talk about Mum.

Bronagh sits forward in her chair. 'I think I was jealous,' she says, like it's only just occurred to her. 'Sarah was off in a new town with a new, arty group of friends and, honestly, I don't think I liked it. Since I moved to England at the beginning of sixth form, I'd always been her go-to. When her mam died, she moved out of Sunnyside and into my parents' house so she could finish her A levels. We were like sisters. Fought like it too sometimes. But now there was this bunch of mates who were only getting the best of her. You know, that beautiful creative side.'

I know that side.

~~And the other side too?~~

'Maybe if I hadn't been so petty… If I'd carried on going to visit at the weekends… Maybe she wouldn't have gone so far off the rails and…' She dabs at her cheeks with a napkin. 'There are so many maybes with Sarah.'

'Good girl! Good girl!'

Maybe if Dad and I had gone for Christmas breakfast.

Maybe if he hadn't taken me away.

~~Or the maybe of all maybes, if you hadn't made that call~~

Don't even.

The café is bustling now. The queue reaches the door. Every table is filled.

'Did you know my dad back then too?'

'Sure, they were a cute couple. Matt was moony for Sarah.' Bronagh smiles, and I swear her eyes go a little starry at the thought of this loved-up version of Dad. 'Everyone was moony for Sarah, though. She had this way – I don't know how to describe it – of making you feel anything was possible, that you could be whoever you wanted to be.'

It's true.

The summer before she died, Mum scooped me out of bed at three in the morning, bundling me, Bim the bear and several blankets into the car.

'It sounds crazy crackalackas, but we need more darkness,' she said, speeding away from the house and into the hills, which from the car window in the depth of the night were the humped backs of huge and silent monsters. 'We're driving up up up! And that's good, Iris! Life is good good good!' Everything she said and did was punctuated with an exclamation mark.

None of it made sense, but I went with it anyway, because she was my mum, and she was so sure, and I was ten so what choice did I have?

'Here.' She lifted me on to the bonnet of the car, the warmth of the engine as reassuring as her arm wound around my shoulder. She let me put star-shaped glittery stickers in her hair as she explained the streaks of light in the sky weren't rockets or superheroes but comet debris, most of them likely no bigger than a grain of sand.

I looked up. 'But how are they so bright if they're so small?'

'They're like you.' Her voice was as clear as the night sky, her words carrying the same awesome heat as the flaming celestial shards. 'They're evidence that even the tiniest of things can fill the endless dark with light. *You* do that, Iris.' Her hand on my arm pulled me tighter. 'Scientists call it a meteor shower.' She kissed the top of my head so hard I swear I could feel her teeth beneath her lips against my skull. 'But you know what I call it?'

I looked from the sky to my mother. Each was boundless. Both excited me and sometimes filled me with fear.

'I call it hope.'

Bronagh tilts her head as she looks at me. 'When it was good, it was grand, right?'

'*Hola! Hola!*' The parrot greets a woman as she manoeuvres a buggy into a space between our two tables. She hands her strapped-in toddler a giant chocolate coin. The little boy stares at his mother as she unlocks her phone, then stretches his arm to reach the window, where he draws a heart in the condensation with his finger. Just like that, he puts the simple shape of his feelings on the glass.

Twenty-Five

'Not really *my* problem,' Jonny Filer pipes up from the row behind me. 'He's hardly gonna flop his nob out for me, is he?'

While I was meeting Bronagh on Sunday, the flasher exposed himself to another young woman about a mile from Good Hope Wood. This time he threw in a wank too. The last three days have been rife with messages on the Safe Home group on how best to thwart an attack.

> Poke his eyes.
>
> Punch his throat.
>
> Stamp his foot.
>
> Knee his groin.
>
> Go batshit mental and spit in his face if you must.

'We're all here, Jonny, because this is *everyone*'s problem.' Angeline Daré twists to glare at him, and I don't know who's more pissed off, Jonny because his ex just called him out in front of the entire upper school, or me because I've been forced to admit that occasionally a Dumbbell can talk sense.

'Point well made, Ms Daré.' Ms Clarke, our head, goes on to explain that she called the meeting to discuss 'how we might *all* proceed'.

'My mum told me, if I see him, to just laugh at the loser,' Evie, Queen of the Dumbbells, says from her prime position at the front of the hall. 'It's pathetic.'

'I wouldn't say it's a laughing matter, Evie.' Ms Clark looks across at the school counsellor, Mr Moriarty, who nods in sincere agreement as he makes his way on to the stage.

'Indecent exposure,' he says in a slow I-am-not-embarrassed-by-such-topics voice, 'is too often ridiculed in the press, which can mean neither the crime nor its victims are taken seriously. I want you to know that if anyone here comes to talk to me or any other member of staff about this, they will be listened to, OK?'

'Fuuuuuuuuck's sake,' Jonny mutters as Ms Clark reminds us of the usual ways in which us girls can make ourselves safer. 'It's not like the guy's even touched anyone.'

If Tala's poetry has half the clout of the evil look she blazes at Jonny, I swear she'll be lauded as a twenty-first-century Shakespeare.

Ten minutes later, Jonny's mouth is still zipped as Mr Moriarty explains that those people who choose to expose themselves are likely experiencing a delusional sense of entitlement, and that they may take pleasure in their victim's embarrassment or shame.

'Sometimes there may also be a power-play element to it,' he says, citing examples of well-known actors and comedians who've admitted to sexual misconduct. 'Because even if there was no touching, indecent exposure *is* sexual misconduct.' Mr Moriarty glares at Jonny.

'With all the unsolicited dick pics bandied about this place, most of the boys in our year are probably guilty of

177

sexual misconduct,' I say to Tala as we're swept along in the rabble of students rushing for the canteen when the meeting is declared over.

'Not all of us are morons, Iris!' Dougie sidles up to his poet laureate in the queue. 'Some of us actually give a shit about making a change.'

'Do you, though?' Tala says as she pays for what must be her seventy-third jacket potato of the term and heads to a table. Is it wrong that I'm kind of jazzed by the hostile tone she takes with him? 'Because from all the smutty sniggers, it sounded like most of the boys in there found it pretty amusing.'

Silence falls between them, and God knows, I'm not going to be the one to break it.

Tala starts on her lunch. Jeez, who knew such violence could be committed with just a fork and a baked spud.

'I'm sorry,' she says, sheepishly retracting her cutlery and resuming her usual hushed volume. 'All those rules, though: stick to well-lit areas, project confidence, keep your phone in your pocket so you're not too distracted to check on your surroundings, have your hands free in case you need to fight.' She looks up at Dougie, who's not taken his eyes off her since she sat down. 'You say you want to make a change, but all that advice we were just given was about *us* girls changing *our* behaviour, not you.'

I've never known Tala speak for so long in public.

'You're right.' Dougie's face is sombre, contrite. 'I'll think about it, if there's anything properly helpful I can do.'

'Good.' Tala's face when she smiles at him is so open, so engaged when he says he might have a surprise for her in the next few days. 'Tell me,' she says, but Dougie's all coy brows and, *you'll see, you'll see*, as they drop into a lengthy chat about their plans to head into Birmingham for an LGBTQIA+ book club.

Er, hello? Why hasn't anyone mentioned this to me?

'I spoke with one of the organizers last night.' Dougie steals a spoonful of beans from Tala's plate. Bit gross if you ask me. 'I mentioned your poems and they said if you wanted to practise performing you could do it there maybe?'

'*I'm* performing Tala's poems,' I say. But Dougie just shrugs. And my nails dig into my palms as my veins are flooded with blood that's so suddenly hot I know my cheeks will be burning. 'And I've been thinking,' I rush to continue before they can revert to their private chat about their private escapades. 'I'm not sure if the "I'm Ace" poem is the right poem of Tala's for *me* to be performing at the slam.'

'It's brilliant,' Dougie says. 'She's worked so hard on it.'

'I know that.' I wave a bag of Maltesers at Tala, my eyes to her all, *you want some?* My inner devil to Dougie, *I bet you didn't know these are her fave?* 'But the content is kind of personal?'

'Which is what makes it so powerful.' Dougie's not aggressive in his rebuttal, just matter-of-fact.

'I get that.' From the corner of my eye, I clock the Dumbbells' nudging elbows and sneery pouts, but I'm not taking my gaze off Dougie. 'Tala's had enough aggro from that lot, and I don't want her having to put up with any more for the sake of your slam.'

'I'm not doing it for the sake of *his* slam.' Tala doesn't shout exactly, but something closes my conversation with

Dougie down. 'I'm doing it for me. Because I'm comfortable with acknowledging and sharing the fact that I'm asexual. And because, unlike some people, *I* am not ashamed of who or what I really am.'

For what feels like minutes, but according to the giant ticking clock on the far wall – the only thing I can bear to look at – is just seconds, our corner of the canteen is like Redmond.

Tala, Dougie, the Dumbbells, me.

None of us says a word.

As Tala has proven, though, silence is never permanent.

'Classic,' Evie hoots, though really 'hoots' is too sweet to describe what Evie does, because what Evie does is caustic and mean. 'If anyone was ever going to be scared of sex, it's Redmond.'

'Shut up, Evie.' Angeline casts her eminent Dumbbell some serious side-eye. 'Don't you think of yourself as the "Font of All Things Sex"?'

Evie's eyes round in warning to her hitherto loyal sidekick.

'Surely, if you were the "Font of All Things Sex", you'd know asexuality isn't about a fear of sex, it's about not being sexually attracted to anyone.' Angeline looks at Tala for clarification. 'Is that right? I don't want to put words in your mouth or anything.'

After her eloquent outburst, Tala now looks like she could do with someone speaking on her behalf. Beneath that sheath of dark hair, she nods.

'Well, I think it's cool,' Angeline says, not exactly fronting up to Evie, but there's a definite challenge in the puff of her chest. And while I appreciate she's stepped in to defend Tala, I'm also kind of miffed that she got in there first.

'I'm sorry, Tal.' A minute or so later when everyone's turned back to their own tables and the air is again filled with noise, I slide a conciliatory hand on to her knee.

'It's fine.' No one else probably notices the slight shift in her body, edging her just a fraction closer to Dougie and what feels like a mile away from me.

Twenty-Six

'What did she mean, Nessy?' Frozen mud crackles beneath my boots as I crouch down next to the bassett hound, holding on to her collar so she's no choice but to stick with me and listen. 'Unlike some people, *she's* not ashamed of who she is! You know what Tala was implying, don't you?' Nessy pulls, desperate to join a huddle of beagles scampering and scuffling down by the water. 'She thinks *I* am ashamed. That *I'm* not being honest.'

Nessy's long ears perk and her nose twitches. Her front left paw scratches at the ground. 'Fine.' I release her and she's off. Nothing to concern *her* other than which beagle butt she'll sniff first.

What *is* Tala's problem? She finds her voice and, what, the first thing she does is use it to have a go at *me*?

Indignation sparks through my body with every crunchy step I take along the dark, frosted riverbank. I shout at Nessy to follow, and despite all the warnings in today's stupid meeting about not being distracted by your phone while walking, I scroll as I stomp.

No notifications.

I've not posted an @DoratheUrbexplorer pic in ages and can't really imagine ever wanting to go to a bando after that night with Órla at Matteo's. Dad'd be pleased, but I still don't dare open my mouth in his company for fear of that thick tumble of rage.

'I need cake,' I tell Nessy now as the river bends into the park and we charge, probably a little too fast for her short legs, towards town.

I clip her lead back on as we turn left on to the cobbled pedestrian street, past shop windows jewelled with fairy lights and elaborate scenes of gold-crowned swans, a candy-cane circus and a single, red-breasted robin on the snow-laden branch of a tree.

Nessy's lead goes taut as she keeps walking, oblivious to me having stopped dead, my eyes fixed on the bird.

The robin is hand drawn and beautiful, with a big russet belly and obsidian eyes that follow me as Nessy tugs on the lead, pulling me back on track to The Vault. Once there, I plan to alleviate my woes wi—

(Nice use of 'alleviate', Iris.)

~~Shut up. Shut up. Shut up.~~

I am strong, I tell myself in rhythm to the stamp of my DMs through the thin crust of freezing puddles.

I am.

I am.

I am.

So what if I don't want to divulge my inner feelings to Tala or to the world via poems or canteen diatribes. Isn't the idea that there's no such thing as normal, that it's OK for us not to all be the same?

'And why now?' I ask Nessy, whose claws trip along the paving slabs the colour of thunder. It's not like I'm the one who's suddenly changed. If anyone has mis-sold themselves, it's Tala, right? One minute, she's Redmond, the next she's channelling the confidence of Dua Lipa.

'Closed?' I come to a halt and read the sign on the door. 'It can't be.' But it is. And not just for the evening. Because there's a note taped beneath the sign that says, *Due to unforeseen circumstances, The Vault will cease trading 11th December.*

It can't be shut.

I was here only a few days ago.

What could have gone so wrong?

I bang on the glass of the door. 'Oi?'

My hand is a fist, which is thumping, which is loud, which is dangerous, a do-gooder pushing a buggy tells me as she walks by. 'You're going to smash it,' she says, reaching for my arm, but I snatch it away from her and go to the window, bat at that too.

'You in there?' I shout.

'I'll call the police,' the lady warns.

'They can't just fuck off with no warning!' I'm practically screaming.

Nessy skitters at my feet.

The woman takes a step back, putting herself between me and her son. Like I'm a crazy person.

~~Like your mum?~~

My knuckles smack against the sign.

BANG.

'It's not right!'

BANG.

'It's not fair!'

BANG.

184

'It's not what you do to people who've been loyal to you!'
BANG.

'You can't just decide not to be here!'
BANG.

Nessy is barking now, jerking as I smack at the glass with my fist wrapped around her lead.

'How'–*BANG*–'dare'–*BANG*–'you'–*BANG*–'just'–*BANG*–'fuck'–*BANG*–'off'–*BANG*–'and'–*BANG*–'leave'–*BANG*–'me'–*BANG*–'standing'–*BANG*–'in'–*BANG*–'the'–*BANG*–'freezing'–*BANG*–'cold'–*BANG*–'on'–*BANG*–'my'–*BANG*–'own!'–*BANG*.

'Hey!'

Someone bigger than the woman with the child and the buggy and the judgement grabs at me from behind.

Poke his eyes.
Punch his throat.
Stamp his foot.
Knee his groin.
Go batshit mental and spit in his face if you must.

I raise my leg ready to trample, clomp or kick.

'Iris,' he says.

Know-All?

'Please.' He's quieter this time. And while he doesn't release his hold, it's not exactly his force that keeps me wrapped in my stepbrother's arms but my potent eddy of shame. 'It's OK.' I feel his chin leave my crown as he turns his head away from me. 'I've got this.'

'If you're sure,' the buggy-woman says.

'She'll be fine.'

Of all the statements Know-All has presented as fact, I think this most recent is the least likely to be true.

I'm not fine, am I?

Or strong.

Nessy sits, her long ears covering her head, which is hung in, what, embarrassment? Fear?

After a minute or so of my snivelling, Know-All lets go. 'Classic Iris behaviour. Only you would think it's acceptable to smash your way into a café because you need a hot chocolate.'

'Cake,' I say, twisting away from the gentle hold he still has on me, leaning back against the wall.

'Huh?'

'It was cake not hot chocolate I was after. A raspberry oat slice, to be exact.'

'Oh, well in that case I one hundred per cent get it.' And although it's arched, there's less of Know-All's usual conceit in his brow.

'This is fucked up, dude. Now even *you* are being nice to me. Am I on some screwed-up game show where everyone in my life starts behaving as their opposite?'

'Seriously, this is Iris overload.' Know-All blows on his fingertips to stave off the increasing cold. 'You'd have to be a narcissist to think the entire world had been reconfigured to fuck you over. None of this is a game show. It's just life, Iris. People change.'

'Says the seventeen-year-old who still plays Lego.'

'What can I say? My brain age is seven.'

'That the opening line for your Oxford interview, is it?'

His eyes narrow, and what was momentarily soft between us hardens. He nods at Nessy. 'Don't you need to get her home?'

It's ridiculous, right, that even after he's seen me punching doors and heard me whimpering, that when my eyes prick, I turn away from Know-All, pressing my forehead against the thankfully still-intact window.

My breath forms a wonky circle on the glass.

I could draw a heart in it.

I don't, though.

I draw a cross instead.

Twenty-Seven

On the walk back to drop off Nessy, Know-All and I don't talk about what just happened. Rather my stepbrother seizes the opportunity to give me an insight into the Human Rights Act of 1998. In usual circumstances, I would have cut this short at two minutes max. Not because I don't care about human rights, rather because I don't much care for what my stepbrother has to say about them. But this evening his lecture is the exact white noise I need. That monotone hum of fact after fact lulls my ramped-up heart into a far steadier beat.

My calm is momentary, though, rattled again when we walk down Mr West's street, where his son Adam's coming out of the house with a suitcase and a face full of woe.

'How's your dad?' I call across the hedge.

'Grumpy.' His voice suggests this is a trait passed down the generations.

'And Buddy?'

His shoulders rise, like, *who knows*, as he loads the case into the boot of his car.

'What do you have to say about *Mr West*'s rights then?' I ask Know-All. The bitterness whenever I think about how my elderly friend has been wrenched from his dog tastes like I've been sick and not yet brushed my teeth. 'Or Buddy's?'

Know-All shrugs. 'Funnily enough, that kind of thing isn't on the A-level law syllabus.'

'So what? A moral issue's only worth thinking about if you're going to be marked on it?' The scorn I puff from my nose briefly turns the air to smoke. 'Surely, even if Mr West is incapable of looking after Buddy, he still has a right to see him?'

For once, Know-All doesn't come straight back with an answer. Instead, we're both silent for the rest of our cold walk home.

✦

As soon as we get inside, my stepbrother scurries upstairs to his room.

'Not long till dinner,' Dad calls after him from his aproned position by the stove.

'You have mail, Iris,' Rosa says, dropping the cloth she was – weirdly – using to wipe the leaves of her beloved plant. 'Looks like it might be special.' She holds up the white envelope, which has been coloured with pencilled rainbows and, on the seal, one single stuck-on heart.

'Rollo sending you love letters?' Dad asks.

When I don't answer, Rosa fixes her gaze on me and widens her eyes, like, *well?*

'I'm not with Rollo any more.' I make it clear my answer is directed only at Rosa, keeping my back to Dad as I take the envelope. Such pretty post is hardly Rollo's style. And even if it was, given he seems finally to have got the hint that we're no longer happening, I don't think Rollo will be sending me anything anytime soon. I hadn't clocked when his efforts to engage me in some kind of relationship rescue mission stopped but, thinking about it, there's been no new messages for days.

Rosa's eyes flit from me to Dad to me again. '*New* boyfriend then?' She's in full Linchpin mode now, trying to broker the peace.

The postmark reads Edglington. Órla?

'Not *boy*friend, no.' A moment of wistful wishful thinking.

'Girlfriend?' Dad could do with a lesson or two from Mr Moriarty in how to sound chill when talking to teens about sex. He needs to ditch that quick awkward cough for a start.

I say nothing as I head to my room.

'Dinner's almost ready.' He is such a broken record.

I shut my door and press play on an urbex podcast I can't really hear because my heart is a marching drum.

Inside the envelope are two pieces of paper. One of them has been folded into a blank fortune teller, the other is a note:

> *Maybe our destiny's not written in the stars or by others on a piece of paper.*
>
> *Maybe it's written by us.*
>
> *X*

I let both bits of paper fall to the floor. What Órla's written is a nice idea. But she's wrong. Because when have I ever been in charge of my own fortune? Hasn't my whole life so far been dictated by Dad. He took me from Mum. He stopped me from seeing her. No wonder she—

It wasn't a choice; it was a consequence.

Because she wasn't the kind of person to—

I reach under my bed for the Better Things notebook. And I read about picnics, about swings, about Christmas crafts, about bike rides, about dancing, about notes on my pillow in the mornings, about Mum braiding silky silver ribbons through my hair.

I haven't pulled the curtains. The single light of my bedside lamp makes the outside look eerily distant and dark.

Mum was kind. Mum was happy. Mum was—

~~Remember, Iris.~~

~~She *was* those things.~~

~~But Mum was other things too.~~

There's a knock on my door.

'We can't continue like this, sunshine.' Dad walks, uninvited, into my room.

'Is that what you said to Mum too?' It's a conscious decision to talk to him. So what if something ugly bursts out of me. I'm done with barricading *my* hurt to prevent his.

'Not quite that, no.' He edges forward. 'But if I had, it would have been true. I know it's upsetting, but we did need to change something.'

'Why?' I want to hurl the question at Dad like a fireball, but it comes out weak and pathetic. I sink further into my pillows propped against the wall.

'I think you know why.' He weighs down into the mattress next to me. I stand and sit instead on the chair by my desk.

'Because Mum was ill?' Is this the first time I've said it? The first time I've attempted to give shape to what Bronagh talked about. How Mum was lost to her sometimes. I think now of all the hours Mum disappeared.

The heat of Dad's stare is mild, like the flame of a candle.

'But she mostly had good days,' I say. 'Really really good days.' Is it worth telling Dad about the dens, the bird houses, the treasure trails, the origami, the little boats we'd make from bottles and the maze we made from masking tape stuck to the floor?

'You weren't safe.'

'You weren't there.' I swipe at the flush of tears. It's not my sadness I want him to see but my fury. 'You left us, remember. So how could you possibly know?'

'You told me, Iris.' Tears run in thin, rapid streams down his cheeks.

'I told you?' My head hooks into the memory my heart thrums as hard as possible to escape. 'What did I tell you?'

'That you were frightened.'

'Of what?' But I already know the answer.

He says it anyway. 'Sarah.' Dad gets up from the bed, and as he walks closer and closer, I can see that he doesn't want to say whatever's coming but understands now that some truths need to be spoken. 'You phoned me, remember? You said you couldn't stay with your mum any longer. You said you wanted to come and live with me.'

Twenty-Eight

I pedal faster, willing the wind to whip harder across my face, knotting my hair as I ride my bike through the country lanes lit only by a moon half lost to the cloud.

I promised Dad I'd stay put, but how could I? My entire quota of acting like a normal person was taken up with sitting through a dinner I barely ate. There was no normal left when it came to sleeping, or even lying still in my bed.

I am a traitor.

A teller of tales.

And if I wasn't those things, if I was only the strength and smiles I've always thought I was, then Mum wouldn't be dead.

But she is.

And I'm as much of a fraud as any of them.

The acidic burn in my thighs.

The deep ache in my shoulders.

The searing rip in my heart.

~~You know now.~~

I push against the pedals, relish the smack of my rucksack against my back.

~~You know who you are.~~

Water stinging my eyes, which are searing with speed.

And shame.

~~Never forget the shame.~~

Take the bends wide then wider.

A blare of a horn.

A window wound down.

'I could have killed you!'

~~And wouldn't that have served you right.~~

'What you have to realize is it's not your fault,' Dad said when I said nothing. He was trying to hold me but still didn't know how to hug a porcupine, and my spikes were pushing out further, growing sharper.

Is that what I'm made of?

Spikes?

~~Come on now, let's not forget betrayal.~~

'You weren't safe there, love.' Dad's hand was cupping my head like that was the least dangerous part of me.

~~Clearly, he's not privy to your wicked thoughts.~~

'Sarah's behaviour was making you unsafe. You called me. Can you remember? You called me on her phone while she was sleeping and told me about the potting shed and the stargazing and France?'

'France?'

'She made you France in the sitting room, remember?'

'She did,' I said, like, *what's that got to do with anything?* France is straight out of the Better Things notebook. 'We had baguettes and cheese and Ribena poured like wine. There were flags. It was magic.'

'Iris.' His voice was no longer a broken record but a broken heart. 'She'd painted an entire wall red, white and blue. She'd dragged you out of bed to see it. And, yes, she'd made you a special French supper, but all this was at three in the morning.' Dad asked if I wanted to sit down. I couldn't find the word 'no' because my brain was a jigsaw broken into ten thousand scattered pieces.

You can barely see the church from the road. It's not as tall as the trees and not much wider than the potting shed at Sunnyside. The only clue that it's there is a rusted sign which, like the pathways, is overgrown with branches, brambles and weeds. I dismount, shoving the bike forward, thorns tearing at my thin leggings, tiny but barbed and determined, ripping a hundred jagged cuts into my skin.

~~They should be deeper.~~

~~Bloodier.~~

~~They should be scraping flesh and bone.~~

The moon is disappearing behind the clouds now. In its fading light, everything but the gloom retreats.

It was the opposite the night we went stargazing. As we drove through hills with the windows down and the music loud, the lunar glow had been so fierce. Mum had worried the stars would be diminished in its glare.

'Sing,' she begged, and I tried, even though it was late or early, I wasn't sure which, and I didn't know the songs that she told me were by Kylie Minogue. 'Come on, Iris, you're my rainbow. I brought you with me for colour, not so you could sit there like a sack of grey.'

It hurt, of course it did. But then came more magic: hot chocolate from a flask; stickers in her hair; streaks of light in the sky.

The next day there was a note. I found it on the mat when I returned home, shattered, from school. It was a complaint from neighbours in the village. They'd been woken by our adventure. Mum's speed and volume were unacceptable, they said.

For once, I was pleased Mum was in bed at four in the afternoon. It meant I could destroy the note before it destroyed her. We'd received similar warnings the previous week when we'd had a bonfire in the front garden, throwing on everything from tables to records to plates, which didn't burn, of course, but smashed noisily on the paving slabs. Mum rushed back and forth from the house, eyes and mouth wide with excitement, telling me for the twentieth, thirtieth, fortieth time that the inferno was ceremonial, that this wasn't destruction but an astonishingly glorious new start.

'I love you, Iris,' she said, unbuckling my shoes, tugging off my socks and tossing those on the fire too. 'Dance,' she said. And yes, she was as wild as the blaze but, in that moment, the way she held my hands and swayed me wasn't scary but free.

In that moment.

~~But there were other types of moments too.~~

Shining my torch on the entrance to the church, I see it's open. I'd read it would be, but you can never be sure. Authorities hear about these broken places and think they are dangerous. They bolt locks to their doors and windows. They put up signs. They warn people to steer clear. There is risk of injury or death.

And that may be true, but within the dark and damage, there can be so much beauty too.

'Don't leave me,' Mum said the night after the bonfire as we ate cheese and pineapple in front of the telly and used the discarded cocktail sticks to clean the ashes from under our nails and between our toes. 'They all leave me.' She was drooping, the word we used for the time between the highs of reaching for the stars and the lows of the hollowing beneath the duvet. I went into the kitchen, where I'd already swept up the fragments of the plate she'd dropped the previous night in her hurry to get to the fire. I returned to her, then, with the fortune teller we kept in the Everything Drawer.

'Here,' I said. 'Let's play.'

She picked yellow. She picked three. I unfolded the flap. 'You will be strong,' I read in my very best reading-aloud voice that Mrs Tucker had helped me with in the afternoons when we'd played too much noughts and crosses in the hour since the other kids had gone home.

'You're my rainbow,' Mum said, but her voice was a giveaway; my colours weren't bright enough to save her.

I was a disappointment.

A sack of grey.

From my bag, I remove my phone. The girl in the selfies I take looks weak. Her strength spent. She's lost. And there are no paths or roads on the fortune teller to help her find her way.

It's colder inside the church than out. Darker too when I make my way to the front, where there are three pews still solid and stable.

The church smells. Not the damp wood and urine stench of other bandos, but musty and thick with ancient spice.

I sit down on the front pew and take out my Box of Mum Things, which I'd shoved in my rucksack when I left home.

It's lies.

The fortune teller.

The photos. That one of Mum, Bronagh, Órla and me.

The angel.

The key.

All of it's lies. Everything changed to suit a story. Promises written to conceal the truths I have buried deeper than my bones are buried inside my skin.

You will be strong.

With a pen, I scribble over the eight promises until the paper beneath them is thinned and almost torn.

'It's not your fault, Iris,' Dad repeated earlier tonight when he came to check I was in bed and told me, once again, that I'd done the right thing when I'd called and asked him to come fetch me. 'Sarah's behaviour was dangerous,' he said. 'What you did was brave. It can't have been easy, love, to tell me, to choose to make yourself safe.'

I didn't betray her.

I hadn't packed a bag. It wasn't *that* kind of decision. There was no plotting or forethought, no time to think things through.

I didn't betray her.

It was heat of the moment. It was my mum is scaring me. It was I can't do anything but go.

An owl hoots in the distance. Inside, though, there is silence. I swing my torch across the walls, catching the large window that stands above the door. Warm gold, vivid purple, tranquil

198

blue. The stained glass forms a picture of Mary cradling, protecting, her child.

I couldn't sleep at Dad's when he'd taken me. Every time I closed my eyes, I heard Mum's 'Don't leave me', and felt her hands pulling me from between the duvet and sheets. With Bim the bear clutched to my chest, I crept downstairs, where Dad was sitting in the living room with the TV on mute and his phone pressed to his ear.

I don't know who he was talking to. 'No child should ever have to make that call.'

I was ten years and ten months when my mother collapsed in a potting shed at the bottom of our garden.

'I'm going to find the light,' she'd said.

She'd left me to myself with the TV and a fridge filled with ten cucumbers, ten carrots and ten pots of hummus that were only one day over the expiry date printed on their lid.

I wasn't hungry.

Not for food anyway.

The TV threw a glow across the living-room walls as it grew dark outside, and I began to wonder how the light would find her when it was clearly already fading with the sun. There was a woollen blanket tossed across the back of the sofa, itchy but better than going upstairs for my pyjamas, because if I went upstairs for my pyjamas, I might not be here when she returned.

It was important that *I* was the first thing Mum saw when she came into the house, that she knew I wasn't like the others. I wouldn't leave her. I would always be here no matter how long it took for the light to come.

I didn't betray her.

I turned the volume down on the telly to hear smashing and swearing and screams.

I ran. Without shoes or socks or slippers, I ran down the pathway to the potting shed, where my mother was throwing terracotta pots against muddied bare-brick and wooden walls.

'Mummy!' I shouted, but she couldn't hear me. Couldn't see me. She was in a different place or time. 'Mummy!'

We'd been in the potting shed the week before. When things were calm(ish) and steady(ish) and what she called an even keel.

'Iris, we're going to grow some irises.' Her breath was wispy clouds as she passed me what looked like a handful of tiny onions and then tipped her phone to show me photos of bright violet petals marked with yellow and white. There was a wide bowl and a huge, slit-open bag of compost. She told me to dig my hand right in. 'Then add the bulbs,' she said, pressing hers into the soil, her eyes on my eyes, inviting me to do the same. 'I bought them at the end of the summer. I have seeds somewhere. We'll throw those in too!'

Our fingers touched. After the bonfire, her cool skin and the promise of flowers made me look forward to spring.

But that night, *the* night, her fingers were scorching slithering snakes, coiling themselves around anything liftable then tossing it across the shed.

She grabbed the bowl of would-be irises.

'No!'

But she threw it, and the bowl smashed, and compost scattered, and all those tiny never-grown irises bounced in hard, repeated smacks across the freezing-cold tiles and out through the open door.

'Mummy!' I shouted. 'No!' I told myself it was just like hopscotch when I had to jump to avoid the shards.

I didn't betray her.

I stood on the grass outside, shivering but safe(ish), until she stopped with the throwing and the screeching and fell asleep crying and curled tight in a ball. I slipped her shoes from her feet and put them on mine while I cleared everything away. I scurryfunged. I wanted Dad to come and get me, but I didn't want him to think she was a monster. I just needed a break. I didn't want to never come home.

It was her who chose never.

I promise, I didn't betray her.

If anything, she betrayed me.

Twenty-Nine

Now I know the truth, I can keep living life as perfectly normal. Only the perfectly normal things I most want to do are with my best friend. And any time I have with her is continually invaded by bloody Dougie.

'This place is epic!' He's here now, his eyes flitting about the bothy like Buddy's when he's desperate to take in every single other dog at the park.

'Epically freezing!' Tala says, resuming her usual role of Firestarter as I shoot off a picture of a very wrinkled, very unappealing dried fruit to Órla.

A perfectly normal Iris has moxie. And so, given my decision to be perfectly normal, this morning I finally thanked Órla for my blank paper fortune teller. We've been messaging each other pretty much non-stop ever since.

Órla: Prune?

Me: Close

Órla: ??

Me: Date!

It's a bold move, right? But there's strength in bold. There's adventure. And adventure's what I need after accepting the facts about Mum and what she put me through. Despite what I said to Órla about it not being a good time for pursuing new friendships, if I could have an adventure with anyone right now, it'd be her.

Órla: Now you're talking

Dougie crouches next to Tala and passes her kindling, the dream team battling the cold.

I was starting to think I'd imagined Órla. Her red hair. Her pale face. Her pink lips. And when she messaged me back, my imagination *did* play its part, concocting movie-reel images of the two of us, gentle at first, tentative, a peck, though peck is too hard sounding a word for what I imagined our lips will do. They will be easy-going, an odd way perhaps to describe this thing that will happen between us. What I mean is, it will feel right and our eyes will close and our kiss will be magic and everything everything everything will be wonderf—

'Focus!' Tala nods at Tita Celestina's suitcase, a clear order that I need to crack on with *my* usual role of provider of snacks. In a perfectly normal world, I would be offering up a raspberry oat slice but, with The Vault closed, the only sweet treat I could come up with was a pathetic box of Jaffa cakes instead.

I haven't mentioned yesterday's door-whacking moment of madness to Tala, partly because who would want to admit to such unhinged behaviour, but mostly because it's been difficult to get a word in edgeways. I listen to her and Dougie now, as they back and forth about videos of a Filipino performance poet Tala sent him last night, taken by how swiftly they segue into their shared love of nachos and then on to their plans for next year.

'When I applied to UCL, it seemed like madness.' Tala takes a Jaffa cake and begins nibbling the chocolate from its top. '*Me?* Studying psychology? In *London*? But all this poetry stuff…' She smiles at Dougie, and there's no flirtation, just, I dunno, respect or gratitude or both. 'It's like something's shifted, and such a big change feels a bit more doable now, you know?'

'I've been chatting with this girl, Stella,' Dougie says, accepting a packet of salt and vinegar crisps, which he and Tala then share. 'She's in her second year at Oxford and reckons it's really different to being in sixth form.'

'Experience like no other!' I say, mimicking Rosa, who, last night, once again raised her concerns that if I take a gap year, I might end up side-tracked and not going to uni at all.

'In what way different?' Tala asks Dougie now, removing her puffer, tucking her hair behind her ears.

'Stella says it can be exhausting. Brilliant, but knackering. All these different nationalities, which is cool, right? But for a deaf person who, in crowded rooms might rely on lip-reading because their hearing aids aren't quite as effective, it can be trickier to understand.'

'I hadn't even thought of that,' Tal says. 'Will you get support?'

'I think so. I need to ask at my interview tomorrow.'

'You have an Oxford interview tomorrow?' I put my hand over my mouth so they don't get a view of my half-chewed Jaffa cake.

Dougie nods. 'Tomorrow. Thursday too.'

I'm well aware of the two-day process. Know-All likes to say the longer-than-average interview is due to the more-intelligent-than-average candidates. I like to say it gives those dons a better to chance to tell if house-cat losers like Know-All can cope with even a night away from home.

'My stepbrother's is this Thursday and Friday. If you were anything like him, you wouldn't be pissing about in a bando right now. You'd be at home methodically predicting questions and meticulously planning your answers!'

'You mock, but you could learn a thing or two from Noah's work ethic, Iris.'

I raise a palm to *whatever* Tala's jibe.

'I have *other* things that need meticulous planning.' Dougie uncrosses his legs on the tartan blanket on which he and Tala are squished. 'Newsflash: we have a date for the slam!'

'Shit!' Tala's jaw literally drops.

'Yup!' He stands to take off his coat, revealing his most garish Hawaiian shirt yet – a yellow-base fabric emblazoned with a repeated pattern of Father Christmases swimming, surfing and laid on sun loungers in the shade of exotic-looking trees. 'The seventeenth.' Dougie sits back down and opens Notes on his phone.

'Of December?' Tala's shock has quickly morphed into horror.

'Yup, of December, this Friday,' Dougie confirms. 'My mate Frankie's got last-minute access to The Vault – you know that café that shut down in town? They're using it for pop-up events over Christmas and the New Year. And the seventeenth is our night!'

'But I can't.' Clearly, she's so freaked by the slam being

just three days away, she doesn't even hear the news about The Vault. But then she nudges my foot with hers, gives me that look, the one that surfaces whenever she's tried to talk to me about Mum lately. 'Me and Iris are busy then.'

'No, we aren't!' I am so bright and so breezy, it's almost enough to lighten the dark winter sky outside. 'I don't feel like doing it this year.' Tala's eyes widen, like, *why?* 'Honestly, the slam's much more important than *that*.'

'But we need to remember your mum?'

To be perfectly normal, what I need to do is the opposite. But my stupid head won't let me forget, filling instead with the last time I saw her before she—

'You'll come back to put the angel on the tree when I get one, won't you?' White paint confettied Mum's nails from the carrots she'd turned into stalactites and hung from the underside of the stairs. Through the hallway, there was a trail of the hundreds of cotton-wool balls she'd used for the snow.

I remember her excitement too, how she leaped from one foot to the other, dashing for a box, for some photographs, for a silver key, for *that* angel, for a fortune teller we'd made together a few weeks before. She ran back out to the car and mimed for me to wind down the window.

'Pick.' She didn't seem to notice Dad in the driving seat, rubbing his temples and saying how it might be best if she let us go. 'Pick,' she repeated. It's only now that I remember her shoeless feet on the hard frost sparkling beneath the moonish pale of her bare toes. 'Pick.'

Did she know then that I'd already picked calm? Picked safe? Picked Dad?

I picked pink.

And then I picked two.

Mum beamed as she unfolded the paper. 'You will be strong.'
She handed it over, like she didn't need its promises.

Eight days later, she picked *gone*.

'Leave it, Tal,' I say now when Tala starts telling me
I shouldn't be making hasty decisions.

'You can't let the day pass without commemorating your
mum!' Tala looks to Dougie for back-up, but he's busied himself
with his phone. 'If it's just because you don't want to stop me
doing the slam, then I'm sure we can find a way to do both.'

'I don't want to do both.' I take another Jaffa cake, like,
honestly, this is no big deal. 'She chose not to be here, Tala.
I don't really want to commemorate *that*.'

'Iris.' There's so much sadness hanging in the way she says
my name. So much pity in her tears.

'What a wanker!' Dougie says.

'You what?' I'm about to go raspberry-oat-slice kind of crazy
on him when he shows us his screen.

'Not you, Iris. Jonny.'

Dougie shows us a photo sent to his football-team WhatsApp
group. It's a close-up of Angeline. It's blurred, but her wide
eyes and scream are perfectly clear. Tala takes his phone so
we can see better. The picture is scattered with skull emojis.
Underneath is a message from Jonny: Got intel on the stupid
bints whereabouts. Gave her a little surprise!

'Jonny's sister in Year Ten is on that Home Safe chat you've
all been using.'

'I have *not* been using it,' I scoff.

Tala shoots me a look. 'Go on,' she urges Dougie.

'An alert came up on her phone from Angeline telling everyone her route home, and Jonny read it. Went and hid in some bushes five minutes from her house then jumped out on her. He even took a photo so he could show everyone how clever he'd been.'

'What a dick,' I say. 'Seriously, I need to tell Dad and Rosa about this. For, like, the hundredth time, they said again this morning about *me* going for counselling. As if, with all the sick pricks out there, *I'm* the one who's ill in the head. Poor Angeline, she must have been shit scared.' I can't imagine how much worse it could have been if the person who'd got access to that info had even more disgusting motives than Jonny.

'Dougie.' Tala's thumb is swiping swiping swiping through the hundreds of messages that came into the football chat before that one. 'This group is gross. All these jokes,' she says, though the way she says *jokes* makes it clear she doesn't find them funny.

'I know, right.' Dougie sighs, shaking his head at the meme Tala's opened. If it's got tits or tires it will give you problems, it says above a picture of a large-breasted woman in a wheelchair. Well…damn is the pay-off beneath. 'Nobs.'

Tala shrugs. 'You don't make it clear you think they're nobs in the thread.'

'I never comment, though.' Dougie shifts awkwardly.

'Yeah, that's part of the problem.' Tala looks even fiercer than she did in the canteen a few days ago. 'You might not be the one posting this crap, but unless you're actively calling out the people that are, you're just not doing enough.'

Thirty

'Very dapper!' I nod at the blue suit and crisp white T-shirt hanging from the door of Know-All's wardrobe, ready for tomorrow's Big Interview. The Adidas – equally fresh – are paired neatly next to his packed overnight bag below. 'Thought you'd be hard at it.'

There are no books on his desk. No notes on his bed. The craft table is littered only with bricks.

'Chillin',' he says, and as he adds a tiny translucent block to what I think is a stained-glass window, my stepbrother does actually look pretty chill. 'You?' His eyes move from me to Tala, who's hovering nervously at his bedroom door.

'Ms Poet is suffering stage fright. We're looking for a dummy audience. And while I don't want to call you a dummy the night before you have to convince those dons of the opposite, I was hoping you might do us a favour and come sit in the living room with our dummy parents. You just have to watch Tala here prove that she doesn't need me but is instead very capable of performing her exquisite poetry herself!'

'I don't know why you're making me do this,' Tala mumbles, pulling the sleeves of her black jumper down over her hands.

'Because I'm your best friend and I *know* that you can.' I've been banging the same drum since the bothy yesterday.

It might not seem much but telling Dougie he needed to pull his proverbial ally socks up was just the latest in a series of small moments in which Tala's proven her nerve. 'You've found your voice, now you need to use it.'

Tala's chest rises as her eyes drop.

'Is this something to do with that thing you and Dougie were handing out flyers for this afternoon?' Know-All bends over, picks up some stapled-together paper from his floor. *Magdalen College, Oxford*, it says above a photo of a Lego tower. *Jeez*, talk about obsessed.

'That's the one,' I say, letting slide the fact that my stepbrother appears, from the £7.50 price tag at the bottom of the top page, to have spent real money on brick-by-brick instructions on how to build a university he's not yet got in to.

'Looks cool. Who came up with the name?'

It was Dougie who christened the slam Rhyme's Up, and Dougie again who's redesigned his flyers to include a statement promising all profits from the evening will be split between two charities – Time's Up and White Ribbon. I'd not heard of the second.

'They work with men and boys to end violence against women,' Dougie told us. And he could have been smug about it, like, *hey, look at what a good ally I'm being now*, but instead he apologized. 'You were right,' he said to Tala. 'I've kept too quiet. I've not been doing enough.'

'Apparently,' Tala says now, 'his friend Stella said setting up nights like this should put him in good stead for playing an active role in the poetry society next year.'

'*If* he gets in.' I quickly shift my focus to Know-All before

Tala has the chance to accuse me of sounding snippy. 'What society will you be joining?' I glance over at the completed Central Perk set. 'Or will you continue to live your life vicariously through places and people you create in your room?'

'You *do* remember you came in here asking me for a favour? Insults are hardly the way to get me on board.'

'I'll sort the dishes every night for a week?' There's no way he'll refuse. If there's one thing Know-All and I agree on, it's that Dad's hovering as you load the plates and bowls after dinner is one of *the* most annoying things in the world. Why bother giving someone a job to do, if you can't bear the way they do it? He reloads every single time.

'Two weeks.' His voice is all *take it or leave it*.

What other choice do I have? 'Deal.'

We even shake on it and head downstairs, where it becomes apparent that Know-All and I aren't the only ones to have been involved in a heated negotiation.

'If you want the bloody tree that much, Matt, then have the bloody tree.' Rosa's plumping already plump cushions and shaking her head as we walk in.

'Brilliant.' Dad slaps both hands on his thighs, inevitably squashing the freshly plumped cushions as he sits down. 'I know that old one means a lot to you, love, but you're never going to regret switching to the real thing.'

'Remember the eagle pose!' Rosa says to Tala, encouraging her to take several deep breaths. 'Balance, strength and flexibility. Something you need not just in poetry performances but marriage too.' She shoots Dad playful evils. 'Isn't that right, Matt?'

'Shall we get going?' I move Tala to prime position on the rug and take my seat by Dad on the sofa. 'Go on,' I urge. And she begins.

It's sod's law, right, that the only moment Tala looks up from the carpet as she stumbles her way through 'I'm Ace' is when *I* look fleetingly at my phone which, while silent, has lit up with an alert from Órla. Our text exchange yesterday may have suggested she was game for a date, but we haven't yet set anything in stone. Is this it? Is she giving me a time and place?

It seems not. Rather, she's sent a picture of herself, one arm behind her back, the other raised in front of her, holding a giant burger.

Transformation complete: Official Beef-Devouring Glutton!

I swear it's only because Órla's cute that I'm laughing. That it's nothing to do with Tala forgetting her line. But that's clearly not what Tala thinks when our eyes meet, and she stops speaking and starts crying and telling everyone that this is all a complete waste of time.

'You were doing amazingly, Tal,' I call after her as she hurries into my room and starts gathering her stuff like she's planning to go.

'So amazingly that you were distracted by your messages. Great.'

'We can practise. Over and over. I've found online tutorials and podcasts about public speaking. We don't have to sleep. We can work on it for the next forty-eight hours straight if we have to. I swear, you'll have my undivided attention.'

'And what if I crumble on the night?'

'Then I'll be there. And I can either stand by your side or read it myself, if that's what you want me to do. But at least give yourself a chance, yeah?'

She shrugs, but the arm holding her coat is already lowering, like she's about to drop it, like, deep down, Tala knows she wants to stay.

'Listen to this.' I pull my earphones from my drawer, plug them into my phone and set up a podcast I found about owning the room. 'It's brilliant. You're brilliant, Tal.' I poke the ear buds into her ears, press play and hold up all my fingers and thumbs to show I'll come get her in ten.

Half an hour later, we're back in the sitting room cheering Tala as she gives us her fifth performance of 'I'm Ace'. With each rendition, Tala's looked a little more comfortable, but this one was perfect, and we rise to our feet in a standing ovation, turning over the paddles I hashed together with card, sticky tape and Sharpies while she was listening to inspo in my room. Like the judges on *Strictly Come Dancing*, Dad, Rosa, Know-All and I are all beaming as we each give my best mate ten out of ten.

'It's different here with you lot, though,' Tala says after, when I tell her she has it sussed.

'Only the location.' I put the paddles in her bag as a good omen. 'Wherever you are, Tal, you know I'll *always* have your back.'

Thirty-One

'You sure you don't want to do anything for your mum today, Iris?' Tala says as she pulls up outside my house after driving me back from school. She checks the clock on the dash. 'There's still time for us to go to the bothy. It feels wrong that it's the seventeenth, and you've barely even mentioned her.'

Why would I mention her? Why would I want to dwell on what she did?

I flash Tala the calendar app on my phone. 'The only thing of major importance today, Tal, is your slam!' Sadly, Rhyme's Up is the only real thing of importance in my diary until Christmas. Still no word from Órla on our date.

'*Bon appétit!*' I say in my best French accent, surreptitiously checking my messages – nothing – before sliding my phone back in my bag. 'See, who needs French A level when it comes so easily *à la moi*?'

Tala's brow arches with obvious disdain. 'Your English grammar is impeccable, Iris, but your *Français, ça laisse à désirer.*'

'I stopped listening at "impeccable".' I grin and climb out of the car. 'Which is what *you* will be tonight, my friend.'

She doesn't look convinced. 'I don't know how Mama and Papa expect me to eat anything.' Tala says she's not sure if Tita Celestina and Kristian are celebrating her poetry or her coming out. Either way, since she first performed 'I'm Ace' for them, they won't stop telling her how proud they are and have insisted on a fancy dinner, just the three of them, before this evening's slam. 'I already feel like I'm going to vom.'

'I'll be there with a bucket at seven thirty then, yeah?' I'm only half kidding, Tala looks like she could legit be sick right now. 'Nice and early, like we said, so you can be prepared.'

'Thanks.' Her seat belt catches as she twists her entire body to face me. 'For being there.'

I wiggle my fingers to ward off the rankling cold and stick my head back in the car. 'You're my favourite person in the entire world, Tal.'

'You're my favouriter.'

'You're my favouritest. I wouldn't be anywhere else.'

It's true. When I walk into the kitchen and find Know-All not long returned from, and boring on about, his interview, I would give absolutely anything to already be backstage, deep breathing and eagle-posing with Tala. Instead, I'm stuck with Know-All's gloating and Rosa's gentle interrogation.

'Surely, it can't all have been such a breeze. You were there overnight, love. Were you not flummoxed by anything at all?'

For once, my stepbrother doesn't jump straight in with an answer as cocksure as Buddy's belief that he can catch any tossed ball. 'I dunno,' he says, kind of quiet and weirdly focused on spreading butter to the very edges of two slices of toast.

Rosa doesn't budge from her position by the kettle, just stands there like her whole evening hinges on whether Know-All found something difficult, which, history tells us, he won't have done. 'Well?'

215

'No,' he snaps. 'Just leave it. Everything's fine.'

Rosa places a hand on his back but turns to me. 'How about you, Iris? How's your day been?' Only the way she says 'your day', she's clearly hinting at the same fact that Tala was so hung up on, which is that today isn't just any day but the seventeenth. When will they realize the date is nothing but a number in a calendar? Today has been, and still is, OK. More than. It's almost the end of term. We have the slam tonight. We can get a Christmas tree tomorrow – a real one! And even Know-All should be chill given the interview that's dominated his life for the past three months is now done.

'Are you all right, lovely?' Rosa's hand moves across Know-All's back so she has a full arm around him. His obvious desire to move the hell on from this conversation is sated by Rosa's ringing phone.

'No!' She shakes her head as she listens. 'Seriously?'

'What's happened?' Know-All asks, but Rosa holds a hand up, mouths, '*just wait.*'

'It was your dad,' she says once she's hung up. 'He said they've caught that man who's been exposing himself.' Rosa swallows, but there's no getting rid of the disgust in her expression. 'He's a teacher.'

'What?' Know-All and I say in unison.

'Yeah, at a senior school on the other side of the county.'

'But…' I don't know how to finish my sentence. All I can think is how Mr Moriarty has urged us to go and talk to him or any other member of our school's staff if we had any information. Has this other teacher – this flasher – said the same to his students? Have they trusted him? What if they…

216

I send Tala a link to the article I find, and she messages me a barrage of alternate angry- and sad-face emojis. A few minutes later, my phone beeps again.

Tala: FFS who are we supposed to trust?

My mind flashes to that night in Good Hope Wood. His near-silent approach. His indecipherable smile. The galling swagger of his laugh.

You will be strong.

I believed it. For years I've believed it, walking untouchable in the dark.

I can't look at *that* fortune teller now. I did the right thing scribbling over Mum's scrawled promises, which even she couldn't live by.

I perch on the edge of my bed, scrunch my eyes tight and try not to see his bone-white skin, his hand in his pocket, his—

Saved by the bell.

Or the beep, at least.

Órla: I'm here

I don't get it. To me, *I'm here* suggests Órla is waiting for me. *I'm here* suggests we have a plan. We *don't* have a plan. Sure, we had an *idea* of a plan, we skirted around the possibility of a date. But with Tala's intense rehearsal schedule, I haven't had time to think about where I might take Órla, what exactly we might do.

It's incredible how quickly your mind can tumble into possibility, how alive your body can become with mere thought.

Me: Where's here?

Órla: Here

Me: Here here?

Órla: Hear hear

Me: Seriously?

Órla: Seriously

Órla: I'll be at the train station in 5

Me: WTF!?

Me: So we're going on a date NOW?

Me: And the train? Why didn't you drive?

She doesn't reply immediately, and I don't have time to wait. When I pull into the station car park, yanking hard on the brakes of my bike, Ó.M.G. is already there. Standing in an oversized pea-green raincoat with its hood up, she lifts her hand – the one I've imagined on my neck, my back, my… (check yourself, Iris) – to wave.

'Hey,' she says as I ride closer.

'Hey,' I say as she walks closer still.

Wordless, then, I marvel at the heat of her breath separate from the heat of my breath on the air, imagining we'd be capable of melting ice caps with the force of its combination to come.

And then it comes.

They come.

Her smiling lips barely change shape as she leans in, like it's absolutely to be expected, and kisses me not quite on my lips but nearly.

There are no cellos.

No crescendo.

No tongue.

But it's definitely more than friends. And definitely lovely in a basic not-movie but still for-real kind of moment. A marker in time, which passes too quickly, the length of an inhale, in which I get a sense of the coffee and mints she must have had on the train.

'I'm sorry.' Órla pulls back. 'I didn't mean to... I shouldn't have assumed... I just saw you and...' Her left forefinger goes to her mouth as if it's possible to erase the new picture it just painted of us.

I take it. Her finger, I mean. I don't want her to wipe whatever we are away.

What I *do* want is to kiss her finger. What I want even more than that is to kiss her mouth. But while I thought it wouldn't matter, in all my fantasies of this moment, Órla and I are alone. Here in the real world, there are people who might be looking, who might be noticing that the girl straddling her bike is being kissed by the girl with the oversized pea-green raincoat, already wet with snow.

Snow!

It's light but it *is* falling.

While I don't kiss either Órla's finger or Órla's mouth, I do tell her it's fine that she kissed me. 'More than fine,' I say, trying to sound like I'm not bothered if she ever kisses me again.

Which I am.

Obviously.

I *am* bothered.

Very, very bothered.

'So this is a surprise.' I lock my bike in the rack outside the station and we start walking towards town. 'I thought you'd be hard at it in the gym.'

219

'Slight problem!' Órla stops and pulls back that giant sleeve. 'Accident,' she says as I take in the bright white cast concealing her right arm.

'Shit!' I reach out and touch it. Our gazes diverting then, as if I just touched her skin.

We continue up the hill. 'Worst thing is, this charity-shop coat is the only one I can get over the bloody thing.'

'Don't hate me, but I just thought it was another one of your unusual, I mean *beautiful*, creations.'

'Give me some credit,' she says, unpopping the coat to reveal a jumper with 'SLEIGH WHAAAAAT?' stitched on to its front. 'More my style. And good news is, since *this* happened –' she holds up her duff arm – 'I have more time for *this*.' She points at her handiwork.

'You can still sew then?'

'Well, no, but I'm very good at being a creative director, and Mam is very good at doing as she's told.'

'So what happened?'

'Doesn't matter.' Órla shrugs her shoulders dismissively, stops again, nods at the poppers she's struggling to do back up on her own.

There's something very intimate about dressing her, about my fingers being this close to her chest. I mutter something about the cold making me shake.

'What *does* matter is that not having to go to gym meant I could come here.' Órla takes a hold of my hand to steady it. 'So, Iris Tremaine, what destiny will you be writing for the two of us today?'

Thirty-Two

I check the time on my phone: 4.30. We have three solid hours before I need to be at The Vault to help Tala prep. I pull out the flyer from my bag and hand it to Órla. 'A bit later, we'll go here. But first…' I park her in the doorway of a bar, where bearded hipsters sip craft ale in the window. 'Wait here for a second, would you? I have an idea, but it requires some grovelling first.'

'You're taking the piss, right?' Rollo says when I rush from what I admit is a pretty vague apology for my recent behaviour to a request for an immediate favour. Sure, he's not exactly delighted to hear from me, but this call's already going better than I'd expected. I mean, he answered, which in itself was a surprise.

'For old times' sake?' Even I'm wincing as I say it.

'*Old times*' sake,' he scoffs, and I imagine him shaking his head the way he did whenever I said anything on the cusp of outrageous. 'Iris, it's not even three weeks since you broke up with me. That's hardly old times, is it?'

'For *my* sake then.'

And maybe Rollo hears how much I want this because he tells me to spill. 'You're going all-out on this date,' he says once I've outlined the favour.

'I guess.' I'd forgotten how much louder silence sounds on the phone. What feels like minutes but must only be seconds later. 'Look, I know things didn't exactly end mutually between us.'

'End mutually?' He's actually laughing. 'That's not how I'd put it.'

I'm not going to ask how he *would* put it, but Rollo clearly isn't missing the opportunity to let me know.

'You ghosted me.'

'Ghosted you?'

'What else would you call radio silence after what I thought was a really cool night in?'

A flash of Rollo how I left him sleeping in his bedroom. The sheets not enough to stop goosebumps forming on his skin.

I turn to face the wall, tangled in the discomfort of Órla being so close by as the memory of Rollo's heavy but delicate weight on me burns in my cheeks. Not long after we'd returned home from the cinema – removing our inhibitions as quickly and easily as we'd removed our clothes – he'd said he wanted to kiss me all over, working his way up from my toes.

'It *was* cool,' I tell him now. 'Pretty hot too, from what I remember.'

'So…?' Rollo's voice this evening is as deep and searching as his tongue that night in his room.

'So, what?'

'Was it what I said about Europe? Me coming with you? Is that why you disappeared? Because there was no pressure in the suggestion, Iris. It was just an idea.'

Thing is, there *was* pressure. Just not the kind Rollo was thinking.

222

It wasn't the first time he'd hinted that he thought what we had going was serious. That he might be falling in love.

When someone loves you, they're giving you the power to hurt them.

Is it more dangerous, then, to leave or to stay?

'I don't know if it's worse,' Rollo says, 'that you were just playing to form.'

'Playing to form?'

'All I'm saying is I was talking to Felix—'

'Felix?' What the fuck? 'My exes had a conference about me? Jasper there too, was he? Jack?'

Thank God Órla is out of earshot.

'Just me and Felix. And it wasn't a conference, it was a chat. We like you, Iris. Despite how things ended, I care. I dunno. I just worry that if you keep shying away from people who care about you, you're gonna end up like those derelict buildings you love so much.'

It seems ironic that a derelict building is the reason for my call.

'I'll do it,' Rollo says a few minutes later. 'But on one condition.'

I turn back to watch Órla, who's been diligently reading and re-reading the Rhyme's Up flyer all the time I've been gone. 'Go on…'

'Don't go raising this guy's expectations with your wild romantic gestures then disappear the moment you have him hooked.'

A few minutes later, Órla and I are marching back down the hill.

'We'd normally have to climb to where we're going. Not just through windows either.' I pause outside Tala's favourite bookshop and point up towards the higgledy-piggledy tops of the ancient buildings. 'Seriously, we'd be all over the roofs too.'

Órla wide-eyes me, like, *you have got to be kidding.*

'Fortunately for you, Ó.M.G., I have contacts.' I tap my nose the way people do in movies.

'I had a feeling you were worth pursuing.'

God, she looks hot when she quirks her brow.

'Well, when I say "contacts", what I really mean is this guy Rollo who I went out with for a bit. He works at the bar on the same site so can offer us a much less precarious way in.'

A faceless sing-song of guys is *warbling* its way down the hill. Shoe-horned into festive jumpers, they're bursting with ho-ho-hos and lager. One of them has gone harder on the theme than most with an outfit that makes him appear as if he's being piggybacked by a snowman. He croons into a solo, a loud and highly gesticulated rendition of Mariah Carey's 'All I Want for Christmas'.

'…is you!' Órla joins in the chorus, half whisper, half song, pulling me to her by the front of my coat.

With Rollo, I was the Órla in the couple. The cool one who could charm with love songs and woo with kisses. The confident one who knew and could take what she wanted. The fearless one who at all times was in control of every move.

This, though, with Órla, isn't me in charge. This, though, with Órla, is me falling.

Panicked, I step back.

There's an 'Oi oi!' from one of the beered-up choir now behind me.

Órla flinches, her eyes flitting from me to them to me to them until they land on me in a sad yet spiky stare.

And I know what she's thinking. That I'm ashamed, which is true, I suppose. But not in the way she imagines.

It's not her I'm ashamed of.

It's me.

Don't go raising this guy's expectations, Rollo said, and he had me nailed. He understood my predilection to run.

(Nice use of 'predilection', Iris.)

'Fancy coming under the mistletoe, love?' Ugh. The lech sounds about fifty. And I'd normally be all wisecracks and clapbacks, but I'm stumped.

Órla, though, she's on it. 'Nah, you're all right, thanks.' She doesn't even blink.

'You're too scrawny for me anyway.'

I haven't turned to look at him, but I can picture his face. His sneer's so thick in his jibe.

'Well, that's cool, mate, because you're too dickish for me.'

In other circumstances, I'd swing straight round for a glimpse of that muppet's gobsmacked face. Instead, I keep my head hung, turning only to catch the backs of the *fa-la-la-la-la-la*ing mob as they disappear further down the hill towards the station.

Órla's eyes haven't left me. 'Did that make you uncomfortable?'

'What? The sexist prick?'

'Not him,' she says. '*Me*.'

It's not only Órla's casted hand that's awkward. Her other one, and mine too, dangle empty at our sides.

'Huh?'

'You think I didn't notice how you totally didn't want them to see we were together?'

'That wasn't it, I—'

'It's cool, Iris. I just want to know where I stand with you. I've only had one girlfriend, though I'm not even sure I can call her that. She wasn't out. Everything was secret. We never even went on a date.'

'You *have* been on a date, though?'

Órla shrugs.

'This is your first date?'

She nods. 'Is that pathetic?'

'No!' I shake my head dramatically. 'It's *my* first date with a *girl*.'

'And you're cool with that? Being on a date with a girl? Being on a date with *me*?'

'Yes.' There's definitely fear in the way my heart shudders as I take Órla's good hand. But there's hope too. And, for the moment, feeling both together is OK.

Thirty-Three

'Watch your footing.' Even though Rollo shut the door before heading back to the bar below, I'm whispering. 'Here.' I offer an arm.

The head torch I wrapped around Órla's hat as soon as Rollo snuck us through the staff room into the first of the disused labyrinthine corridors is casting rapid-moving spotlights on the bronze-tiled walls as she takes it all in.

'What *is* this place?'

'You'll see.' As I guide her up the last set of stairs, Órla's boots make small, echoey thuds on the steps. They slow the further we climb. It's only when she sniffs that I notice the slightly animal urine smell of multi-storey car parks. 'Sorry,' I say, like it's me who's weed in the unlit corners of the building. 'I guess I'm used to it. You need the loo before we go in?' I flash my pocket torch on the sign for the ladies; its brass is worn, and only the 'A' and 'S' are still painted white. 'I don't want to be getting up halfway through the movie.'

'The movie?'

'Uh-huh.' I stop outside another door, this one more ornate with carvings in the dark wood and handles which would once, when polished – when cared for – have shone. 'I'm nothing if not conventional when it comes to dates…' I take Órla's hand and lead her through.

Otherwise pitch-black, the room reveals itself piece by piece in the yellowish-white circles of our torch beams. The vast room before us would once have been decadent, its decor reminiscent of a cartoon crown. On this side, *our* side, the door is painted gold. Deep-red walls run down into a burgundy carpet, threadbare with footfall and dusty with time. Numbered seats, upholstered with velvet in the same regal tone and folded into their backrests, climb upwards in alphabetically ordered rows.

Órla tips her head back, her torch exposing the panelled ceiling, then down to the backrests of the chairs, where ancient ash and cigarette butts spill from shell-shaped trays. She turns slowly, her jaw dropped at the battered grandeur of it all. Behind us, a huge pair of curtains is closed, concealing what would once have been a screen.

'A cinema?'

'See, predictable first-date stuff, right?'

'Hardly!' My torch isn't on her, but I can hear Órla's smile, her thrill at the place, which is inevitable really because it's beautiful. Grimy, sure, but one hundred per cent beautiful.

'It's so…'

'Romantic?'

Órla's grip tightens. Our palms have now forgotten the cold. 'Yes!' She sounds so sure yet so surprised.

'Snacks?' I cast my light to the top of the auditorium, where there's a hatch marked 'KIOSK'. 'The menu's a bit limited, but I got us the VIP package.' Two bags of crisps and two glasses of Coke sit on the counter. I owe Rollo big time.

To my ex's credit, his reaction when I rocked up with a girl was chill too. Sure, he'd whispered, 'What? So you're gay now?' But Rollo didn't so much as arch an inquisitive brow when I mumbled about not yet being sure of a label.

'I dunno,' I said, my cheeks warm with the uncertainty. Isn't this something I should know? 'Bi, maybe? Or pan?'

'Cool.' Rollo shrugged then reminded me to send him a text once we're done.

'What else does the VIP package involve?' Órla takes a sip of her drink, her eyes lit by my torch as they scan the vast room, clearly wondering what possibilities it holds.

'Pre-cleaned seats – Row F, twenty-three and twenty-four – and a pick of two of Pride.com's *Ten Romantic Lesbian Movies to Watch for Your Date Night*. Big up Google!'

'Deffo. Google led me to some very cool photos of you.'

I dread to think.

'Speaking of which…' Órla puts her drink on the floor and pulls out her phone. 'Don't we need to get a picture for your Insta?'

I see in her quickly dropped smile that I've been too slow to say yes.

'Oh.' There's a wisp of something like disappointment or nervousness in her tone.

'Not because I want to keep us a secret.' I don't know how to express what I need to say without sounding corny. 'Honestly? After the shitstorm of my life the past few weeks, being here with you feels kind of magical.'

She puts her phone away. 'Go on.'

'Posting online's always been a sort of validation of what

I'm doing, like other people seeing it makes it more real. But tonight, it being just the two of us, somehow it already feels real enough.'

Órla's laugh as she sidles her way along Row F doesn't sound like a piss-take, it sounds like relief. 'That's pretty emotionally exposing for a Capricorn!'

'Oh God, I'd forgotten you were one of *them*.'

'One of *them*!?'

'An astrologist!' The way I say it must turn it into an insult, because Órla twists to glare at me, dazzling me with her light. 'Jeez, you want to turn that thing off?' I shield myself from her torch, wedging mine, pointing upwards, between our two seats, then sit side-on to face her. 'Seriously, you're blinding me!'

'With my torch or my devastating good looks?'

'Both.' I reach across and remove the light from her head, taking off the beanie too.

'OMG, Ó.M.G.! Your hair?'

'Bold, huh?' The long red braids are gone. What's left is practically a buzz cut on the sides, though the top is inches longer. The curls are swept away from her face, highlighting all those beautiful angles of her nose and cheeks and chin.

Órla slides herself around so she's leaning on her left shoulder, her face within touching distance.

Without thinking, I reach for the longer strands on top, rubbing the ends between my fingertips, which draw an invisible line then from Órla's hair to her cheek, which is warm and soft and beautiful. My touch is gentle. A contradiction to my heart, which thunders so deep I swear it might burst through my ribs.

Somewhere, several floors below us, there are people drinking, revving themselves up for the weekend. They'll be shouting over the music, which they can't really hear but can feel through the bass vibrating the floor.

Here, though, it is quiet.

'I can hear you breathing.' I resist the urge to put a hand to her chest.

Her lips open, my fingertip slides from her cheek on to her tongue, between her teeth. She bites. Not hard, but enough to keep me there.

Wanting.

This, right now, is hotter than any other body to body contact I've had. Ever. Until.

Ringing.

'Órla! The first rule of cinema? You *have* to turn off your phone!'

'Sorry!' Only because my finger's wedged in her mouth, it comes out like, 'Shorry.' And then it's awkward, you know, figuring out what to do with her saliva on my nail. I mean, should I lick it? That's the kind of thing that could be a turn-on if the vibe was still seductive, which it's not, because Órla is now talking to someone I assume is Bronagh, and that pretty much busts the mood.

'Sorry,' she says when she's done, clearly this time because my finger, which I've wiped on my jeans, by the way, is no longer near any sensual part of Órla, but is instead tapping at my iPad, trying to set up a film. 'Mam's gone into overdrive with sorting meetings and phone calls, trying to work out plans for next year.'

231

'Next year?'

'My year out.'

And my brain must be all kinds of hypocritically haywire because, despite balking at Rollo's suggestion that he comes to Europe with me, my head – and, yeah, my groin – is a flutter with the ridiculous notion that Órla and I could year-out together.

'Though Mam might as well call it a year in.' Órla's face hardens. '*In* a gym. *In* a routine. *In* a timetable that's even more gruelling than—'

'Hey.' All my fluttering dissipates with seeing her so changed. 'The only place you're *in* now is this cinema. With me.'

But Órla's not for soothing. 'Talk about overbearing mothers. Honest to God, I swear sometimes, I wish she'd just—'

'What? Take some pills and die?'

Órla's face creases, like, *what the hell just happened here?*

'I'm sorry.' The words need to fall faster to make the mood lighter to show me as brighter—

'Tell me,' Órla says.

'It's too much.'

'Not for me, it isn't.' She sits back, her good hand on the armrest between us, the other weighing down on her thigh.

'That's what worries me. There's something about you, Órla Mary Gamble, that makes me spill way more than I normally would.'

'Of course there is. Pisces are empaths, which makes us very good listeners.'

I roll my eyes.

'OK, well, if you refuse to believe in the power of my birth sign then we can just put it down to my name.'

'Your name?'

'There's a fada, an accent, above the O. With it, Órla means golden princess.'

'Hence your Olympian destiny.'

She shrugs, like, *whatever*. 'Without it, Orla is the Gaelic word for vomit. So maybe –' she cocks her head, confidence in her theory bolstered now – 'with you, I'm not meant to be a golden princess. Maybe I'm here to help you *vomit* your truth.'

'Eeeww.'

'Better out than in.'

'Can I turn off the torch?'

Órla doesn't look convinced.

'It's easier to vomit in the dark.'

'OK,' she says. 'But don't you dare let go of my hand.' The touch between us is different this time.

Not sexy.

Safe.

Our quiet is even quieter in the dark.

'Rollo, you know that guy you met earlier, he warned me I'll end up like these places if I don't sort myself out. And I get what he means but, honestly, these buildings, the abandoned places, they're *already* where I feel most like me.'

Órla had asked me not to let go of her hand, as if *she* were the frightened one.

'All the name stuff. Iris means Goddess of Rainbows. But if I'm a fucking rainbow, I should be technicoloured, right? And until a few weeks ago, I really thought I was.' The words are a swirling rush on my tongue. 'But everything's topsy-turvy. I thought Mum loved me, but she killed herself. I thought I loved Mum, but I asked Dad to take me from her. I thought Dad was a stickler for truth and reason, but he's lied to me for years. I thought it would push people away if I got sad or angry, but I'm kind of both right now, and yet you're here.'

'I am.'

'Before I discovered the truth about Mum, I must have blocked out half of our lives together. I only remembered the good stuff. But, thing is, it wasn't just good, it was incredible. I really believed *she* was incredible. And she made me believe *I* was incredible too.'

'To be fair, I don't know you that well, but you do seem quite incredible, Iris.'

Technicoloured Iris would have soaked up the compliment, but, in this darkness, my uncertainty deepens and roars.

'If I'm so incredible, then why did Mum choose to leave?'

A siren wails somewhere beyond our black cocoon.

'Iris.' I can tell from the rickety catch in Órla's voice that I'm not the only one crying.

'I love that you made me a blank fortune teller. But without that strict instruction to be strong, I don't know who or what I'm supposed to be.'

The heat of Órla's breath as she presses her cool forehead against mine is a shock that sends me from deep in my head to deep in my body. 'You're not the only one who doesn't know who they are.'

What the fuck is wrong with me? How can I leap from melancholic to turned on? 'You think?'

'I don't think.' Her lips form the words against my skin. 'I *know*,' she says, her mouth edging closer to my mouth. The only thing separating us is the nerve it takes to make that final move.

The dark around us is physical now.

Charged.

The quiet is thick with anticipation.

My palm on her jawline.

Hers on my thigh.

I can only live this moment once, I think, before thinking stops and a sweet, hot unravelling begins. If it's my tongue or her tongue first, I don't know, but now it's our tongues. Our fingers. Our breath. Our heat. Our push. Our pull. Our soft. Our hard. The clash of our teeth then the brush of her eyelashes against my cheek. Everything mindful. Everything wild. Our bodies catching each other clumsily in the dark. When her cast hits my arm with a lumbering whack, I don't care if there's a bruise.

Who knows how many seconds, minutes pass, all I know is, there will be no movie. Not when there is this.

'The time?' Órla's sharp collarbone tastes of cocoa and salt.

Her wrist twists against my shoulder as she turns to illuminate her watch. 'We have half an hour,' she says, and I hear her. But hearing isn't the most powerful of my senses as my back arches, pressing my chest into hers as she lets out a small moan and our lips come together again, and I am nowhere but these two seats with her.

When you kiss someone like Órla, time moves too quickly. Every second presses you further into the moment you're with them until you can't imagine ever not being this close. They know, maybe more than you do, exactly who you are.

'I could do this for hours,' I murmur into that bit of her neck that meets her... 'What's this even called?'

'Décolletage?' Órla pulls ever so slightly away, her hands moving from my shoulders to the crack between our seats where I'd wedged the torch. 'Me too on the for hours front, by the way,' she says, the light too bright after so long in the black. 'But –' she shows me her watch – 'we have to go.'

'Shit!'

Órla shifts her legs to the side as I clamber for my iPad, which has slipped from my lap to the floor. 'Chill,' she says, and from her pocket she whips the flyer I gave her earlier. 'I read this thing very thoroughly while you were on your mission call with Rollo. The slam starts at eight. I even checked the map. It's got to be a ten-minute walk max. It's seven forty. We have ages.' When she drops it to reach up and take a hold of my shoulders, the flyer flutters to the floor, and despite the ticking clock, I can't help it, I bend down to kiss her once more.

'I said I'd be there for half past, so enough with the lips already.' I wipe my mouth with the back of my hand like this might erase the magnetic pull Órla has on me. But she tugs at my sleeves, wanting more. 'I'm serious.' Just one then. 'Stop.' And another. 'Right, I'm not even looking at you because your fucking gorgeousness makes a swift exit impossible.'

'Consider me off-limits then.' She attempts to cover her face with her cast. 'You go.'

'You're not coming?'

Órla shakes her head. 'Sounds like this is a big night for your friend. Maybe it'll be easier for you to focus on her if I'm not there!'

'Wow! Seems you're as wise as you are sexy.'

Her smile's so broad it's easy to believe that I will never have a single problem again. 'I'll get our stuff together and wait for you in the bar downstairs.'

After one last, lingering kiss, I bolt to The Vault, vibrating with rainbow colour, ready to bathe Tala in all my glorious light.

Thirty-Four

'Too late.' The usher's a dude I vaguely recognize from primary school, but he's not letting old connections sway his power. 'You can stay here and watch with everyone else, but you're not going up there.' He jerks his head at the staircase that leads to what used to be an upstairs seating area when this was a café. It's now serving as backstage, which is exactly where I need to be if I'm going to fulfil my promise to Tala.

Her and Dougie's phones both go straight to voicemail.

Crap.

I look around, desperate for another way up. But while the tables have been shifted around to create a performance space and the framed prints that were hung on the walls have been replaced with pages roughly torn from books, the crux of the building remains the same. I've been here enough times to know there isn't one.

Rosa, sitting with Kristian and Tita Celestina, pats the empty seat next to her. 'C'mon,' she calls. 'They're starting any minute now.' It's not only me who gets the message. The audience hushes, almost but not quite silent with that dimmed-light buzz of anticipation. Just the odd rustle of snacks and a series of muffled coughs as the air thickens with the wait.

'Welcome, everybody, to Rhyme's Up!' Rema? I didn't know she was into poetry. But she's there on the makeshift stage with Dougie, who stands next to her at the mic, which isn't dissimilar from the many mics emblazoned across his shirt. Together – her voice, his hands – they intro the night, the charities, the idea that it's up to all of us to end violence against women, that the pen is mightier than the sword, and performance poetry and signing can be even mightier still.

Two people, maybe in their early twenties, one Spanish-looking in slim-fit dark-wash jeans, a plaid shirt and with an obligatory beard, and the other porcelain-skinned in a 1950s floral swing dress and with vintage curls, walk on next. Only they don't just walk, they strut, in a way only people who own a room can.

It's not just their confident entrance that gives them gravitas, it's their whole demeanour. Their aura, I guess you'd call it, an innate quality that means whatever they say will be heard.

They move slowly across the stage, possessing every inch of it, the guy talking, his voice a boom without the mic, and the girl signing, each of them somehow maintaining collective eye contact with the crowd. For the next five minutes, if they were to hold out their palms, we would all crawl right in.

Rema and Dougie are back on stage. 'Next up, Dougie will be joined by this evening's debut performance poet, Tala Fischer.' My heart is like Buddy's tail thumping against Mr West's kitchen tiles when he gets a whiff of a dog biscuit. Only while his rhythmic thwack is the beat of expectant joy, mine is less optimistic. Because, well, I don't want to be mean or anything, but how can Tala – even the new Tala – follow the previous act, who set the bar for charisma so exceptionally high?

When I spot her, side of stage, my entire body trembles. Rosa squeezes my hand, this smile on her face like she's so sure everything is going to be OK. The smile on *Tala*'s face couldn't be more different. It's fixed. Fearful. Fake.

She and Dougie step forward and take their positions a couple of feet apart.

Her hand tugs on the mic, which remains a bit too tall, pushing her on to her tiptoes as she says, '—'.

Ugh.

What she says is lost to a high-pitched echoey squeal. There's a communal wince, several hands over several ears, and awkward laughter from Tala as her head practically spins for help, which comes, finally, from a scrawny white dude, who looks in desperate need of some sun. Tala closes her eyes as he fiddles with the mic.

And I'm rising from my seat ready to go rescue her, but Rosa holds me back. 'She'll be all right.'

My best mate's chest rises and falls, rises and falls, her eyes still shut even when the technician leans in close and tells her, I'm assuming, that she's good to go.

Tala's feet don't move. Not for five seconds, not for ten, not for thirty. And I know this because I'm counting them up up up in my head.

Someone at one of the front tables squirms in their seat. Someone near the back begins to mutter.

Tala, it seems, is oblivious. Apart from the breathing, she is perfectly still.

Until.

Her hands go to her hair, pushing it back from her face so it's tucked firmly behind her ears. It's an everyday movement but executed with such deliberation that when her fingers are done and her eyes pop open, Tala has the attention of every single person here.

Dougie mirrors her.

It's not just their stance that's different from our rehearsals, the poem is too.

'Enough,' she says, pausing to allow the word – the title – to root itself in the room before continuing:

We have all walked with a key pressed between our fingers
as we turn around corners where the danger lingers
yeah, in the dark, in the shadow, but so too in the light
because as girls we learn quickly it's not only at night
that we must
    KEEP our gaze down.
    DON'T catch anyone's eye
    DON'T smile
    DON'T frown
       just blank face
           and   walk   by
men quickly, though
       s l o w   d o w n
a little because we MUSTN'T look fearful
of them in their suits or their hoodies with their jeer full
of bants about
our legs

241

or our tits

or our mouth

or our eyes

or our arse

or our arms

or our nose

or our thighs

or our dress

or our shoes

or our hair

or our skin

or our refusal to engage or let their words seep in

to something like an everyday normal conversation

in case *our* tone or *our* look is mistaken

for interest

or *dis*interest

and then we're a *slag* or a *prude*

or a *stuck-up bitch* with a bad attitude

for not taking the words in the way they were intended.

Which was…

What?

Tell me.

Cos now *he's* the one offended?

By the gall of us wanting to walk the street

without constant fear of the men we might meet.

Oh, he's heard it before, this feminist stuff

and I take his point

not   all   men.

But ENOUGH.

ENOUGH.

Because when there's a list of victims killed by men in
  one year that's

                118 murdered-women long

Sober women. Drunk women. Jogging women. Sex-
  working women.

WHATEVER *they* were doing, *they* did nothing wrong.

Then ENOUGH.

Enough.

And yes

ALL MEN

can play their part in seeing this violence isn't inflicted
again
and again.

Tala is no longer soft or hesitant, she is fury.

I stand. Rosa stands. Tita Celestina and Kristian stand. The
girl in the hat in the corner stands. The old lady with the shawl
and the glasses I want to call spectacles stands. The couple with
their matching shirts and ties and waistcoats stands. Everyone –
even the belligerent usher – stands.

Clapping's insufficient. I whistle and stamp my feet as Tala
and Dougie take their bows and head backstage.

'Tal!' Before the usher has the chance to block me, I'm
storming upstairs and throwing myself at Tala. 'You. Were.
AMAZING. Like, totally, unbelievably amazing.'

'Thanks.' She moves out the way of the next poet, who's
clutching his notes while doing neck rolls, readying himself
to go on.

'See!' Dougie grabs hold of Tala from behind, spins her round, and the electricity they're firing is ramped up so high, they're barely touching the ground. 'I told you you could do it. C'mon, over here.' He pulls her away from me, in through a door to a room which was once just a loo but now looks, when I follow, like a dressing area. 'I've only got a couple of minutes before I go back on with Katya, but, Tala, you were awesome.'

'*You* were awesome,' she says, and they get caught in this little schtick of 'No, *you* were awesome', 'No, *you* were awesome' that if we weren't in the midst of post-performance hype, would be very annoying.

Thankfully, some guy with a clipboard and a pen behind his ear gives Dougie the sign that he's due on stage.

Once he's disappeared, I open my eyes and arms wide, beckoning Tala in with my fingers. But even though she comes close, whatever we're doing right now is not a hug.

'You coming to watch the others then?' Tala's words as she wriggles free of my hold might form an invitation, but it's hardly a warm one. It's like the second Dougie was out of here, all that pumped-up jubilation was gone.

My mouth squirms into the pained, grimacing-face emoji. 'I left Órla at the Old Cinema with Rollo. God knows the crap he's feeding her about what I'm like as a girlfriend.'

Tala turns to the mirror leaning against the wall. The thirteen giant bulbs flanking it give her skin a warm glow that clashes with her expression, which is ice. 'Maybe he'll tell her that you're about as reliable with boyfriends as you are with best friends, i.e. –' she picks at her nails and juts her chin up to face me – 'that you're not very reliable at all.'

'Tal.' I make a grab for her hand, but she shakes it away.

'You promised you'd help me prep.'

'We got carried away.' And it's all kinds of awful, but even now I go weak-kneed at the thought of it. 'I'm sorry.'

'I'm sorrier,' she says. 'Our relationship might be platonic, Iris, but I didn't think that made it second best. But for you it is. When did Órla even get—'

'It's not like that, Tal, I—'

'You know what?' She puts both hands up, like, *stop*. 'Forget it.' She turns her back on me.

'I'm sorriest,' I say to no one but my reflection when she's gone.

Thirty-Five

I'm out of breath by the time I get back to the Old Cinema, which is, of course, the only reason why I can't speak when I walk in to find Rollo leaning across the bar, his lips so close to Órla that he's practically French-kissing her ear.

'Ah. So, she *does* return.' Rollo winks as Órla gives him this look, like, *see.*

'How'd it go?' Órla's smile is the glimmer of fresh hope I need right now.

Tala was livid. Quiet, sure, but somehow her disappointment was screamingly loud.

'She did great,' I say, but without enough oomph for Órla to hear me.

'What?' She stands up from her stool, our faces almost touching.

I look down at the shards of peanuts crunched into the sticky carpet by boots and stilettoed heels. It doesn't take much to destroy something.

'You all right?' Her hand is a relief on my wrist. 'Drink?' She holds up what looks like a lemonade, gesticulating to Rollo that she might want another, but I shake my head and suggest we get out of here.

'Too many people,' I shout. Tribes of revellers are rabbled around every table. A couple of blokes, too recently doused in aftershave, are standing within breath-smelling distance, and I swear one of their thumbs just brushed my thigh. 'Somewhere more private.'

Órla nods, like, *I hear you*. And, sure, she's on to something with her siren grin that suggests she knows what I'm thinking but, truth is, while I do want to be alone with Órla, I want to be far away from Tala too.

'OMG, Ó.M.G.!' My shriek reaches embarrassing heights of excitement as we emerge from the bar. 'Snow!' Heavier than earlier, it's settling now, a silent dusting of magic that conceals all the dirt with light. I stomp my DMs into the very fine layer it's made on the path while opening my mouth and trying to catch the tiny flakes on my tongue.

'C'mon, Elsa.' Órla tugs at my elbow. 'If you're taking me somewhere *more private* we'd better get a move on…The last train's at ten forty-five.'

'OK, OK.' I swipe a shimmering crystal from the tip of her nose. 'How much do you trust me?'

'That depends on whether I should believe Rollo or not.'

I don't ask.

There's no traffic, but Órla presses the button on the pedestrian crossing and waits an age for the man to turn green.

Suited commuters spill from the station slinging chiding looks at an ambush of Christmas partygoers. From their teetering walks and yowling cries about the cold, I'm guessing the short-skirted girls and ankle-skimming-trousered boys got well into their celebrations on the train.

I go to the bike rack, unlock mine and point at the handlebars. 'Up for a ride?'

'Are we flirting right now, or do you actually expect me to sit on that?'

'There'll be a helmet.' I offer her mine. 'And very good road sense.' I can see from the slight curl in the corner of her mouth that she's softening. 'And a whole lot more of these.' I lean the bike against the wall and kiss her.

'OK,' she says as I pull away. 'I'm obviously far too weak and easy to bribe. But what about this?' She holds up that bloody bulk of a cast.

'You never did say what happened.'

'A very boring tale, which I shall tell you later. For the moment –' she smiles suggestively – 'there are more important things…' And we're kissing again. My body flushed with hot despite the cold.

'Maybe it'll work better if you take the seat,' I tell her a few giddied seconds later. 'Your good hand can hold on to my waist. It'll add a little precariousness to the journey, but I promise you're in safe hands.'

'Not according to Rollo.'

I roll my eyes and clip the buckle of the helmet beneath her chin. 'Screw Rollo.'

'From what I hear, you already did.'

'Ha! Touché, Ó.M.G., touché.' I straddle the bike between the seat and the handle bars then twist to help Órla clamber on. 'Maybe this isn't such a good idea,' I concede. 'Bronagh'll kill me if you break anything else.'

'We're doing it!' Órla shuffles into position and I begin to pedal.

After a few starter wobbles, during which Órla howls like Buddy when I went over to help Mr West keep him calm on Bonfire Night, we're off, rallied by the occasional warning horn. Órla squeals in response and I wave. A few minutes later and, with the freezing wind and snow whipping through my unhelmeted hair, we careen, both whooping, along the dark lanes lit only by my weak white lamp.

'You liked it then?' I ask when we come to a less than perfectly controlled stop outside the bothy.

The snowflakes are larger now, turning the hillside as white as it was that afternoon that Tala and I first came here. We took shelter from the cold but risked soggy jeans to make snow angels. When I stood up to look at mine, a robin flew down from the roof of the building and landed in the place where my angel's heart would have been.

'Liked it?' Órla dismounts, using the torch on her phone as she wanders up the just-visible path away from me. 'I loved it. Wish I could have taken a video to send to my coach.' She turns back to face me, her eyes wide with the buzz of rebellion, following the beam which she swooshes across the bushes, through the trees and up the ivy-clad walls of the bothy. 'What on earth are we doing *here*?'

'You know what?' I run to catch her. 'I'm not really sure.'

I'd sworn I wasn't coming. And yet.

I swear, it's nothing to do with it being the seventeenth of December and everything to do with the privacy, with the cold that brings bodies together for warmth. With the supplies I keep stashed for those days and nights when I've come here to think about Mu—

'We going in or what?' Órla urges me into the bothy and, with her shoulder against my shoulder, helps me shunt the door closed in an effort to defeat the Arctic chill.

'Might take a bit more than a shut door to get us toasty.' She jigs up and down on the spot. 'What about that?' She nods at the fireplace.

'Not my skill set. You could try, though?' I unlock Tita Celestina's case and pull out the tub of firelighters, along with packets of crisps, roasted cashew nuts, some apples that are a little over, and a Tupperware stuffed with breadsticks.

'Romantic!' Órla's toe nudges the candles. 'You come here often?' Her knees press deliciously close to mine as she crouches down bedside me on the stone floor. 'Tell me, lover, who else have you lured into this wicked lair?'

'Just Tala.' I catch on the 'just', because Tala isn't *just* anything.

~~Shame you made her feel like she was *just* a friend.~~

I sit back on the nest of blankets, watching Órla poke ineptly at the fire, my thoughts growing hotter than those flames will ever be. 'Hey, there is another way we could get warm.'

It always surprises me how different kisses can be. Even with the same person. The same two pairs of lips can create an entirely new sensation. And not just lips. A hand that was on a jaw or elbow last time, might rest now on a back or thigh. 'Rest' not quite the right word, though, because even though Órla's hand isn't really moving, there's the rush of blood beneath its touch.

'So many layers!' She counts each item – still very much on my body – coat, jumper, T-shirt, thermal vest, and then – in principle only – bra. Her fingers inch ever closer to my skin.

250

When I lie back, and Órla is above me, there's no spotlight, but I'm as exposed as Tala was on the stage tonight.

She runs her hand over my hip, and a shot of something volcanic blasts up and through my spine. 'What next?'

The flop of hair on the top of her head falls on to my cheeks as she straddles me. 'Maybe this,' she says, her thumb edging down to the belt of my jeans.

With blankets below and on top of us, Órla and I are a bubble. The kind you blow through a small plastic hoop. Its thin surface beautiful in how it lets in only the tiniest fragments of light.

One wrong move, though, and it could pop.

We are slow, then, ever so gentle in how we hold each other, which is close but wanting closer, willing the spaces between us to completely disappear. Fully clothed, none of our skin is touching now, and yet every inch of my body burns.

And the kissing.

Fuck.

Me.

The k   i   s   s   i   n   g.

Yielding and taking.

Delicate yet mind-blowingly fierce.

Our clothes a rumpling barrier but no rush to remove them because this is enough for the moment, anything else might be too much to handle when I'm already throbbing with the heat of her hand on my edges and the separateness of our bodies now blurred.

'Órla?' Her name is all I can manage; there's a question in there, though. A *should we*, a *can we*, a *how do we* that

251

I've been googling since we started messaging again earlier this week.

Twelve sex positions for lesbians
How do lesbians have sex?
A guide to how to sleep with another woman for the first time
Ten women talk about having sex with another woman
Should I experiment with another girl?

All the tips in all the articles on all the websites, all of their words, and all of their pictures too. They're a flood in my head, only they're not liquid because they don't flow, they block, and I can't—

'Órla?' I pull away.

'You OK?' Her bright eyes swill with concern. 'We can stop.'

And I don't want to but I do want to. I smile but I wince.

'I'm sorry,' I say. 'I've been…' My voice trails off as I unravel myself from her, not completely but so our lips and mouths and legs come slightly apart. She still holds two of my fingers. 'I've been reading, you know, what to do, how to…'

Órla tilts her head. 'How to…?'

I ram my eyes shut and spit the words out before they burn the inside of my cheeks with my naivety and shame. 'Satisfy you.' I open one lid slowly, squinting as I try to figure out if Órla now thinks I'm some kind of novice, or perv, or just wildly presumptuous for ever thinking she might want to do any more than that hot hot kiss. 'Confession: I feel like a born-again virgin.'

She laughs, not quite at me, but almost, and squeezes my hand. 'When were you last a virgin anyway?'

'Oi!' I snatch my fingers from her grasp and playfully flick her wrist. 'I don't know exactly what Rollo told you, but if he was judging my sexua—'

'It's nothing to do with Rollo,' Órla says, rolling on to her back and staring up at the ceiling of the bothy, partially lit by an upended torch. 'Although you can relax. He was actually very nice about you.'

'Oh?' I must buy him a beer.

'What I mean is the whole virginity thing is just a stupid construct anyway. I'm not saying things can't change, but the way I feel at the moment, I am very unlikely to ever have a real-life penis inside me. Does that mean I'm forever a virgin? Gym, tampons or masturbation probably tore my hymen years ago, so that test of my sexual innocence is a no-go too. What is sex anyway?'

'I suppose that's what I was researching. Pathetic, huh?'

'Not pathetic,' she says, turning her head round to look at me. She smiles. 'Studious.'

'No one's called me that in a while.' I lie on my back too and shuffle closer, casting my eyes towards the window, where snow is forming a soft barrier between us and the outside world. 'C'mon then. Tit for tat.'

'Tit for what?' Órla gives me some flirtatious side-eye.

'I've divulged my embarrassing sapphic homework. I reckon it's your turn to tell me something equally cringe about you.'

'Nice use of "sapphic", Iris,' she says.

It's OK, I tell myself as my heart clenches with the odd crash of my present and past.

'How cringe do you want me to go?'

'Like, one hundred per cent.'

She holds up her right arm in its cast. 'Will this do?'

'I don't get it.'

Órla lays her arm back down by her side. 'Would you think I was mad if I told you I broke it on purpose?'

'You what?'

'Oh, mate, from your tone I'm assuming that's a yes!'

I sit up, reach a hand out to Órla as an invitation for her to do the same. 'I don't understand.'

She crosses her legs and sighs. 'I needed a break,' she says. 'No pun intended.'

I shrug, like, *that is not sufficient explanation.*

'You know how hard it is being a gymnast?'

'From the training schedule on your fridge, it looks insane.'

She nods. 'At the level I'm at, it means I can't be anything else.'

I still don't get it.

'I punched a wall five days ago, Iris. And look.' She holds out her damaged arm again, points at the cast. 'Blank.'

'What's that then?' I ask, scrabbling for my phone and shining the torch on a red line on what would be the back of her hand.

'That's where Mam wanted to sign it, but I stopped her. Nothing like flagging up the fact that you have zero friends *and* zero life than your mam being the only signature on your cast. At least if there aren't any on there, it looks like an aesthetic choice.'

'You must have friends, Órla. And you definitely have a life. You're headed for the Olympics for fuck's sake.'

She rolls her eyes. 'What if I just want to head to the shops on a Saturday afternoon? Or a bar on a Friday night? What if I want to be something other than the golden bloody princess?' Her face is different when she's angry. Her jaw is squarer. Her eyes are narrowed, and in a brighter light her frustration might be mistaken as mean. 'I want to be a student, a real one, who spends time in school and studies more than two subjects because she doesn't have to worry that an extra A level might screw up her chances of gold. I want to sew,' she says, that changed-face softening again as she snuffs out a kind of laugh. 'Didn't think that one through when I gave the wall a walloping.' She shakes her head. 'I want to be someone's friend. Don't look at me like that,' she says.

'Like what?'

'With pity!'

'It wasn't pity, it was disbelief. You must have friends. What about at gym?'

'Coach favours me so much the others kind of hate me. And at school, everyone got bored of asking me along to stuff and me always saying no. I love gym, but I'm not sure it's very good for me any more. Mentally.' She tips her head on to my shoulder and heaves another colossal sigh. 'You know what I mean?'

I hear the clatter of the shards of china and glass I'd swept up in the potting shed as they tumbled from the dustpan and into the bin. Mum was still down there sleeping. Dad would soon be on the other end of the phone.

I know what it's like to want to leave something you love that's hurting you.

'I know,' I say to Órla.

I know.

I know.

I know.

'Don't tell anyone. Mam thinks I slipped on some ice.'

A familiar thread of panic tugs at my stomach. I've felt the sharp end of secrets. 'I'm sure Bronagh would unders—'

'I mean it, Iris.' Órla's head juts upwards, her glare as intense as her tone. 'Not a soul.'

Thirty-Six

Everything is fine.

Honestly, repeat after me:

Everything.

Is.

Fine.

Sure, Tala was kind of mad, but she'll get over it. Just like Dad has already got over last night when he had to come and pick me up in his pyjamas because we pretty much got snowed in at the bothy. Dad does always insist I should call him in an emergency. We were cutting it close for Órla's train *and*, given the mood Tala was in earlier, I could hardly risk tapping up my best mate for a lift. So it really *was* an emergency.

'Oh!' Dad did a double take as Órla climbed in. 'When you said *us*…'

'Change of plan.' I hoped that would be enough of an explanation. I didn't want to get into either why Tala and I hadn't done our usual candlelit vigil or what I'd been up to with Órla instead.

'Never mind *change* of plan, it seems to me there wasn't a sufficient plan in the first instance. What were you thinking conducting an exploration in weather like this?'

Conducting an exploration? The Stickler can make even the most exciting things sound drab. 'It was hardly an exploration, Dad. I've been to the bothy a million times before.' Cheeks burning with embarrassment, I slunk lower into my seat, grateful for the dark interior of the car. 'Órla and I just wanted somewhere quiet to hang.'

Hang? Is that what we're calling it?

Órla's WhatsApp was accompanied by her low giggle from the back.

Although Dad seemed chill when I left to walk Nessy the basset hound this morning, to ensure things are definitely sweet between us, when I get back, I suggest it might be the perfect day to buy our first real tree.

All three members of what Rosa likes to call our *blended* family look up and over their croissants with something somewhere between suspicion and disbelief.

'You're suggesting we all go together?' Know-All is more confused by this than he apparently was by any of the fancy-pants questions at his interview.

'I assumed slash hoped *you'd* be too busy for such ventures.'

'Unnecessary, Iris,' Dad says. 'And surely, with mocks on the horizon, *you* should be too busy too.'

'I admit, it's pure avoidance strategy.' ~~Your forté, Iris.~~ 'Visiting a garden centre, even if *he* –' I point faux menacingly at my stepbrother – 'does decide to come along, has got to be better than studying communication accommodation theory.'

258

Bonus: everyone knows it's easier not to stare at a silent phone when your head's preoccupied with picking the perfect blue spruce.

'C'mon, Dad. It's the eighteenth.' I flash him the date on my phone then ask Alexa to play a Christmas playlist. 'Alexa, next,' I say when it kicks off with 'Last Christmas'. I fix a grin and hope no one will catch my inevitable wobble whenever I hear that song.

It was Mum's favourite.

But Mum's no longer here, so, like Alexa, I move swiftly on.

'Actually, it would be nice if we all went as a family.' Dad glances hopefully from Rosa to Know-All to me. 'I'm sure your brother could do with a brea—'

'*Step*brother,' I say.

Know-All raises a middle finger discreetly behind the coffee pot, so it's only me who is reminded that I'm not too old to go on the naughty list.

But an hour or so later, I'm pretty sure I am *not* on the naughty list. Not Dad's anyway. God knows what list Tala would put me on – she's still not messaged! As the two of us – Rosa and Know-All ducked out because, obvs, yoga and homework – now traipse from tree to tree, examining their needles for rich colour and shine, Dad's face is alight with the camphor smell of a real Christmas.

'You're kidding me, right?' I watch him take a bauble from his pocket, hang it from various branches, then – with a foldable ruler for fuck's sake! – measure the distance between said hanging bauble and the branch below.

'You're testing the tree?'

'We need to know there's sufficient space for the decorations to hang freely.' He says this like it's obvious, like it's perfectly normal to treat a Christmas-tree purchase like a military exercise in precision. 'This is the One.' His smile is the broadest it's been since he had to tell me about—

~~We are not even thinking of Mum today.~~

Half an hour later, I'm wedged into the back seat, my fingers hanging over the skin-scoring netting. Dad's whistling along to 'White Christmas' as it plays on the radio. Through the window, gardens are thick with last night's snowfall. A flash of red breast as one small bird takes to the sky, which is otherwise clear and deep blue.

We come to a standstill at a junction. Both Dad's whistling and the music stop.

'Did you manage to look at that list Rosa sent you?' His eyes stay very much on the road ahead. He doesn't need to specify what list. We both know he's referring to the grief counsellors Rosa believes would be helpful no matter how many times I remind them I am fine.

'It's OK to be angry, Iris,' Rosa said a few days ago when she found the T-shirt and fabric pens Mum had wrapped for me *that* Christmas in the outside bin. She'd brought the present back inside like it was worth keeping, like there was a chance I'd actually want to *fill it with rainbows* as Mum had suggested.

I'm not angry. Like they've told me a hundred times, Mum was ill. What kind of monster would I be if I begrudged her that?

'Not yet,' I say to Dad now, reaching for my phone, which I've done my utmost to avoid looking at because as much as

I want to read any messages from Órla, I don't want to be reminded that there's zilch from my best friend.

There's nothing like being forced into a corner, though: either I check my phone or continue *that* therapy conversation with Dad.

I pull my beanie further down over my forehead so I'm only just able to see the video of Tala's performance that someone's posted on YouTube. It was up by the time I got home last night and has just hit two thousand likes. Funny how I was one of the few people who ever saw Tala as celestial, but now the whole world appears to be stargazing, realizing she's not simply *a* star, but *the* star: the sun. For those few minutes in the clip, everyone in the room revolves around her.

Maybe Tala's distracted by the attention. Maybe it's too much and she's had to put away her phone. Maybe that's why she doesn't pick up when I call her. Or reply to my suggestion that we go Christmas shopping. Or watch a movie. Or bake cookies. Or talk books. Or, in the WhatsApp I send when Dad and I get home, go through our notes on language and gender.

Inspo for your next raging feminist poem?

The two little ticks remain depressingly grey.
Scroll through Insta.
I *even* flick through Facebook.
On an Urbex forum, that prick @SuCasaEsMiCasa is still banging on about his search for a bando for his Christmas party. No one's replying. Everyone decent in the community

261

knows you'd never risk the damage that would come with a rave.

As requested, I send a selfie to Órla. No tit pics or anything, just me attempting a sexy pout.

'Knock knock.'

I have just enough time to drop my phone and pick up my textbook before Dad appears to tell me they're off out. 'If you're free this afternoon, though, love, you're welcome to make a start on the tree.'

✳

Rosa's laid all the decorations in ascending size order on the floor.

Mum's were a mishmash of sparkle and glitter in one giant cardboard box that looked like it had played its part in a hundred house moves. We'd push and pull it from the understairs cupboard every first of December.

Even that last first of December.

That year, there was no tree. Instead, we taped tinsel to the frames of paintings, draped fairy lights across the sofas and made wreaths with the corks Mum kept in a bucket beneath the sink. The wine bottles they came from were thrown into tubs by the potting shed. She'd forget to clear them away sometimes and I'd take them out in the morning, careful with how I handled them, even though it would take more than the clatter of glass to wake her.

'Is it the tree?' Mum said when Dad put the coffee he'd made for himself down on the kitchen table, took her hand and told her in a voice I'd not heard before that I was going to stay with him for a while. 'Because I can get one.' Mum's eyes skitted from the floor to the ceiling to the walls. 'I'll need a lift, though, Matt, because there was a small incident with the car.'

A few days earlier she'd driven into a hedge.

'I think you're supposed to do the lights first.' It's not like Know-All's huge or anything, but somehow his presence takes up the entire doorway between the living room and the hall.

I look at the ten or so felt forest animals I've already hung on the spruce. I'd stalled on the fox, its colours and texture the same as the mask Mum made for Dad. I'd gone to my room, pulled it from beneath the bed and – for reasons I don't know – couldn't quite bring myself to let it go. It's still heavy in my hands now.

Know-All's eyes land on it. 'You're not hanging that on there, are you?'

'Of course not.' I toss the fox mask on the sofa and start removing the decorations from the tree. 'Fuck's sake.'

'Easy.' Know-All comes over and steadies the branches, which fling backwards and forwards as I snatch the rabbits, mice and hedgehogs from the tree. 'I can give you a hand if you like?'

'Whatever.' Like *his* helping hand is something I need.

Ten minutes later. 'Teamwork makes the drea—'

'Don't!' Though I admit we have done a pretty sweet job on the lights. 'You sound like my dad.'

'Is that such a bad thing?' Know-All reaches for the drummer drumming from the 'Twelve Days of Christmas' collection Rosa bought last year.

'Er, not if you don't mind being a forty-odd-year-old Stickler with a penchant for over-zealous caution and rules. Honestly, it's like you oscillate between Lego-obsessed toddler and boring old man.'

'Unlike you who remains steadfastly on self-obsessed cow.'

It's a good job he's laughing as he says it.

'It's bigger than Mum's artificial one.' Know-All stands back to admire our efforts once we're done. The uppermost branch droops to the right under the weight of a giant, glittery gold star. 'You think it's a bit sparse?'

I shrug like I'm not sure.

But he's right.

Why does he always have to be right?

'We could *make* the last few decorations.' He says this quietly, like despite his bottomless knowledge, my reactions are something of which Know-All's unsure.

'Make them?'

When he nods, I imagine him fetching cardboard and glue. What I don't expect is to follow him upstairs, where he promptly tips an entire tub of Lego all over his bedroom floor. 'It's easy,' he says, grabbing a pure-white skyscraper from his shelf and pulling the bricks apart, quickly reassembling them into a sphere. He scrambles in a drawer for some googly eyes and snatches an orange cone from one of his Lego City sets he was mad on when we first met. 'Snowman!'

'That's actually pretty awesome!'

I swear Know-All looks as chuffed by my compliment as he was when a teacher first asked if he was considering applying to Oxbridge.

'You try.' He offers me a handful of bricks.

I keep at it for almost an hour. There's something meditative in the construction. As I trawl through the bricks for the right size and colour, it's not that I don't think about Tala ~~or Mum~~, but the high-pitched buzz of panic mellows with the business of my hands.

'That's the best bit,' Know-All says when I admit how calm it makes me feel. 'It takes my mind off the studying.'

'I didn't think anything took your mind off studying.'

'I don't think you realize…none of those top marks come easily to me.'

'Unlike arrogance!' I'm only half joking. 'You know how much pressure comes with having a stepbrother who gets straight nines?'

'Probably less pressure than having a step*sister* whose attention-grabbing antics mean the only way *I* get noticed is if I don't let those straight nines slip.' A peachy circle piece he steals from a castle above his bed becomes Santa's nose. 'You might be fun, Iris, but you're not always the most straightforward person to live with.'

'Well, you might be straightforward but you're not always the most fun.' We both have these fixed smiles on our faces as if all this is just bants. 'Seriously, though.' I take the one-stud white piece Know-All's offering and clip it on to the side of my brown sphere. 'You know the expression, all work and no play…'

'Don't,' he says.

'What?'

His exhale is a puff of frustration. 'My interview.'

'Oh God, seriously? Any opportunity to turn a conversation into a precis of how well you performed at Ox—'

'No, actually, I didn't.' Head already in his hands, Know-All slumps on his bed.

'I thought you smashed it?'

'Mostly.' He rubs his eyes.

I'm baffled. Know-All's run through his interview, like, a thousand times, and his answers to questions about how he'd handle a theoretical case in which an unborn baby died after his mother was stabbed have all been annoyingly eloquent and on point.

'Go on…' I say.

'The interviews themselves were fine. It was the rest of the time that was difficult.'

'The rest of the time?'

'The night between the first and second interviews. Some of the other candidates went out for drinks, but I couldn't…' He repeatedly pulls off the head of a Lego scientist, then clips it back on. 'I felt too awkward.' My stepbrother glances up then, his brow arched, like, *you got me*. 'Looks like I'm not the only Know-All, eh? You always said I should get out more.'

'C'mon. You smashed that interview. You know you did. And you'll get used to the social stuff. You just need to get some practice in something other than sourcing the right brick.'

Bang on cue, he digs me out a small 'brown plate'.

A few minutes later, Know-All holds up a snowflake. Approximately three hundred seconds ago it was a car.

'That was kind of fun,' I say as we loop thread through what he tells me is a technic tile, a black piece we've attached to the top of each of our baubles for its handy-sized hole.

'It was,' he says, side-eyeing my decoration and laughing. 'Even if your Christmas pudding does look more like a turd.'

Thirty-Seven

'Sorry.'

The two cockapoos look up at me from a perfect 'sit' in their porch. I compensate them each with a pig-in-blanket dog treat, which looks less like our human version of the festive delight and more like a shrivelled witch's finger. The dogs momentarily forget to be peeved.

Dad reckons I give the dogs I walk too much emotional credit. 'They don't feel things like we do, Iris,' he said only yesterday when I mentioned how tragic it was for Buddy that Mr West had arrived home from hospital to a house without him in it.

But after a briefer Monday morning walk than usual, Dumble and Hovis certainly look like they're feeling hard done by.

I turn the key in the lock, wipe their paws with the kitchen roll Leonard and Nitin always leave out for me, and apologize again for this morning's too-brief trip to the park.

'I've got to hurry. It's the last day of term!'

Dumble's head cocks optimistically.

'I know, right? Whoever heard of Iris Tremaine desperate to get to school?'

Thing is, I need to see Tala. It's not that she's still giving me the silent treatment; we finally exchanged a few messages late Saturday night and even spoke on the phone on Sunday morning. But she was quiet. And not Redmond type of quiet, more like every sentence she spoke to me was suffocating in the words she was choosing *not* to say.

Inspired by the video someone in Friday's audience posted on YouTube, she's set up her own TikTok and YouTube channel, with not only 'Enough' but 'I'm Ace' and a new poem 'According to Me'. All three pieces are evidence that Tala selects her words carefully, that she gets the muscularity of them, how one might be a prod in the belly, whereas another is a full-pelt punch.

'Angeline's helping me with it,' Tala said when I asked her how she's filming the performances. I offered to go over and be director's assistant, but my best friend was too busy working on 'something new'.

I assumed she meant poetry, but when I get to school there's a rustling chatter among the students that reminds me of the wild sweep of night-time creatures in Good Hope Wood.

Every so often I hear Tala's name.

I find her by the boys' changing rooms, sitting cross-legged with Dougie and holding a clipboard out to Angeline, who's signing her name on what looks like a time sheet with hourly slots throughout the day.

'What's that?'

'Only the best idea ever!' Evie barges past me, grabbing the pen from Angeline and putting herself down for 1 p.m. 'You don't know?'

My heart is sticky with a new kind of ache. Evie of all people knows Tala's business before me? Hurt trickles down my throat so my voice, when I say 'no', refuses the casual tone I was after and instead comes out like a pang.

'Tala's organizing a prote—'

'Tala can tell me herself, yeah.' Just looking at the satisfaction rippling across Evie's face is enough to bring me back on form.

'If she wants to. Seems to me she chose to keep you out of the loop.'

Every inch of me lurches with hate. 'What do you know about Tala's loop?'

'I *am* here you know.' Even the way Tala stands is gritty.

'Leave it, babe.' Angeline passes the clipboard back to Tala then shunts Evie to the other side of the corridor, where Know-All is silently watching from his position by a Year Nine physics display on Changes in Energy. Evie, Queen of the Dumbbells, sidles up to him and bites her lip in gruesome anticipation. As always, she's baiting blood.

I turn my back on them.

'So?' I ask Tala, attempting blasé but achieving only accusation.

She shrugs like it doesn't count for anything that she's clearly up to something big without me. 'We're expanding Rhyme's Up beyond The Vault.'

'What does that even mean?'

'Dougie and I want to start a conversation. Not just in poetry, but in our everyday chats here in school.' She points at a poster stuck to the wall.

OH, BROTHER,
WORD ART THOU

challenging language
and
questioning masculinity

'Oh, Brother, Word Art Thou?'

'It's a play on words.' Dougie's on his feet now too. 'You know, the Clooney film, *O Brother, Where Art Thou*? The point is in th—'

'Clever!' I know it's rude to cut him short, but the luminescent glow of those orange pineapples on Dougie's turquoise shirt is too off mood to bear looking at right now.

'We've all heard the crap that gets slung in there.' Tala nods her head towards the changing rooms, where some of the boys are known to toss around hardcore bants with as much aggression as they kick around a ball at break. 'Maybe if we talk to them—'

'Count me in.' I get it now. 'When it comes to telling a dick he's a dick, I'm your gir—'

'It's not about starting a war, Iris. We don't want a fight. We want change. We want people to understand the onus is on all of us to make girls and women safe. We're having a sit-in. We'll stay here in pairs, trying to start open conversations with students and staff about how this violence affects all genders.'

''K.'

She might be a star, but Tala's eyes are full white moons when she looks at me.

'Give me a slot then.' I hold my hand out for the time sheet, which Tala presses with a flash of nervousness against her chest.

'I need people who are going to turn up.'

How is everyone else so steady on their feet when the ground just shook beneath me.

'I'll be there, Tal. I'm all in. I love shit like this, big, grand gestures that make people sit up and listen.'

'Big, grand gestures? You *are* good at those!' She laughs a laugh that's not a laugh but exasperation. 'Your big, grand gestures feel like something in the moment, but…'

'But what?'

'Tala's Best Bits.'

'That I gave you for your birthday?'

She nods.

'What about it?'

The corridors are usually a sweaty burst of students at this time of the morning. Today, though, it's as if the noise has been reeled in, hanging bystanders on tenterhooks as Tala stands on a different kind of stage. I watch as, suddenly aware of the attention, her new boldness sinks into her old timid self.

She looks up at me through hair fallen across her face. 'Do you remember what you said when you gave it to me?'

I shake my head. 'No.'

'When the Dumbbells make you feel small, I want you to remember how much I love you.'

'The *Dumb*bells?' Evie screeches somewhere behind me. 'What the actual fuck?'

272

Tala unclenches the hold she has on the clipboard and, for a second, I think she's going to pass it over, that she's remembered it's *me* she's talking to, that I'm the one who's always been on her side. But she hands it to Dougie, pulling her shoulders back and inhaling as she turns to face me. 'Iris, sometimes it's *you* that makes me feel small.'

My heart hangs unbeating in my chest. 'I made a mistake. And I'm sorry. I wouldn't have missed the prep for your slam if this thing with Órla wasn't serious.'

'So what *we* have *isn't* serious?' She smiles then. But even counting all the times the Dumbbells packed on the mean with her, I've never seen Tala's face look this bruised and sad. 'I don't count enough for you to put *me* first?'

'Of course you do.' I reach out, but Tala wraps her arms around herself like I am something from which she needs protecting. 'I love you, Tal.'

'I know you do. But that doesn't mean you'll do what's right for me. And I love you too,' she says. 'But that doesn't mean I trust you to stick around.'

Thirty-Eight

There are no carol singers at Edglington station, just boards warning passengers to please take care on the platform. The snow is gone today, leaving a precarious layer of ice. The back of my bike slides out as I wheel it to the road, where thick grey slush banks against the curbs. I can barely feel the clips of my helmet when I fasten it beneath my chin.

As I walked out of school this morning, I called Órla and suggested meeting at Birdies.

'You know it?' She'd sounded surprised when I told her I'd been there with Bronagh.

'So you met up with Mam?' she says now as I sit down next to her in the same spot as the woman whose son had drawn that perfect heart on the glass.

Órla fiddles – *shit*, does she feel awkward? – with those few long red curls remaining after the Chop.

'*Hola!*' The parrot lifts alternate legs on its perch like it's dancing. 'Good girl! Good girl!'

In a movie, this kind of quirky addition to a scene would diffuse any mounting tension, but Órla ignores the bird and widens her eyes at me, like, *well?*

'I wanted to ask her about Mum,' I say, my palms searing with the difference in heat between the scorching mug and my December'd skin. I sip my drink: tea. After this morning, a hot chocolate would be too sweet.

'You didn't, you know, say anything about…' Órla glances down at her cast.

'It was before you even…' I quirk my brow as I look at it too. 'You still haven't told her then?'

Órla shakes her head. 'God, no. She'd kill me.'

'Bronagh seems cool, Órla.'

'You don't get it.' Her gaze drops like she's been let down. 'It's not only *my* life that's consumed by gym. She's given up so much. You know, I'm the reason she works part-time? She couldn't hold down a full-time position with having to ferry me to all my training, and she's always telling me that of course it's worth it, but…'

A bell chimes as someone dressed as Santa walks through the door.

'*Hola! Hola!*'

'Merry Christmas!' Santa says to the bird.

Órla leans forward, a hand on my knee. It's the first time we've touched since I arrived. There was a moment when we met outside where we might have kissed, but the memory of all that other kissing that would have been too much for broad daylight made a peck inadequate and so we'd just said hi instead. I lay my mug-hot fingers on top of hers now and something lulls between us as they entwine.

'You know that's the parrot Mam thinks is my nan?'

I nod.

'Thinking about it, we probably shouldn't even be talking about you-know-what in her presence.'

275

'Bad girl! Bad girl!'

'See.' Órla pulls her purple velvet armchair closer, but I think it's less about wanting to be near me and more being out of earshot of the bird.

'Are you decided then?' *Jesus*, even I'm talking in whispers. 'That you're giving up, I mean?'

Órla wrinkles her long nose and shakes her head. 'But the more I'm off timetable, the more ways I think to spend all these hours I'm not trapped at gym.' She increases the pressure slightly on our pressed knees. 'Speaking of being off timetable…' A beat passes between us, and she wide-eyes me when I don't immediately divulge my reasons for bunking off school.

'Tala,' I say, though it's not really Tala that's the problem, is it?

It's me.

'Oh, please God, no.' Órla's hand and knee jerk away from me as she half stands to look out of the window. She raises two fingers in the most half-hearted wave I've ever seen. 'What the—'

'Girls!' Several heads turn as Bronagh's voice cuts through the low hum of conversation in the café.

'*Hola!*'

'Afternoon.' Bronagh winks at the bird and wends her way through the tables before sitting in the empty chair beside Órla, who looks somewhat aghast.

'What are you doing here?'

'Well, that's a grand way to greet your mother now, isn't it?' Bronagh rolls her eyes in my direction as if seeking support.

276

I smile but stay quiet, fearing if I tell Bronagh it's nice to see her too, my shin will bear the brunt of Órla's foot.

'When you messaged me, Órla, that youse was meeting up, I just wanted to pop in to give Iris here something.' She shakes her head when Órla's stony face doesn't soften. 'I found this, pet.' From her bag, Bronagh draws a clear plastic sleeve. Inside is a picture. 'It's of your mam when *she* was seventeen. Can you believe the likeness?'

I stare at Mum with hair piled into a loose bun, her eyes looking directly into the lens.

'I don't see it,' I mumble.

'It's just something about the pair of youse,' Bronagh says, tapping a pink-Shellac'd nail on Mum's face. 'I cannae quite put my finger on it. It's more than looks.'

My tongue curls into the back of my teeth as I think about what Bronagh just said.

> *Can you believe the likeness?*
> *It's more than looks.*

About what Tala said.

> *Your big grand gestures feel like something in the moment.*
> *But that doesn't mean I trust you to stick around.*

About what Know-All said.

> *You might be fun, but you're not always the most straight-forward person to live with.*

'You can add it to those others I gave you.'

When I don't say anything, I see a twitch of doubt in Bronagh's smile.

'I don't have to dig out any more if you don't want them. I'm sorry, Iris, if I've ups—'

'No, no, no. It's helpful.' I lift the photo closer. 'I see the resemblance now.'

Bronagh and Órla are talking, but their words are drowned by the crashing wave of truth as it breaks over me: the things that made me leave her are the things about *me* that push others away.

~~You got it, Iris.~~

'Iris?'

'Iris?'

'Iris?'

When I look up from the photo, Bronagh and Órla are both fixed on me.

'Are you OK?'

'Yes,' I say. 'Sure,' I say. 'I…'

'I'm going to the loo.' Órla juts her chin in the direction of the bathroom, her eyes kind of maniacal and her good hand gesturing, *come with*.

But that truth has made me too heavy to move.

'Would you leave it, Mam?' As she stands, Órla bats Bronagh's hand, like it's a wasp, away from her hair.

'What do you make of her new do?' Bronagh is unfazed by her daughter's dismissal. 'Catherine – Órla's coach – is gonnae be beside herself. She'd have her entire squad as identical as you and your mother there.'

Órla lets out a sigh. 'Will you want another drink on my way back through?'

'I'm good.'

~~Are you, though?~~

With Órla gone, I keep my head down, examining the photo. Bronagh's gaze on me has the same slow burn as midsummer sun. I catch how she tilts her head, and I know she's about to ask me a question. 'Any idea what's up with Órla?'

I do. But what do I do with it? With the knowledge that someone is not OK? For so long with Mum I pretended it wasn't happening.

Tala's words when I told her I loved her this morning are jolting shots to my sullied brain.

But that doesn't mean you'll do what's right for me.

What *is* right?

Now, I mean. Here.

Órla was so clear that she didn't want Bronagh knowing what she did to her hand. But she doesn't get it. How we build layers around our secrets after we bury them. So it's not only the secret itself but the effort of holding it that weighs a ton.

I look down at my lap and say it. 'She punched a wall.'

'You did what now?'

'To get out of gym. She punched a wall.'

Fuck.

Know-All was on to something when he said I was self-obsessed.

I was talking before I was listening.

You, Bronagh just said.

Not *she*.

You
You
You
did what now?

I know before I turn round that Órla's behind me. And I know before I turn round that the shimmering bubble that only a few minutes ago surrounded us has now burst.

Thirty-Nine

'Iris?'

I don't look back, just grab my bike, hurling apologies as I collide with Christmas shoppers, my wheel skidding on the plastic of their dropped carrier bags on the ground. On the corner, Santa – coffee spilled down the white trim of his suit – is in a blusterous row with his elf.

How did I ever think I'd get it right?

The thin rain is almost ice on my hands and face as I ride along the high street and then on past the houses with illuminated reindeers in their shadowed gardens, their fairy lights desperately twinkling good cheer in the blue-grey haze of the setting cloud-smothered sun.

As if I'd be any better at not hurting people than *her*.

The dark has won by the time I reach Sunnyside. Any smudges of purple pink in the sky have gone.

Of course, I made Tala feel like she's not good enough. Of course, I betrayed Órla. Of course, this is how I act because, like Bronagh said, it's more than my looks that makes me similar to Mum.

I drop my bike by the gate and head straight for the potting shed, for the cupboard in the corner where Mum kept her 'occasional boost'.

'Noisy little things,' she'd say as the Chardonnay and Rioja miniatures clattered against the party of full-sized bottles in the supermarket trolley. She didn't drink all the time. But the highs sometimes clamoured for higher, and the lows meant she was looking for something – anything – to drag her mood up from where it had wilted on the floor.

Dad sanitized the house but hasn't yet made it down here, where the walls are still soil-and-mud grimy and shelves remain littered with sharp-edged tools.

In the cupboard, my fingers push through thick matted cobwebs that swathe bottles and jam jars with handwritten labels that say *Peppermint Oil – aphids*; *Garlic Oil – slugs*; *Baking Soda – mildew*; *Vinegar – fruit flies and weeds*. All that effort she went to to avoid chemicals. To be so kind to the earth.

There they are. At the very back. An attempt to hide them from everyone, including herself.

I line the six bottles up on the brick ledge by the window, take the first and unscrew its cap.

Why not? They're what she passed down to me.

Like Sunnyside and…

What?

Exactly what else did she pass on?

My neck corkscrews and my tongue snarls and my throat smarts with the acrid burn of gone-off wine.

'Fuuuuuuuuuuuuuck.'

I take another.

Because this is how it's meant to be, right?

Like mother, like daughter.

Youse are so much like her at seventeen.

And another.

Cheers to Bronagh.

And another.

Cheers to Órla.

And another.

Cheers to Tala.

And another.

Cheers to Dad.

The cobbles are hard and lumpy against my knees and elbows when I crash to them.

My head lolls to the side. A flowerpot has also toppled. It has cracks running down its middle, like me.

You will be strong.

'Ha.' It's funny, what we become.

I thought the Box of Mum Things was my inheritance but nah ah ah. My inheritance is all of this... I roll on to my back and reach my arms into the air, waving them in wonky, whirling circles, grasping for the hard facts of the potting shed and Sunnyside. But they're untouchable. The only inheritance I can really feel is her unreliability and its fallout: filthy loneliness and milky shame.

I need to be rid of it.

All of it.

Then maybe that nasty pushing-people-away side of me will be gone.

I press the backs of my legs into the floor, but my head spins anyway, round and round and round and round until I claw my way outside to air that's bitter harsh in my lungs and on my skin.

Big gulping breaths fight against a heaving stomach. Nothing, not even air, wants to stay down.

Eyes squeezed tight so every inch around me disappears everything

black	dark
black	dark
black	dark
empty	

and

still.

And it works.

Except for one single sound.

Light and full and sweet and soft, it starts in the suthering trees but comes closer, closer until its vibrations shiver my flesh and spine.

'Now?' My laugh is dribble and spit on my chin. 'You come now?'

My vision, when I open my eyes, is blurry, but the shape on the path in front of me is definitely a bird.

It hops. Its feet a tiny scratch when it jumps on to my palm. Its legs skinnier than toothpicks. Its belly as red as blood.

But it sings.

'Why?'

It sings.

'Why?'

It sings.

'Why? Why? Why? Why? Why?'

It keeps on with its song, even when I stand, even when I shoo it, even when I stamp my foot and scream and tell it it's too late, shout that if it loved me, it would never have flown in that too-far direction, which meant it could never come home.

Like the potting shed and Sunnyside and everything else about my old fake life, the robin needs to be gone.

My phone is lead in my hand as I message @SuCasaEsMiCasa.

You wanted a place to host a party?
I'll leave the front door open.
I've started already.
Tell everyone nothing's off limits.

I type as the blurred bird keeps singing.

Just do your worst.

Forty

Bodies make silhouettes in the windows. They began arriving in pairs an hour or so ago. But the pairs quickly became clusters, and the clusters became gangs way bigger than I'd imagined would be up for a Monday night party. There are too many of them, oozing through the front door like in this footage I saw once of a vet squeezing maggots from a dog's back. It makes me want to puke is what I mean.

And I'm not the only one. A guy is throwing up in the garden. A mask dangles on elastic around his neck.

I hate him.

Thing is, I hate myself more.

I brought them here. @SuCasaEsMiCasa played his part, sure, but I gave him the house for what he dubbed his Masquerade Brawl.

'Cheer up, love.' Even with his face half concealed by a Batman mask, this bloke looks too old to be at this party. He winks a dirty come-on and raises a bottle of beer, all the time slouching backwards, his shoulders crumpling my childish artwork that Mum so proudly stuck to the drawing-room wall.

What I should say is 'fuck off', but instead I lean into the darkness until my nose is pressed against his masked nose and the slow leak from his sweaty nostrils wets my cheek. My tongue pushes inside his mouth, searching for a taste as rancid as I feel. But the mix of beer and cigarettes isn't grotty enough. I reach further, full stretch, pulling the webby tissue attaching my tongue so taut it might rip.

Let it tear, I think, forcing it now, pressing myself into him so we're hard against the wall, my fingers clawing pins from the crayoned pictures so they float to the floor. I feel his groan more than hear it. Feel his dick too. Rigid on my hip. And his hands, already up and inside my coat, my jumper, my T-shirt, not soft like Órla but still too gentle for what I deserve.

'Harder,' I urge into his throat, into his neck, which smells of aftershave and sweat, and I bite him then, because what I want is blood.

'Oi!' His palms whip from inside to out, bearing down on my chest as he pushes me away. 'Mad bitch!' And I stumble, grabbing his beer and necking it, as I wander the house for someone, anyone. Seriously, give me any filthy ragbag who can match me for rank.

Two guys in the kitchen, one in a harlequin mask, the other with horns like the devil, are shotting something. I don't care what. Their heads tip back as they each take their turn.

'Me now.' I snatch the bottle from one, the glass from the other, pouring then swallowing, pouring then swallowing. 'I'm game,' I tell them. 'For anything,' I tell them, wanting the worst because wouldn't that be confirmation of what I deserve.

'Easy,' says the devil, whose hair's protruding from his mask like the bristles of a manky broom. 'Maybe you've had enough. You're gonna get yourself hurt.'

I give him these eyes, like, *yeah. Bang on. Getting hurt's exactly what I'm after.*

'You here with anyone?' It's the other one, removing his clown mask to reveal a face like a bull terrier, those too-small eyes scanning the room like he's some kind of hero who wants to save the drunk girl from disgrace.

'Forget it.' I take one last shot of their poison, revel in its harsh and satisfying burn.

It's working.

The drink, I mean.

Everything's buckled and blurred.

The volume's cranked.

Floorboards shudder underfoot.

I need to get out, but the pack's too thick and is heaving towards me, masked faces surging. The air is closing in.

A thud-in-the-bones bass pounds rhythmic and hard.

Every inch of the house is shaking.

Or maybe that's me.

'Dora!' Hot breath and saliva in my ear. 'A little worse for wear than in your Insta profile, but it *is* you, right?' A hand on my waist. If I was generous, I'd say it's spinning me round but, really, it's more like yanking. 'I'm Isaac.' His mask is simple but creepy, bright white with thick black eyebrows, thin goatee and moustache.

I'm up in his face trying to figure him out. 'SuCasaEsMiCasa?'

'That's me!' He's shouting now. 'Drink?' He takes my hand and leads me to the hall, where cans are stacked by the coat hooks. Mum's Barbour jacket is soaked in what looks like lager on the floor. 'Get one while you can,' Isaac says, laughing. Only his laugh's not infectious like Mum's or Tala's or Órla's. It's mean. 'Some of the guys found a socially inept fuckwit dressed as a fox in the garden and are waterfalling him with beer.'

'Waterfalling?'

But Isaac's already penetrated the pack of revellers in the dining room, where the chairs and tables have been pushed back to make space for the dancing bodies and their monstrous clumping feet. I slump against the door frame that's slick with their enthusiastic sweat. Their arms around each other's waists, they crash into the walls, knocking down then trampling on pictures, their boots shattering the glass.

'Look!' A girl, masked as a cat, points to the window, where there's a different kind of thud.

Not inside but out.

Trying to get into the action.

Or to get away from the dark.

The robin.

'Stop!' It starts as a whisper. 'Please.' To the bird, yes, but to the hordes too. They're wrecking the place, which is what I wanted but the robin...

She needs to get to the light.

Heads back, mouths open, the throng cackles like all this breaking and snaking is normal, like all this carnage is OK.

And still the desperate robin thwacks at the glass.

'Stop.'

'C'mon on, Dora.' Isaac's hands are clawing me into the crowd. I elbow him, sharp, furious, but he's quick up in my ear. 'Watchit!'

I run to the window, pulling at the catch, at the frame, but *shit*, it's painted shut.

'STOP!'

Isaac's all, 'Is she shouting at me or that fucking bird? Nutjob.'

'Stop it. Stop it. Stop it.' My voice is a siren, a plea.

Her small body beats against the pane.

I will it to smash.

'Stop!'

To save her from her own free will.

'Please.'

The bird makes one last strike and slips pathetically down the other side of the glass.

Outside, my kneecaps grind the leaves into mulch that soaks through my jeans as I twist in gnarled circles searching for her.

In the near distance, at the end of the drive, car doors slam like hard, fast endings.

My palms scramble in a wild goose chase across the floor.

But the robin is gone.

I watch the mob through the window.

This is Christmas.

This is people, festive and dancing and kissing and, probably, upstairs fucking.

This is happy. Like Dad and Rosa and Know-All and Tala and Órla might be if I left them well alone.

Voices in every direction.

Bodies on every floor.

In the bush, even.

A flit of a creature.

Of life of brown of red of chest of wing

      of   h   e   r

u

p

      a   n   d

f   l

             y

      i

             n

                   g

a   n   d

alive

She makes her way to the sky.

We did that once.

Mum and me.

Mummy and Iris.

Iris and Mummy.

'Iris,' she'd said, her voice all buzzy…buzz…buzzy…like me at Christmas. Old me, I mean. Old Christmas, I mean. Christmas before she—

Then though, that night, it wasn't Christmas, when she woke me from my bed, put trainers on my feet and tied the laces. When we got to the landing, I'm sure we went up not down. Up? Not down.

'Shh!' She put a finger to her mouth. 'Secret room,' she said, unlocking a door that looked like it led only to a cupboard. But there were stairs.

The key lies, where it did then, in the small gap between

the skirting and the floor. The staircase was always narrow, but my grown body shrinks it now smaller and smaller, gathering dust as I climb.

It smells like she did.

Cigarettes and perfume.

Paint and glue.

Masks – fifteen, maybe twenty, maybe more – hang from ribbons from the rafters of the pitched roof. Not all of them are finished, though even the ones with patchwork faces are beautiful. Owl. Bear. Mouse. Rabbit. Badger.

On a small workbench there is one in progress. Brown wool at the top of its head blends into vibrant red, curving towards a black and pointed beak.

The moon casts light through a round window with the circumference of a Mum-sized body. It opens easily when I lift the catch.

Just as she taught me on that roof-topping night, I heave my torso through to the sill outside, dragging my bag after. The roof pitches up and away from me. (Like Mum did.) Its chimneys stretch for the moon, which is out now, pushed through cloud to a clear sky pricked with stars.

'It'll be quieter up here,' Mum whispered all those years ago. I was sleepy. But like it does tonight, the icy blast cut through the haze. 'It will be easier to breathe.'

The cool slate of the tiles as I manoeuvre myself from the windowsill to the roof is momentary relief on my palms which, like the rest of me, are livid with shame.

Music from the party skims the slate tiles, agitating the wintered air.

My head may have stopped spinning, but the shock of cold can't shift the thick truth of who I am and what I've done.

You will be strong.

I thought I was silver linings and bright sides but, turns out, what I am is stupidity and betrayal.

I thought I was a looking-up person.

But, right now, all I can do is look down.

How would it feel? Not when I smash into the ground, but after. How would *that* feel?

Would it be like the darkness that followed the meteor shower Mum and I watched huddled on the bonnet of the car? None of the burning shards of comet, though. None of the hope. None of the moving from one atmosphere into another.

Just the empty aftermath black.

Imagine.

It's bliss. Isn't it?

Because it's nothing.

It's no more.

It's I'm done with this shitty life and this shitty me and this inability to be anything but a hurricane.

It's farewell to the girl who tricked herself into thinking she was happy.

It's the end of pretending, and the acknowledgement, finally, that she's not.

Forty-One

Tala: Iris, are you ok?

Could I actually say to her: *You know what, I don't think I am.*
Be *that* frank.

Tell her that in the haze of time I've laid on this roof, the thing that's become most clear is that I hate myself.

That I no longer believe the lie inscribed on a paper fortune teller seven years ago.

That all of it's utter crap.

I type, but not to Tala.

Google: what is the quickest way to die?

It doesn't tell me, though. Not straight away. What Google tells me instead is a number.

What Google tells me instead is someone is waiting for my call.

'Whatever you're going through,' the website says, 'a Samaritan will face it with you.'

I couldn't.

Could I?

Me?

Strong, stoic Iris.

Call a fucking *helpline*?

I've scaled fences, crawled through drains, squared up to bolshy boys and seedy men who thought they could keep me down. Do I really need to spill my guts to a stranger?

The faceless bodies on the driveway have been dancing in endless circles like my head. But, 'Just found a neighbour snooping,' Isaac's shouting. 'Party's over. Time to go, before they call the cops.'

My voice, when I say, 'All you have to do is fall, Iris,' disappears into the night.

I look down at the
        d
            i
  z
       z
                 y
                         i
            n
                   g
  w
       h
  i
      r
  l
      i
  n
      g

d

r

o

p.

Old Iris would be safe up here.

Old Iris would climb down, no hassle.

Old Iris would not be afraid of heights.

~~Thing is, if you're not old Iris, which Iris will you be~~
~~now?~~

I dial the number.

'I'm scared,' I whisper when someone answers. 'I think I want to die.'

The voice on the other end doesn't gasp or scream or tell me I'm silly or that I'm a self-obsessed cow who shouldn't say such terrible things.

What she says is that her name is Emily and, 'No pressure, but if you'd like to, you can tell me your name too.'

'Iris.'

'I'm glad you called us, Iris.'

I don't know what I expected, but it wasn't this. It wasn't someone who isn't shocked or appalled by my secrets. It wasn't someone who talks to me in a normal voice, like despite these unspeakable things I'm actually speaking, there's a chance it will be OK.

'Is it that you want your life to be over, Iris? Or is it the way you're feeling right now that you'd like to end?' Emily talks slowly. Not the way people talk slowly when they think you're stupid, more like she's talking slowly because she wants me to take my time.

Even with time, though, I don't know what to say.

But Emily is OK with my silence.

When a few minutes pass of me not having any answers, she asks, 'How do you feel?'

'Angry,' I say. 'Sad,' I say. 'Stupid,' I say. 'Sorry,' I say. 'Alone.'

'Is there anything in particular that's happened to prompt these feelings? Or have you been feeling this way for a while?'

'My mum died.' I draw down into the rawest depths of my gut. 'Suicide.'

Emily doesn't say 'how terrible' or 'how shocking'. All she says is 'hmmm'.

'It'll be seven years on Christmas Day.'

She doesn't sharp-intake disgust when I laugh either. Like, actually laugh. Because it's funny, right, how this is the most wonderful time of year and yet, here I am, sitting on the roof at Sunnyside, where my mum took her own life, wondering if it would be better for everyone if I did the same.

'How old were you when she died?'

'Ten.' The night he told me, I still just about fitted on Dad's lap.

'That's young.'

Which is true, but I was me, right, even then? Just a younger version of this fucked-up, not happy enough me.

'It's my fault.'

'What makes you think that?' It could so easily be nosiness, but Emily's voice suggests not curiosity but exploration, that what she's asking isn't for her but for me.

'I told my dad to come and get me. I left Mum on her own and went away.'

'What was it, do you think, that made you ask your dad to get you?' There isn't any judgement in her tone.

How do I explain the bonfire?

Or the glass?

Or the French flag painted on the wall?

Or the other adventures which I loved but left me shaky?

Or the fact that Mum's effect on me was sometimes the same?

'I loved her. I promise, I loved her. I didn't want to leave.'

'What *did* you want, Iris?'

'To be safe.'

'Do you think she might have wanted you to be safe too?'

Mum's hands as she gave me the Box of Mum Things, how they were shaking but she tried to hold them still.

'My friend reckons when people die, they come back as birds.'

'And what do *you* think?'

'Is it mad that I thought I saw her tonight? As a robin?'

'Do *you* think that's mad?'

'A few days ago, I might have done, but now... Everything's muddled. What was quiet is loud. What was truth is fiction. What was strong is...' My throat closes as my heart roars, and it literally hurts to speak. 'I don't think I can cope.'

'So don't,' Emily says.

My noise, then, is animal. Thick and guttural, long and loud, and soaked in a seven-year dam of tears. 'Fuck,' I say. 'Sorry,' I say.

'What are you sorry for?'

'Crying? Swearing?'

'Sometimes it can help to say these words when our feelings are overwhelming.'

I exhale a puff of, *you reckon?* 'I wish my dad knew that.'

'He doesn't like you swearing?'

'Swearing. Feeling. Exploring.'

'Exploring?'

'I go to abandoned buildings, places where…'

Emily allows the ellipses to turn into silence, then lets the silence be.

'…where I can settle.' The first time I went to the bothy without Tala, my whirring eased to a quiet lull. 'Dad thinks it's fucked up. Sor—' I stop my apology. 'I guess I like how everything's just a little bit broken, but you can still see how lovely it must once have been.'

The toe of my shoe pokes one of the slates on the roof. It slips an inch or so before I stop it. My heel is the only thing preventing it from sliding and crashing to the hard ground below.

Does Emily know she's doing the same for me?

'I thought I was special.'

'What was it about you that you thought was special?'

If my life were a movie, there'd be a shooting star right now to prove me right. At the very least, there'd be an aeroplane I could mistake for a fucking sign.

As it is, there's nothing but an ordinary night sky.

'When Mum died, all these people, all these grown-ups, said how brilliantly I was doing, wasn't I happy, hadn't I adjusted well. And then they whispered to Dad, or to each other, how it was a miracle, really, given everything I'd been through, just how happy I could be. Everyone loved me because I was a survivor. But it was a lie, wasn't it? I'm chicken shit.'

Below me, the music comes to an abrupt stop.

'You sound pretty cool to me, Iris. I'm sure people love you for reasons other than you being happy.'

The bones of the house stop shaking.

'I've let everyone down.' I tell her about Tala, about Órla, and then, about Mum. 'She must have hated me for leaving. That must be why she took those pills.'

'Do you want to tell me about her?'

I do. I tell Emily the good things, the bad things, the amazing and magical things. I tell her what Mum told me about me being her light.

'It sounds like you were very special to her. Like you're special to lots of people. We can make mistakes and still be special. We can be sad and still be loved.'

'But how could I have been her light if she chose to leave me?'

I hear Emily's inhale-exhale. 'Have you thought perhaps both things can be true?'

The longer I really look at the sky above me, the more and more stars appear.

'You said just now you were chicken shit. But you called us, didn't you?'

I don't get it.

'You called us, Iris. That takes some strength.'

'But if I was strong, I wouldn't need you.'

'Do you remember what I said just now about being both? You can be strong and need help. You can think you want to die and love your daughter. You can grieve and be happy. You can let someone down and be their best friend.'

The night Mum and I watched the meteor shower, she taught me all these big new words. 'Celestial' and 'asteroid'. All this time I'd forgotten the other word she taught me too.

'I can see the Big Dipper,' I tell Emily. Even though there's no one else to see it, I point, as Mum did, at the eight brilliant white stars. 'Mum told me how the Big Dipper is so bright, so obvious, some people think it's a constellation.' She'd shaken her head, like, *we always plump for the obvious.*

'Is it not?' Emily asks me from her far-away end of the phone.

'Mum said it's an asterism. A group of stars *within* a constellation. Maybe it's just the bit we see most easily so it's the bit everyone can name. But on a clear night, if you look hard enough, you can see so much more.'

We lie together, Emily and me. I mean, she's not here on the tiles, but she's beside me in the way that counts.

'Thank you.' I pull the loose slate clean of its neighbouring tiles, tuck it safely inside my bag so it won't fall. 'The night's a bit clearer,' I tell her. 'I'm going to sit here for a bit. And then, I promise, I'll climb back down.'

Forty-Two

As loose and raucous bodies spill from Sunnyside, I send Tala a string of messages.

> Think I need to take a look at that list of counsellors Rosa gave me
> OK right now but at Sunnyside and need to get home
> Love you

There are so many stars. Thousands, millions even. And yet no matter how much I try to un-see it, my brain is locked on the Big Dipper.

It's normal, isn't it, to look for the familiar, for patterns. It's why we spy human limbs in electricity pylons and faces in the bark of trees. Our brains make sense of objects before we're allowed to see them for what they truly are. It makes the world safer, I suppose, if we think we know what to expect.

Which is fine in theory.

But what if we go too far?

A car screeches up the driveway.

A man shouts, 'Isaac, time to go!'

Protests from under the porch. 'Still got a few bits I want to grab, mate.'

I keep looking up, urging those eight standouts to pale so I can see the rest of the constellation. If I nail it with the stars, maybe I'll stand a chance with people.

Like Mum.

I was so sure her death was all about me.

The word 'Mum' is an asterism.

But Mum – Sarah – was a constellation. She was a friend, a daughter, a woman who was an artist, who had hobbies and feelings, some of which had everything to do with her family, and some of which were hers alone.

Maybe her reasons were a constellation too.

Maybe there is no one why.

Maybe there isn't an answer.

The only truth is, I'll never know for sure.

But she is more than her illness and her suicide.

And *I* am more than the same eight predictions on our paper fortune teller.

I am a constellation too.

My phone beeps.

And I know what Rosa would say, because she says it to all of us all of the time: 'Be in the moment, not on your mobile.'

But.

I open the notification with my eyes wide shut.

Órla: You're a dick, Iris a. Because you told Mam b.
Because I went to your house and you weren't there so
I have to put these words in a WhatsApp instead of saying
them to your face.

This is it, isn't it? The big heave-ho.

It beeps again.

I can't stand to look. But I can't stand *not* to look even more.

Órla: You did me a favour. Mam was cool. Said I can take as much time as a I need. A whole year out if I want to…

Hit call.

'Órla?'

'Iris?'

'Are you for real? What you said?'

'About you being a dick?' Her voice is dead serious.

'Oh, I meant the oth—'

And then it's not because it's laughing and crying and telling me how Bronagh was raging, and not about Órla maybe giving up gym, but rather about Órla not being open with she how she felt. 'So after I told her everything, Mam was cool.'

'Isn't that exactly what I said earlier.'

'Don't push your luck, mate.'

From the ground, 'Isaac! C'mon!'

'Where even are you?'

'I'll tell you tomorrow.' And I will. But, 'I've got to go.'

Men shouting.

Bottles smashing.

A robin – my robin! – flying.

The bird-ghost settles on the chimney pot, her black eyes watching me as the maniacal laughter pierces the otherwise still and quiet driveway below.

'C'mon!' Isaac's voice is scorched with vicious delight. 'Back the car up as close as possible. I've dumped everything I want to take by the front door. Books, records, art and shit. Could be worth a fair bit on eBay.'

To Isaac, these things he's taking are stock. To me, they're my childhood. They're my mum.

'I'm sorry,' I whisper to Sunnyside as if the bones of the house know it was me who let this vermin in.

Isaac, with that creepy white mask around his neck, heads back inside while his mate runs, arms spilling with what I guess is Mum's stuff – *my* stuff – to his car at the end of the drive. He chucks everything, like it's nothing, into the boot. His stereo's booming, but the music is squashed down by the closed doors. Windows rattle. Tyres screech. He's hurrying as if, for his kind, manhood is measured in speed.

'Change of plan,' Isaac calls, coming out through the front door with his arms full not of easily moveable and sellable objects, but a fox.

A six-foot-tall, blue-suited fox.

It's not just the fox mask that's familiar.

The Adidas too. And the brown hair. And how clear it is – from his drooped and swaying posture – that this bloke can't handle a party.

Noah.

Even with Isaac's grip on both of his shoulders, Noah's body's slurred. Like, if he were a sentence, he'd slide off the page. His head lollops so all I can see of the fox mask is its orange-brown ears.

'Oi!' I shout.

'What the fuck?' Isaac's mate tips his head back and points at me as I clamber across the tiles to the chimney. Even when I pull myself up to standing, the robin doesn't move.

'Let him go!' I scream at Isaac.

'Well, well, well.' He shunts Noah further up the drive and away from the house so he can better see me. His mate roughs his hands on Noah too so they're flanking him. As if he even stood a chance of running away. 'It's the resident nutjob,' Isaac says to his crony, who laughs, though not like he finds what Isaac says funny, more like he knows it's better for him to do whatever Isaac wants and expects him to do.

'Took you to Niagara, didn't we, Foxy?' There's that nasty laugh again, as Isaac mimes pouring drink after drink into Noah's mouth.

'Leave him.'

Isaac pulls Noah's mask an inch or so away from his face. When he lets go it snaps back with an audible smack. 'What is it with you? First you wanna save a pathetic little bird, now you're coming over all soft for a fox. Have a thing for him, do you?'

'He's my brother,' I say.

Noah's head lolls to one side as he looks up in my direction. Beneath the nose of the fox mask, I see a smile.

'What kind of fucking saddo gets this pissed on a few beers?'

'The same kind of fucking saddo who taught me that while trespassing alone would never result in a criminal record, taking stuff from the sites you visit is theft.'

Noah raises two weary thumbs.

'And who's gonna give a shit if I take anything from here?'

'Me.' I want it. Sunnyside and everything in it. I want it so I can learn about the constellation that was my mum.

'And how you gonna prove I took anything?'

I hold up my phone. 'I've been here a while, Isaac. Enough time to film you and your mate taking stuff from *my* house to your car. I'm sure the police aren't the only ones who'll find it interesting.'

'Whad'you mean?' Isaac's still cocky, but you can see how the pluck his crony gleans from being in his company is waning.

Noah's left side slumps a little as Isaac's mate loosens his hold.

'*Take nothing but photos, leave nothing but footprints.* The mess in the house is one thing, but if I post videos of you stealing too…'

The crony's already gunning it to the car.

As Isaac tosses his mask towards the bushes, he releases Noah, who drops with a *thwump* to the gravel below.

Doors slam. An engine starts. The car hot-wheels it down the drive, its headlamps pitching zigzagging beams of light in the dark.

*

Moving slowly through the hallway into the sitting room, it becomes clear just how much damage has been done. Pictures Isaac didn't think worth putting on eBay are skew-whiff on the walls. Cigarette butts have been ground into the mantelpiece and tables. A clutter of bottles litters the beer-tacky floor.

It stinks, appropriately, like the morning after.

'EvenIdunnohowtocleanthisup,' Noah says in one long drawl as we wait for Tala to collect us. Thin dribble leaks from the corner of his mouth down his chin.

I wipe it away with my sleeve. 'What are you even doing here?'

'Big brother.' Noah sways from side to side as he points a finger at his own chest.

'Huh?' I brush sticky crumbs from the sofa and guide him down.

'Saw what happened with Tala and Evie.' He mimes an explosion then burps and puts his head in his hands. 'Wanted to check you're OK,' he says when he's able to lift it again. Even in his smashed state my stepbrother must sense my surprise at this stab at sibling protection. 'We're family.' He smiles, and even though the words are slurred, the meaning behind them is sharp.

Of all the facts Noah has ever cited, strange as it is to admit, *we're family* is the one I'm most convinced is true.

'And it was you who said I'm Jack boy! Dull boy no-play boy. Get wilder, you said.' He waves his arms in the air and grabs the mask from where I'd laid it on a cushion. 'Wild Fox!'

'How did you even find out about the party?'

Ignoring my question, he attempts to pounce, but the sudden energy makes him retch.

'Maybe Lego's a better pastime for you than drinking.'

How someone who's vomiting into his own trainer can look so smug, I don't know, but Noah manages it. 'As always,' he gloats between heaves, 'I was right all along.'

Forty-Three

'Bloody hell, Iris,' Dad says as he opens the window, flooding Sunnyside's sitting room with December sun. He's not stopped shaking his head since we arrived for this morning's clean-up mission.

'I'm sorry.' I've lost count of my apologies over the last nine hours. I started the second I saw Dad and Rosa, who were waiting for us when I walked and Noah staggered through the door.

'Me too,' Dad said as I muttered it the first time. I'd expected a bawling, but what I got in the kitchen at 2 a.m. was a hug.

And I know I should have just enjoyed it for what it was, but, 'So *this* is how you hug a porcupine, is it?'

Dad pulled back and took me by the shoulders, scanning my face for clues as to what the hell I might mean.

'That book! The one on your bedside table? You think I'm a porcupine? Too spiky? Too tricky to hold?'

'No,' he said, his arms right back around me, full and warm and tight. 'Rosa bought that book not because of you but *me*. She says I'm a tad…' His torso twisted as he turned for confirmation from his wife.

'Tetchy?' Rosa laughed. 'Fractious, maybe, about rules?'

'Abitofaprick!' Noah doubled over in helpless giggles. 'Geddit? Porcupineprick!'

It can't just have been me who expected a *language, Noah, please*. But Dad swerved his usual parental clapback. 'You'll be relieved to know I'm working on being less restrained! I might even have a surprise for you on Christmas Eve.'

I was too tired by then to probe. And now? Well, now I'm too busy, rubber-gloved for scrubbing toilets and mopping floors. There's a team of us. Dad, Rosa, Noah – who's kind of useless – and Tala, who came armed with a fresh batch of palitaw. 'Mama thought it might help.'

'Your mama's an angel,' I tell her now as I take my second cake from the tin. 'And so are you. You sure you have time for this? You know, with everything you're working on with Dougie and Angeline?'

'You scratch my back…' She tickles my shoulders with a feather duster. 'I'll help you with this today, and then tomorrow, we can find you a job with Oh, Brother Word Art Thou.'

My heart mad-dogs in my chest. 'You'll let me help you?'

'Well, we could do with someone to mop the floor before we sit and protest on it.' Tala smiles wryly and nudges my bucket of water with her toe. 'I was going to ask Evie, but I'm not sure she's as keen on working with me since everyone's now calling her a Dumbbell.'

'Whatever you need, I'll do it, Tal. I won't let you down.'

'Ditto,' she says. And I shrug, like, *you never do*, but Tala's eyes glaze with tears, and she takes my hands. 'I can't even imagine how hard the last few weeks must have been for you, Iris. I'm sorry. I should have given you more slack.'

'Don't be silly. You're the best.'

'You're bester,' she sobs.

'Actually, you and me, together, *we* are the bestest.' I'm sobbing now too.

An hour or so later, we all sit down for sausage rolls, though Noah still can't stomach anything but salt and vinegar crisps.

We've moved the table and chairs back into position in the dining room. If you can get past the lingering smell of inebriated bodies, it's quite nice to sit with my family in the place I so often used to sit with Mum.

I don't know if I believe in bird-ghosts or ghosts of any kind at all. But I do feel Mum here. I catch a glimpse of her many-ringed fingers holding out a scone, and I hear her voice asking, *Cream first or jam?* And as Tala talks about her plans for the next slam, I smell the sprouts Mum spooned on to my plate, pretending not to know I'd hide them in my shoe. They are flashes. Real and unreal. Gone but present. Fleeting yet somehow they stay.

'Could we come here on Christmas morning?' I ask when there's a lull in conversation. 'Like Mum wanted. It doesn't have to be for long.'

'Sure. That would be nice,' Dad says, and his voice might be convincing, but his eyes are bothered and torn.

'What?'

'Will it not upset you?'

'Maybe. But if it does, I think that's OK.' Mum named me for rainbows. I'd only ever thought about them being made of colour, but what they really are is the combination of light and rain.

Noah rubs his temples. 'Can I have more paracetamol yet?'

'Here you go, party animal!' Rosa pops two tablets from a packet in her bag.

'I still don't get how you found out about the party?' I toss Noah his fourth – and what Rosa insists is his *final* – bag of crisps.

'There's a reason why you call me Know-All,' he says with this look of absolute superiority and leaves it at that.

While Rosa goes to fetch him some water, I pass Noah my phone. 'When you get that place at Oxford, you will be OK, you know.'

'If this is how partying makes you feel, I can't do it, Iris.'

'Look,' I tell him, and it's not just the glare from my screen that makes his face brighter. 'See, you don't have to party! You just need to find your people!'

'There's a Lego Society at Oxford?'

'Yup! No need for any wild drinking to find you some mates. Less of a hangover with blocks too!'

'I'm just so grateful it's only a headache you're dealing with.' Rosa places the drink on the table, ruffles his hair. 'That kid Isaac sounds like pure trouble. Kudos to you, Iris. I don't think *I'd* have had the wherewithal to think of filming him.'

'And you reckon I did?' I tear a palitaw in two and pass half to Tala. 'The most recent video I have on my phone is of Buddy chasing a squirrel in the park.'

Dad double takes. 'But you said you told Isaac you had the footage?'

'I was worried he was going to hurt Noah.' I hold Dad's gaze and smile. 'Sometimes you have to lie, right? To protect the people you love.'

Forty-Four

'I know I did it the other night when I called the Samaritans, but I was pretty much anonymous then. This woman I've booked to see after Christmas, well, it'll be face to face.'

'It's still just talking.' Tala turns off the engine and twists to look at me on the verge of a meltdown in the front seat of her car. 'You've been doing that with us all day.'

She has a point. Tala, Órla, Dougie and I spent the last few hours of Christmas Eve at the bothy devising a survey on sexual harassment we want to pitch to every year group at school. 'The subject might have been different,' Tala says, 'but when Dougie asked us about our own #MeToo experiences, the awkwardness I felt was kind of similar to when I first called Switchboard.'

'Switchboard?'

'It's an LGBTQIA+ helpline.' Tala opens their page on her phone to show me. 'You know what *I'm* like speaking to people—'

'I know what you *were* like.' I'm laughing, but maybe Tala hears the smidge of too-much-change-to-handle sadness that hasn't yet fully thawed.

'I'm still me, yeah? Just like with all the shit that's happened lately, you're still you. We're just expanding.' She clicks on the photo I sent her earlier of the counsellor I spoke with briefly yesterday. I'd found the picture on her website, and I know, I know, don't judge a book by its cover, but…

'She looks kind,' Tala says. '*I* didn't have the words when I first phoned Switchboard, but these people, they're trained to get your story out of you. Not in a bad way. They're there to help.'

It wasn't Dad and Rosa who brought the counselling up again. It was me.

'There's something I just don't get,' I said to my stepmum on the night after the big clean-up at Sunnyside, when she came into my room at bedtime. I'd shown her the Better Things notebook, read the memories I'd written about Paris in the living room, stargazing in summer, making ball gowns from bedsheets and whirling in a waltz across the kitchen floor. 'Mum did all these grand gestures. Like, she loved me so much, there was no limit to what she would do to make me happy. But how I remember it, she didn't put up a protest when I left with Dad.'

'I know it might not feel like it.' Rosa's fingers were cool on my forehead when she pushed the hair from my eyes. 'But I wonder if letting you go with Matt was Sarah's grandest gesture of all. She *did* love you, Iris. So, so much. Your dad says she would have done anything to make you happy. Even if that meant you living somewhere else. It was never meant to be permanent. Sarah was sick. Matt just didn't know how sick. And he's sorry.'

I thought of the roof, then, of those thick, snaking thoughts of jumping, brief but so bullish and sharp. 'Am *I* sick too? Is it hereditary?'

'We don't think your mum was ever diagnosed, lovely. But it's something we need to understand better. Whatever happens, though, you're not on your own.'

As I get out of the car now, I take Tala's stack of library books from where I'd balanced them between my boots in the footwell and lay them on the passenger seat. 'You reckon our lives will *ever* be like these?'

Tala looks at me, like, *huh?*

'All nicely tied up at the end. You know, where there's an epiphany and then everything's fine.'

She shrugs. 'I don't think there's ever really an ending. Happy or sad or somewhere in between, our stories will go on and on and on.'

I let out a big sigh. Today's been good, but, *God*, it's also been hard.

'Let me know how you get on with your dad.' Tala waves crossed fingers through her open window as I brace myself for what's about to come.

I've been summoned, see.

'Home by three thirty, please, Iris,' Dad said this morning, before sending at least five reminder texts throughout the day. I'm expecting, at best, a family dinner, at worst, a lecture on all the reasons why my recent behaviour has got to change. What I'm not expecting is Buddy in the back garden in a tug of war with Dad. Despite his best efforts to hold the world's best poodle back, he can't stop his giant paws from pummelling me in the core.

I drop to my knees for a full-on Buddy hug. 'What's happened to you, Bud?' I look up at Dad, whose broad grin is lit by the last of the Christmas Eve sun.

'His coat?'

I nod, running my palms across Buddy's tight-curled fur. It was always black. Now, though, it's almost entirely concrete grey.

'The guy at the dog rescue said he thought it was grief. Because of the sudden separation. You should have seen him when I dropped by Mr West's on the way home.'

I can imagine. Buddy lolloping and rearing. Slipping and sliding about the place as he ran wild through the hall. 'Crazy?'

'No.' Dad squats beside me. 'The opposite. It was like he sensed Mr West was fragile.' He plays with Buddy's ear. 'Your tail was wagging, wasn't it, boy? But otherwise you were as gentle as can be.'

Buddy sits, then raises his paw.

'So does that mean he can move back to Mr West's? Should I walk him over there now?'

Dad shakes his head. 'Mr West still isn't great. It's not just his hip. It's his confidence. You know, he was struggling even before the fall. He said he can't imagine ever really being able to walk Buddy again.'

'But Buddy can visit him?'

'Well, when I spoke with the dog rescue about adoption, you being able to take Buddy to see Mr West regularly was part of the sell!'

'Adoption?'

Dad holds his hands out, like, *ta-da!* 'Merry Christmas, Iris!'

'What?'

His voice, his face, his stance, everything is like Dad can't quite believe it himself. 'What can I say? Somehow Noah convinced me that Buddy needs you more than I need a hair-free sofa.'

'He's a poodle, Dad. He doesn't moult.'

'Which was, of course, one of my many persuasive arguments,' Noah says from where he's standing now with Rosa by the kitchen door. 'That and your human right to a pet, obviously.'

I can't believe it.

'But what about ringworm?' I ask. 'Lime disease? Fleas? The risk of pneumonic plague?' I'm not even kidding, Dad actually included that in his list of reasons why we shouldn't get a dog after a pit bull terrier infected four Americans with the disease in the summer of 2015. 'Thank you!'

'See,' Dad says, faux glaring at Noah. 'Not so much a porcupineprick after all.'

I throw my arms around Dad.

'It's a big responsibility, Iris.'

'You won't regret it, I promise. I'll feed him, walk him, do everything I can to keep him happy.'

'You know,' Noah says, 'research shows Buddy might play a part in helping Iris feel happy too.'

For once, I want to hear more, but Buddy's off around the garden, his grief-grey pom-pom tail going full pelt. He runs in circles before barging past Noah and Rosa through the back door.

'Buddy!' I chase after him, but he's too quick and I can't keep up. By the time I catch him, Christmas is already ruined.

'My blue spruce!' Dad rushes into the sitting room after me, just in time to witness Buddy launching himself at the

Christmas tree. As both dog and blue spruce topple, I'm not sure if it's Dad who's yelping or Buddy.

'Noooooo!' I swear the world moves into slow motion. Lights flicker. Lego baubles smash. Pine needles scatter like confetti across the floor. 'Buddy!' The dog, separated from us by the Christmas tree that's wedged now between the table and sofa, dips his head in what I briefly think is shame. But what he's actually doing is lapping at the water seeping from the toppled stand. 'What have you done?'

'Done', though, isn't the right word, the right tense, because Buddy's still *doing* it. He jumps across the knocked-down tree and snatches the star from its top.

'Iris, get him out of here!' Dad shouts.

'I'm sorry.' My heart rolls in my chest as I make my way through the carnage to grab his collar. 'I guess that's it then? He has to go?'

'Only to the kitchen while we clear up.' Dad's laughing. 'I don't want him getting broken glass in his paws.'

'So he can stay?'

'He's one of us now.' Rosa pats Buddy's bum as I drag him through to the kitchen. 'And we stick with him, foibles and all.'

Forty-Five

'Do you think it was the smell?' Dad's sitting on the sofa with a red tissue-paper hat cocked on his head. Rosa went all out at our Christmas breakfast this morning, party poppers and crackers and indoor fireworks. An effort, I think, to distract Dad from the loss of his tree.

'Smell?' Noah glances at Buddy, sprawled on the rug beside him, and sniffs as if we wouldn't already know if the poodle had let out one of his ginormous farts. Seriously, he's totally pushing the boundaries of 'foibles and all'.

'The spruce.' Dad's expression can only be described as forlorn. (Nice use of 'forlorn', Iris.) 'It smelled so good,' he says wistfully. 'I wonder if it was that that excited him.'

It's been like this since last night. It will seem like we've moved on, but then Dad will reignite his sadness about what we've euphemized as the Fell, offering up another cause or consequence of Buddy's Christmas-tree misdemeanour.

'Just one year,' he says, his eyes fixed on Rosa's artificial tree we rescued from the for-the-dump pile, bodging together the few remaining decorations that weren't destroyed in the Fell. 'For one year, I wanted real.' He sighs. 'I guess it's not meant to be.'

'Don't be so sure.' I rush to the kitchen, returning to the

sitting room with Rosa's pride and joy pot plant. 'If ever there's a plant ripe for celebration, it's this one.'

'Iris.' Rosa stops poking the log burner. 'Hold on.'

'Hear me out,' I say, taking centre stage and holding the yucca aloft. 'We've all mocked Rosa for her failures, but this here is evidence that if we persevere, we can succeed. I mean, look at it.' I place the plant carefully on the table. 'It's thriving. It's so green and so…' My fingers run the full length of the leaves and my jaw drops. 'Plastic!'

We all turn to Rosa, who's chewing her lip, her mouth clamped shut, trying, I think, to contain a guilty laugh.

'Oh! My! God! That's why you wouldn't let us water it, isn't it?'

Her giggles begin to spill.

And they're infectious.

'It was one less thing to worry about,' she says between actual snorts. 'I was trying to give myself a break.'

'But why not tell us?' Dad's thumbing the plant now as if he still can't quite believe it.

Rosa sits down on the rug, crossing her legs in a pose that usually makes her look so strong but right now makes her look like a defeated child. 'It sounds so stupid, but I've always thought I *should* be good with plants. I'm a vegetarian who practises yoga and meditation. Every night I light candles while writing a gratitude journal. I'm obsessed with avocados. For some reason, being green-fingered seemed to fit with everything I think I am. And yet…' Rosa points at the yucca, down-turning her mouth. 'All the time you believed it was real, I could convince myself it was too. Pathetic, isn't it?'

'I think I get it.' I sit down and wrap an arm around her shoulders. 'We're not always the person we expect ourselves to be.'

'All the more reason to use it, I reckon,' Dad says, pulling a couple of the smaller surviving baubles from the artificial tree and hanging them on the artificial plant.

In the late morning, we take the yucca to Sunnyside. Tala, Tita Celestina, Kristian, Órla and Bronagh come too. When everyone is gathered, I take out my Box of Mum Things. In the bottom is the angel Mum gave me the last time I saw her. She wanted me to come back and put it on her tree.

'It's a bit grand for my fake shrub,' Rosa says, kind of sheepish.

'Mum was hardly one for convention. She was always grateful for an opportunity to jazz up anything. And I reckon she'd like this combination.' I place it carefully on the yucca. 'Like I do,' I whisper to Rosa only. 'It's her, and it's you.'

'C'mon,' she says. 'I have something to show you.' She leads me outside, squeezing my hand tighter when she feels me stiffen at the sight of the potting shed. 'I spotted them when I was out here clearing up the other day. And I wasn't sure then, but...' She's pointing at the right side of the shed, where there's a huddle of violet blooms. On a gardening app on her phone, she shows me a photo of the same tiny flowers. They're the ones Mum and I had tried to grow. The bulbs and seeds that had scattered when she threw the pots on the floor.

'Irises?'

Rosa nods. 'Iris reticulata. They blossom in the winter.' I copy her as she bends and puts her nose to the petals. 'Even in the hardest of climates they bloom.'

'Will you wait here for me?'

Rosa nods, and I run inside to grab my bag.

By the time I'm back with my stepmum, my face is wet with tears. I place the Box of Mum Things and the box with her ashes next to the flowers.

'You want me to get your dad? Or Tala?'

'No,' I say.

Memories rush at my skin.

The lightness of feathers.

The heavy weight of love.

Mum did love me. So much.

But for reasons I'll never understand, she left.

I don't know the *why*. Or if she came back to me as a robin.

What I do know is that I can't predict what's going to happen. That all I can really feel is the now.

I made a paper fortune teller for Mum and me this morning. I take it from my bag and, leaving six of its squares blank, commit to two fates for the both of us.

You are loved, I write.

And then:

You are free.

Resources (UK)

GRIEF

Cruse Bereavement Support

cruse.org.uk
Helpline: 0808 808 1677
Twitter: @CruseSupport
Facebook: facebook.com/crusebereavementsupport

A helpline run by trained bereavement volunteers, offering emotional support to anyone affected by grief.

The website also offers an instant messaging service.

Child Bereavement UK

childbereavementuk.org
Helpline: 0800 02 888 40
Email: helpline@childbereavementuk.org

The charity supports children and young people (up to the age of 25) when someone important to them has died or is not expected to live, and parents and the wider family when a baby or child of any age dies or is dying.

Live chat is also available on the website.

Winston's Wish

winstonswish.org
Helpline: 08088 020 021
Email: ask@winstonswish.org

A charity supporting bereaved children, young people (up to the age of 25), their families and the professionals who care for them.

They also provide specialist support when someone important has taken their own life.

An online chat service is available via the website.

Grief Is My Superpower

(In association with Winston's Wish)

Podcaster Mark Lemon talks with different guests about their experiences of grief.

Available on Apple Podcasts and Spotify.

Griefcast

cariadlloyd.com/griefcast
Twitter: @thegriefcast
Instagram: @thegriefcast

A podcast exploring grief and death. In each episode, writer and comedian Cariad Lloyd talks to a different guest about their experience of grief.

Available on Apple Podcasts and Acast.

Good Grief

goodgrieffest.com
Twitter: @GoodGriefFest
Instagram: @GoodGriefFestival

A virtual festival of love and loss that offers online events normalizing the conversation around grief.

MENTAL HEALTH SERVICES

Samaritans

samaritans.org
Helpline: 116 123
Email: jo@samaritans.org

A free 24-hour helpline offering listening support to people and communities in need.

Shout 85258

giveusashout.org
Text 'SHOUT' to 85258

A free, confidential 24-hour text messaging support service for anyone struggling to cope.

Mind

mind.org.uk

A charity providing advice and support to anyone experiencing a mental health problem.

The website has information specific to young people aged 11–18.

Young Minds

youngminds.org.uk
Twitter: @YoungMindsUK
Instagram: @YoungMindsUK

An online resource offering advice and information about what to do if you're struggling with how you feel.

LGBTQIA+

The Asexual Visibility and Education Network

asexuality.org

An online network for the asexual community alongside an archive of resources on asexuality.

Stonewall

stonewall.org.uk
Telephone: 0800 050 2020

Information and support for LGBT communities and their allies.

Switchboard

switchboard.lgbt
Telephone: 0300 330 0630
Email: Chris@switchboard.lgbt

An LGBTQIA+ helpline offering a safe space for anyone to discuss sexuality, gender identity, sexual health and emotional wellbeing.

An online chat service is also available.

SEXUAL ASSAULT

Rape Crisis England and Wales

rapecrisis.org.uk
Helpline: 0808 802 9999

The umbrella organization for a network of independent Rape Crisis Centres. All member centres provide specialist support and services for victims and survivors of sexual violence.

A live chat helpline is also available on their website.

Rape Crisis Scotland

rapecrisisscotland.org.uk
Helpline: 08088 01 03 02
Text support: 07537 410 027
Email: support@rapecrisisscotland.org.uk

A national helpline with support and information for anyone affected by sexual violence.

Childline

childline.org.uk
Helpline: 0800 1111

A free, private and confidential service where you can talk about anything.

ENDING VIOLENCE AGAINST WOMEN

End Violence Against Women

endviolenceagainstwomen.org.uk

A leading coalition of specialist women's support services, researchers, activists, survivors and NGOs working to end violence against women and girls in all its forms.

White Ribbon

whiteribbon.org.uk

A charity working to end violence against women by engaging with men and boys to make a stand against violence.

CONFIDENCE

How to Own the Room

A podcast in which comedian and writer Viv Groskop talks with inspirational women about the secrets of brilliant speaking.

Available on Apple Podcasts and Spotify.

The podcast is a companion to the book *How to Own the Room* (Bantam Press, 2018).

Resources (US)

GRIEF

Dough Center

dougy.org
Email: help@dougy.org
Podcast: Grief Out Loud

A peer support group that provides a safe place where children, teens, young adults and families who are grieving can share their experiences before and after a death.

Their podcast Grief Out Loud is mix of personal stories and tips for supporting children and teens.

MENTAL HEALTH SERVICES

National Alliance on Mental Illness (NAMI)

nami.org
Helpline: 800-950-NAMI

NAMI provides support to individuals and families affected by mental illness. Use the website above to find an organisation in your State to help you.

National Suicide Prevention Lifeline

suicidepreventionlifeline.org
Helpline: 988

A national network of local crisis centres that provides free and confidential emotional support to people in suicidal crisis or emotional distress 24/7.

LGBTQIA+

The Trevor Project

thetrevorproject.org
Helpline: 1-866-488-7386

A free and confidential 24/7 support service to LGBTQ young people. Text, chat, or call any time to reach a trained counsellor.

SEXUAL ASSAULT

RAINN

rainn.org
Helpline: 800-656-HOPE (4673)

A national helpline with support and information for anyone affected by sexual violence. An online chat service is also available on their website.

ENDING VIOLENCE AGAINST WOMEN

National Coalition Against Domestic Violence

ncadv.org

An organization dedicated to supporting survivors, holding offenders accountable and supporting advocates. Further resources can be found on their website.

Acknowledgements

Sure, I'd heard of Second Book Syndrome but – what with being a glass-half-full person – I naively assumed that, rather like excruciating childbirth, it wouldn't happen to me.

Thing is, just as perineal massages and hypnobirthing CDs won't guarantee you'll easily push out a baby, extensive research and 20,000-word outlines won't guarantee you'll easily push out a book.

Fret not, all the labour analogies will cease here, not least because my brilliant editor Katie has taught me the great benefit of reining it in.

My point is, writing a second book under contract was painful. The publication of *The Sky Is Mine* was truly one of the best moments in my life but, as Iris learns in *We Are All Constellations*, nothing is ever all good or all bad. As I read reviews – everyone told me not to do it but, seriously, who has that kind of willpower? – my usually optimistic, silver-lining'd head was awash with self-doubt, and what had started as an exciting new project was suddenly shrouded in dread.

I have, then, a lot of people to thank. Because, honestly, I don't think I was the easiest wife, mother, friend or writer to live and work with.

Here we go…

First off, thanks to everyone who read and supported *The Sky Is Mine*. For those of you who took the time to post a review or message me, you don't know what a boost it was to my battered confidence to learn that readers had enjoyed the book. Discovering that Jennifer Niven was one such reader was a dream. *All the Bright Places* was the inspiration for me writing YA. So, as I struggled my way through a messy first, second and third draft of a new book, I intermittently replayed the Insta reel of Jennifer talking about how much she loved Izzy and was immediately lifted. Thanks, Jennifer, you are proof that sometimes it really is good (or fantastic, even) to (virtually) meet your heroes.

Huge gratitude to my editors, Katie Jennings and Molly Scull, who had to read a significant amount of dross and a lot of apologetic emails before we finally reached a point at which Iris was able to shine. Thank you for recognizing that within that first 100,000-word draft – again, sorry! – there was a story worth pursuing, and for being so patient as I killed both my nemeses and darlings. Lesson one: Cull. Lesson two: Cull. Lesson three: Cull. I really am grateful for all the time and thought you've given this book which, with your help, has become something I'm truly proud of.

To the rest of the team at Rock the Boat: Shadi Doostdar, Kate Bland, Lucy Cooper, Mark Rusher, Paul Nash and Laura McFarlane, thank you for turning all those words into something tangible and for then getting that tangible story into people's hands. And for the beautiful cover, big thanks to Anna Kupstova for her stunningly emotive illustration and Hayley Warnham for the eye-catching design.

Thanks to my agent, Hannah Sheppard, for your guidance and encouragement, and for telling me to just hit send when I was too deep in writerly despair to know for myself what was and wasn't working.

It seems fitting that one of my greatest allies in writing a book with constellations in its title is called Stella. And funny too, that as I wrote and rewrote (and rewrote again) a story in which a robin is so significant, Stella Duffy enabled me to grow my wings. Shall we raise each other up? Yes, let's. Yes, let's. Yes, let's.

Writing is inevitably a very solitary activity but, thanks to my writer friends, especially Susie Bassett, Sandra Dingwall, Sara Emmerton, Tess James-Mackey, Liz Pike, Ko Porteous, Louisa Reid, Ciara Smyth and Kate Weston, I never really feel alone. Sharing WhatsApps, lunches and plot holes with you is even more of a tonic than a spoonful (or two) of Nutella, which, quite frankly, is saying a lot.

Special thanks to Tat Effby, whose puns are as good as her cakes. When it came to Rhyme's Up and Brother Word Art Thou, I couldn't have done it batter myself. (See.)

It's no coincidence that the Samaritan Iris speaks with is called Emily. Emily, with you, running is never just running. It's laughing, ranting, sharing and grounding. (And, yes, usually, some peeing too.) Thank you for keeping me sane during lockdown and in the process of writing this book.

Kate, thanks for exploring old memories with me.

To my early readers, Jodie Elderkin, Sara Emmerton, Tess James-Mackey, Louisa Reid and, obviously, Mum, your feedback and encouragement were invaluable and kept me going when I genuinely felt like giving up.

Andi, Reno, Elliot Jacobs, Alicia Milligan, Mia Schartau and Evie Smith, thank you for offering such insightful thoughts and suggestions.

Thanks to Shane Curteis for sharing so much about Filipino culture. Here's to celebrating Christmas in every month with a 'ber' in it!

Very grateful to Chris Schurke, who answered all my questions about exploring and whose photography first inspired Iris's love of abandoned places.

Jayne, thanks for being my go-to doctor, not only when the children have ailments but when my characters do too. Yes, it's great to have a medic as a sister-in-law, but what's even greater is that for me that medic is you.

Richard Dunhill, you are not only a generous teacher and listener but a generous reader too.

To all the Samaritans, especially those in Shrewsbury, thank you for listening.

Dad, thanks for telling everyone you meet on the slopes that I'm an author. If I'm ever a bestseller in Canada, it will be entirely down to you. I love you and, even though you've not yet arrived, am already crying at the thought of saying goodbye in May.

Mum, thanks for reading more drafts and extracts than anyone else. I could look at all the dictionaries in the world and still never find a word to perfectly describe how much I love you. So, for the moment, millipons will have to do.

Monty, thank you for teaching me about history, space and architecture and for being so patient when you have to explain, for the tenth time, about the Big Bang Theory. At eleven, you already know so much more about pretty much everything than me. Our talks give me so much inspiration. And our hugs give me so much joy.

Dolly, thank you for making me laugh every single day. The rush I get from being your mum is nothing to do with the sugar in your delicious bakes and everything to do with your infectious humour. Clever, courageous and kind, you are a wonder. I love you even more than you love Dadadonk. P.S. I really really *really* hope that these heartfelt words win me Parent of the Week.

MDH, thanks for your unwavering faith. I know your ultimate ambition for me has nothing to do with me writing books and everything to do with me bouncing my way across four giant red balls before standing on a ten-foot podium while jumping or ducking to avoid a swinging robotic arm. In the absence of an appearance on *Total Wipeout*, I hope this will do. You are funny, thoughtful, sensitive, clever and handsome. Oh, and you make fractions and parallel parking sexy. This eclectic mix is a wonderful constellation. It is, in fact, my most favourite constellation of all.

Amy Beashel lives in Shropshire with her husband and two kids. Her debut novel *The Sky Is Mine* was nominated for a CILIP Carnegie Medal 2021, longlisted for the Branford Boase Award 2021 and shortlisted for the Bristol Teen Book Award 2020. Incidentally, she is also the fastest woman in the world on a space hopper.